Stalky upset a c⋯⋯ ⋯mall boys among their own cooking ⋯⋯ ⋯cTurk raided the untidy lockers as a terrier digs at a rabbit-hole; while Beetle poured ink upon such heads as he could not appeal to with a Smith's Classical Dictionary.

Minor scuffles these, compared to the anguish provoked when the boys let a dead cat ripen beneath the floorboards of a neighboring dormitory, or when they take it upon themselves to reform the school bullies. Unholy in every intention, fiendishly subtle in their strategy, Stalky & Co. are probably the most appealing pests ever to roister through an English public school. But they have a certain poignancy, too, as the narrative follows the prankster schoolboys into their later, less carefree lives as soldiers of the queen.

Kipling's vigorous description of a late nineteenth-century boarding school immortalizes a system of education which has all but vanished. Amplified by a new introduction, glossary, and bibliography by Steven Marcus, professor of English at Columbia University, this edition will be particularly valuable to students of turn-of-the-century literature.

RUDYARD KIPLING

STALKY & CO.

With a New Introduction by
STEVEN MARCUS

COLLIER BOOKS
NEW YORK, N.Y.

This Collier Books edition is published by special arrangement with Doubleday & Company, Inc.

Collier Books is a division of The Crowell-Collier Publishing Company

First Collier Books Edition 1962

TO
CORMELL PRICE
HEAD-MASTER, UNITED SERVICES COLLEGE,
WESTWARD HO, BIDEFORD, NORTH DEVON, 1874-1894

Library of Congress Catalog Card Number: 62-18994

Introduction

Stalky & Co. is a fantasy and a celebration. It is an idealized recollection and re-creation of Kipling's experience at school. It celebrates a period of life and a way of life, or culture. The period of life is what was once called boyhood. The way of life or culture is that of the English Public School, in this case the United Services College, founded in 1874 by a group of army officers who wanted to provide their sons with an education suited to their class and family, but who could not afford to send them to the more expensive schools. Most of the boys who attended the United Services College were soldiers' sons, and many of them had been born in India. At the College the boys were prepared for the Army Entrance Examination for most of them were, in their careers, to follow in their fathers' footsteps. By extension, then, *Stalky & Co.* celebrates the way of life of the British Army—of its officer class—and of the Empire which it helped to administer and rule. This Empire and its way of life have ceased significantly to exist (and there is reason to doubt whether they ever existed in the manner that Kipling would have us believe). As a result, *Stalky & Co.* is the celebration of a dead culture, a culture that may seem to many Americans as remote and strange as that of Sparta or the Roman Empire.

Whether the period of life—boyhood—which *Stalky & Co.* celebrates still exists is perhaps something of an open question. It is certain, however, that our modern conceptions of childhood and adolescence are very different from Kipling's and the nineteenth century's conceptions of boyhood and youth. The very change in our idea of them—and a change in ideals and values as well. One of the many uses to which a book like *Stalky & Co.* may be put is that it helps us define and understand ourselves by showing us what, in part, we no longer are. No reader of this book will need to be convinced that in our time the period of adolescence is undergoing a

5

crisis and disturbance of peculiar intensity; or that this crisis is nothing if not one of value and of the authority of value; or that what is being registered so painfully, explosively, and honestly in adolescence is expressive of a general social condition. Among its many other qualities, *Stalky & Co.* will be understood to possess the quality of speaking with intimacy and relevance to this situation.

No doubt this is weighty significance to place upon a book that has for generations been an almost exclusive possession of schoolboys. And there can be little question that its appeal will continue so long as readers enjoy jokes, gags, japes, comic plots and revenges, and the life of free-wheeling fantasy. Yet, we should note that if *Stalky & Co.* has been a much loved book, it has also been much hated. The strong word here is accurate, and we should not mistake the matter: It has been hated precisely for its values, or what its values have been taken to be. The school life that it describes is harsh, cruel, and often brutal, and Kipling has been accused of siding with the cruelty and justifying the brutality. The boys are being trained for a life in which force and violence are to be met every day, and Kipling has been charged with affirming the domination of the weak by the strong. The boys are to become part of the governing caste of the British Empire, and Kipling has been accused of uncritically supporting—and as being the propagandist of—the moral values of imperialism and the imperialist system.

These accusations are in one degree or another substantially true. It would be pointless to deny them and almost equally so to try mitigate them. It might, for example, be argued that although the British Empire was a bad thing, it was still, as George Orwell once remarked, a great deal better than the younger empires that have supplanted it. However true and useful Orwell's remark might be, to introduce it into a discussion of *Stalky & Co.* would act more to distract the reader's attention than to extenuate Kipling. The point to be grasped is that among and alongside all these bad attitudes which seem calculated to outrage the values that most educated persons today affirm—values which can be roughly summed up in the term liberal democracy—there exist other attitudes and values whose absence from contemporary life we all feel and are probably the worse for. These values are described by old, obsolete words like honor, truthfulness, loyalty, manliness, pride, straightforwardness, courage, self-sacrifice, and heroism. That these virtues exist as active and credible possibilities in the world of *Stalky & Co.*, and that they seem not to in ours—or if they do, appear almost solely in corrupted forms—must give us pause. Such a fact may serve to remind us that the moral benefits, conveniences, and superiorities of modern democratic society have not been acquired without cost. Part of this cost seems pretty clearly to have been paid by a diminution of the older masculine virtues. These virtues were felt to exist in the societies of the past, and that they existed in conjunction with the injustices of class, the inequities of inherited privilege, and with all the offenses against human dignity of which the social past is grossly guilty, should act to increase our awareness of the tragically paradoxical character of social progress. In the moral life of history there are apparently no gains without losses. Few books urge us to confront this contradiction more barely and boldly than *Stalky & Co.*

Yet it would be an oversight to consider *Stalky & Co.* solely from the point of view of social comment and in isolation from its place in literature. It belongs to a genre of literature peculiarly characteristic of the modern era. This literature is concerned with the discovery, examination, and commemoration of childhood and boyhood—especially one's own. It begins with Rousseau's *Émile* and the poetry of Blake and Wordsworth and is carried forward in the English and American novel, most notably in Dickens, George Eliot, and Mark Twain. Although a serious concern with childhood is a common feature of all modern culture, in no other culture has that concern been so central and intense as in the culture of the English-speaking world. In no other language does the word for boy have the kind of resonance that it does in English. *Garçon, knabe, muchacho,* are good enough words in their way, but they do not take away the winter of desolation or make the buds unfold or cause one's moral being to rejoice in the way that the word boy does. In what other language is there such an epithet as "Oh, boy!"—an expression of the very essence of spontaneous delight. Or in what other language are lines such as

> Shades of the prison-house begin to close
> Upon the growing boy

thought of as expressing the very essence of sadness, and of the human condition. In *Stalky & Co.*, when the triumvirate are publicly rubbing in their revenge on King's house, one of the masters who is being mercilessly imitated overhears what is going on and murmurs to another " 'It's not brutality,' . . . as though answering a question no one had asked. 'It's a boy; only boy.' " Clearly the word is being used here in a metaphysical sense and as descriptive of a metaphysical state. In short, boy is one of the sacred words of the English language; boyhood is—or for one hundred and fifty years was —a priestly state or condition; and the literature of boys and boyhood has had, for a secularized era, something of the aura of doctrinal or holy writ.

One of the chief characters in which the boy appears is as a schoolboy. English literature is particularly rich in the literature of school (as opposed to America, where the boy tends more often to be regarded in his relation to nature). This unique richness is in accord with the unique importance that education has been given in English tradition and history, and with the unique English feeling for the experience of education—a feeling which may be summed up in D. W. Brogan's epigram that England is the only country in the world where being a schoolboy is an end in itself. This does not mean that going to school is not also a means to an end, or, as we say today, a preparation for life. It does mean, however, that school is first and foremost an experience, like all other experience, and that it is to be thought of, judged, and respected as such. It also means that the best way to ensure the success of educational means is to insist upon them as ends; conversely, the surest way to destroy belief in the value and reality of any effort is to make clear that it is not self-justifying or autonomous. Finally, the statement implies that since being a schoolboy has such a special weight and significance, much of one's later experience as a man will itself be justified in the degree that it bears out or is in accord with the values of one's earlier experience. As we see in *Stalky & Co.*, the names that the boys give themselves at school are the names by which they greet and recognize each other for the rest of their lives. And for the rest of their lives—no matter what their age—they think of themselves as "Old Boys," not graduates or alumni as we think of ourselves, neutralizing the sex in one case and fleeing from the language in the other. The brute emotion, the unabashed sentimentality of that phrase "Old Boy" is still another indication of the fierce importance with which the English experience of school has traditionally been felt. Such a phrase also reveals the direction in which character will be distorted by an unremitting application of its idea.

Stalky & Co. is a classic of this sub-genre of literature. That it emerges from and refers to a literature which deals with life at school we learn from the book itself, where such popular works as *Eric; or Little by Little* are mentioned only to be held up to comic contempt. These tales as the reader might suspect, were largely didactic and moralistic in purpose. They dealt with good little boys from home who fell prey to the infinite temptations to immoral behavior at school and who, on the very brink of irredeemable corruption, were saved only by an intervention of moral reform, corporal punishment, or religious conversion. Usually it was a combination of all three. Odd as it may seem today, these books probably served a purpose in their own time. But by and large they served it badly and falsely, and one of the intentions of *Stalky & Co.* is to alter the picture of life at school presented in these books and to set the record straight.

One of these books, the most famous of them, is significantly not mentioned in *Stalky & Co.* Thomas Hughes's *Tom Brown's Schooldays* is a work of considerable historical importance. The story of a boy's experiences at Rugby during the early years of Thomas Arnold's headmastership, it records with sharp realism the terrible, inhuman life of an English Public School before Arnold's reforms were instituted, and the salutary effect on mind, spirit, and morale that those reforms had when they took hold. It is a work of high victorian seriousness and moral earnestness, dedicated to the liberal, humane, responsible, and intelligent values which Dr. Arnold's educational ideas and reforms were founded on and which it was his purpose to instill among his students. In its own minor way, *Tom Brown's Schooldays* is a distinguished book, and though it is carefully not mentioned in *Stalky & Co.*, it is always there in the background. Kipling could not in fact have written his work without the precedent of *Tom Brown's Schooldays;* and *Stalky & Co.* may be described as both anti-*Tom Brown* and *Tom Brown* revived. Kipling may have had this in mind when he once referred to *Stalky & Co.* as a moral tract.

All ideals become corrupted in practice, by application to practical life, and the longer any practice persists unchanged, the more corrupt it will grow—this, incidentally, is one of the sounder arguments for the necessity of constant criticism and reform. By the late victorian period,—1875-1900—the high ideals of Arnold and *Tom Brown* had succeeded in penetrating and reforming much English thinking about school and school life. They had succeeded so well and had been so thoroughly assimilated that they seemed will on the way to turning into their own corrupt opposites. And the forms that cruelty, injustice, pettifogging, and hypocrisy take in *Stalky & Co.* are, by and large, the forms of corrupted victorian idealism. In such a context, the anti-*Tom Brown*ism of Stalky, M'Turk, and Beetle takes on meaning. The boys' disdain of organized games, their refusal to be moved by petitions in the name of "the honour of the house," their systematic flouting of appeals to their sense of moral decency and honesty (as in the "combined" work that goes on in their study), their contemptuous disregard for the entire prefectorial system, even their inconsistent anti-clericalism, are in considerable measure a result of their revulsion from what today we would call the phoniness into which these ideals and values had descended. That the boys are not opposed to these ideal in themselves, that their rebelliousness is in fact intuitively directed by their feeling for them, is among the major burdens of message which *Stalky & Co.* communicates. It is in this sense that we must think of it as a *Tom Brown* revived.

It should be clear by now that in *Stalky & Co.* we are faced with a moral situation of some complexity and probably of deep-seated contradiction. This situation is represented most forcefully in the variety of attitudes we find both in Kipling and the boys taking authority, and institutions—that is, institutional authority—and toward the social system which the institutions serve and whose nature they express. That a writer's attitude toward social and institutional authority should be complex, ambivalent, and even contradictory is no more than what we, in the modern world, have become accustomed to expect. But to find this attitude in Kipling may be something of a surprise, since the side of his writing that has drawn the most conspicuous attention in the last thirty years is the side that maintained a friendly or affirmative, not to say submissive, attitude toward authority. And if we use the word authority, then we must also use its derived form, authoritarian, for almost all criticism of Kipling boils down to the accusation of authoritarianism. That there is an impulse toward it and a streak of it in him, no open-minded reader will deny; but that this impulse is checked by other and opposite impulses which, working together, make for a condition of moral stress and ambiguity the open-minded reader will also see. Why these countering impulses should have been overlooked is an historical question of some complexity. The fact of their having been overlooked, however, may serve to indicate the distance that separates our own age and attitudes from Kipling's.

We find these attitudes represented in the boys' relations with the various masters and with the Head. The modern reader may find the open and mutual antagonism between the boys and masters disturbing because of the book's assumption that this antagonism is natural and proper, and because of the directness, intensity, and ferocity with which the antagonism is enacted on both sides. We don't believe in the propriety or inevitability of such antagonism today; we believe in the cooperative and conciliatory virtues, and distrust the powers of our own aggressiveness so thoroughly that we have almost forgotten how to deal with them—and in the forgetting we have, among other things, palpably increased the likelihood of the world's being blown up. In addition, we are troubled by the kind of freedom that a situation of outright and assumed hostility provides for both sides. All questions of fantasy notwithstanding, the free-wheeling aggressiveness and baiting by both boys and masters in *Stalky & Co.* would today undoubtedly be regarded as pathological conduct. And with a certain justness, for such behavior made sense only within a certain context. This "context" is the Head, and what he stands for. He represents, for both boys and masters, an authority which can be believed in and trusted. He is a court of appeal to which one resorts with faith, and a source of justice whose verdicts one accepts with trust. He represents experience humanized into wisdom, benevolent intelligence, and responsible power. We may think of him as a surrogate for God, as the perfect substitute father for all his orphaned charges, as the idealized voice of society—for he is all these, at least in the eyes of the boys. Whether he or anyone could ever actually embody such qualities and powers is not immediately to the point; what matters is that the boys believe he does, and that, through his conduct toward them, he is able to sustain their belief. Because of this he is able to sustain in them the belief that life itself has certain values, and that one's career in life may have as its legitimate purpose the extension and enlargement of those values.

With this we come to the secret life of *Stalky & Co.*, and to the secret which Kipling, like all distinguished writers about boyhood, has grasped. It is that boys live a life which is passionately moral. Half of the intensity, difficulty, and refractoriness of boys may be traced to the fact that their passionate moral demands on life seem, in the sad course of things, bound to be frustrated and betrayed. As the reader of *Stalky & Co.* will soon discover, boys are by nature moral casuists of genius; they are religious fanatics for justice, and the last true believers in the divinity of law. Boys slavishly worship tradition, blindly reverence ritual, and are the untamed partisans of precedent. They are individually and in aggregate the most naturally conservative, if not reactionary, social grouping—they *want* to believe in the doctrines and ideals that have been officially handed down to them. And we can, without exaggeration, say that every liberal or radical has within him a boy who once found out that "they" were telling him lies, who discovered hypocrisy, sloth, and double-dealing in his elders and superiors. The failure of conservatism has always been a moral failure.

This is not to say that boys devote all their time to inspecting each other's moral fingernails, or that they are not naturally disobedient and do not chafe at discipline and restrictions. That they are and do is written large on every page of *Stalky & Co.* Neither can one say that their ardent moral life can be approached directly and in morality's own terms. When Beetle once complains that King has been unfair, Stalky reproves him: "You've been here six years, and you expect fairness. Well, you *are* a dithering idiot." And after they have exacted retribution on the school bullies, Stalky dryly remarks, "If I knew anything about it, I swear I'd give you a moral lecture." Living in an age and atmosphere in which they have been shot at with moral bullets since infancy, the boys are preternaturally gun-shy of all the cheapened and canting terms of value. (The great creative genius of the Victorian age, Dickens, was almost unable to use the word "moral" in any but an ironic sense—so debased had its currency become.) When the Head chooses to punish the boys, he tells them he is about to perpetrate and howling and flagrant "injustice." Only in this way can he distinguish his moral decisions from those of the lesser masters, which are always of course "just.'" At a later moment he makes this characteristic distinction in regard to the boys' misbehavior: "I can connive at immorality, but I cannot stand impudence." Given the world of 1880, the Head can make sense only by standing these terms on their heads; and only a man who has the intelligence and courage to do that can reach the moral world in which boys live. Today a gifted teacher of youth would be forced to do something very similar with words like tolerance, cooperation, equality, getting along with the group, and love.

Kipling understood that the moral life of boys is at once extremely primitive and simple, and extremely sophisticated and complex. The virtues to which boys most avidly give themselves are the primitive, ancient, classical, masculine ones—what were known in the past as the heroic virtues. They boys in *Stalky & Co.* are being prepared for an arduous military life, and there is no mistaking the connection between their fantastic exploits at school and their heroic exploits on the Northwest frontier—such is clearly Kipling's intention. But we should realize that there is a heroism in *Stalky & Co.* superior to physical conquest and martial prowess, though it co-exists with them. By common consent, the most heroic deed in the book is the Head's saving of a boy's life by sucking the membranous film of diptheria from his throat. The point of such heroism is in its disregard of self, in its self-sacrifice. And we might recall that the ideal of self-sacrifice is not foreign to the soldierly tradition—at least in its older style. It was this ideal which moved Don Quixote to assert the superiority of the profession of arms to the profession of letters. By means of it we can account for the extraordinary affection in which the English still hold Nelson. It was this ideal that Ruskin—the same Ruskin read by M'Turk —had in mind when he declared that the soldier's trade is not slaying, but being slain. In an age like our own in which the military tradition has suffered a degradation which has put it almost beyond redemption, it might be useful to recall that in the past, intelligent men were able to see something noble and humane even in this most destructive mode of human behavior.

Yet these values and ideals, though they are a constant presence in the lives of the boys in *Stalky & Co.*, are never to be discussed, as we learn in the episode, "The Flag of their Country." There the brash, vulgar, and jingoistic Conservative Member of Parliament violates the reserve and offends the soul of every boy in the school by speaking about patriotism and waving the flag in their faces. "In a raucous voice he cried aloud little matters, like the hope of Honour and the dream of Glory, that boys do not discuss even with their most intimate equals; cheerfully assuming that, till he spoke, they had never considered these possibilities." The complexity and sophistication of the moral life which Kipling depicts in *Stalky & Co.* has to do with the fact that the values which inform it are precisely those which are never to be explicitly referred to—like the true name of God, they are too sacred to be spoken—except in parody, joke, or absolute understatement. "Don't you want to die for your giddy country?" M'Turk quizzes Stalky. "Not if I can jolly well avoid it," is the ritual answer.

This quality of indirectness leads us to observe that modern readers will find a certain obscurity and difficulty in reading this book. The obscurity exists in the speech of the boys and is a result of the fact that they speak elliptically and in code. All companies of boys have an argot, a lingo, a code by which they exclude others and help to identify themselves. The code of speech in *Stalky & Co.* is exceptional because of its severity, economy, and power of compression—with all of these attributes in Kipling's prose as well. The danger and weakness of any code is that it tends to become excessively limiting, rigid, and self-referring, and to exclude the user from large areas of experience. In *Stalky & Co.*, however, the code in which the boys speak resonates and is confluent with the life for which they are being trained and with its code. What used to be known as the life of an officer and a gentleman, was regulated by a strict and complex code. The mastery of this code of living is the object of the education described in this book. By means of it the boys were to learn, supposedly, to rule a vast, primitive colonial Empire, successfully and with relative decency; they were being taught to play what Kipling elsewhere called "the Great Game." The weaknesses of such a conception are manifest: To think of life as a Great Game is to run the risk of never growing up; it is also to run the risk of thinking that there are, in the end, winners and losers in life, a more subtle and profound moral danger. But the strengths of such a conception are too easily by-passed: If life is a Great Game, then there are certain rules of play or conduct which are not to be violated; to violate them is to do worse than lose—it is to put oneself out of consideration altogether. The history of the twentieth century has seen the steady attrition of this ideal; and one of the bitterest accomodations that thoughtful and feeling persons, especially young persons, have had to make is to a world in which this ideal possibility of human conduct is not merely violated and flouted, but made to seem irrelevant, foolish, and naive.

Kipling's consuming interest in a code of life brings us

finally to the two modern writers in whom his influence is largest—Ernest Hemingway and Isaac Babel. Both were permanently preoccupied with the heroic code; both took as their central concern the problem of how man is to confront with honor the tragic life of violence that has been his inescapable fate in modern civilization. Like Kipling, both were strongly involved with the life and ideals of boyhood, with conceptions of masculinity and manliness, and with adventures and the life out-of-doors, these latter, our twentieth century equivalents for the nineteenth century idea of nature. Both were deeply influenced by Kipling's style as well, with its incisive force, speed, and dramatic economy. Hemingway's indebtedness to Kipling is unmistakeable and important. Babel's is less well-known but in its way even more interesting.

In his "Reminiscences of Babel," the Russian writer Konstantin Paustovsky tells of their first meeting. It took place in Odessa, shortly after the Revolution. Paustovsky was working in the editorial offices of a magazine called *The Seaman* which had recently published one of Babel's stories. One day Babel was brought to the magazine's offices to meet the editors. He arrived carrying a volume of Kipling under his arm, which he put down on the table but kept looking at it impatiently throughout the polite general conversation. At the first opportunity, Paustovsky remarks, "Babel switched the conversation to Kipling. Writers, he said, should write in Kipling's iron-clad prose; authors should have the clearest possible notion of what was to come out of their pens. A short story must have the precision of a military communiqué or a bank check. It must be written in the same straightforward hand one uses for commands and checks. Kipling's hand was just like that." He then concluded with this unexpected statement. "Here in Odessa," he said with a note of irony, "we don't produce any Kiplings. We like a peaceful, easy life. But to make up for it, we'll have our home-grown Maupassants." He then left the office. Paustovsky watched him from the window. The moment Babel was out in the street, he "opened his Kipling and started to read as he went. Now and then he stopped to give passers-by a chance to go round him, but he never once raised his head to look at them."

It is, of course, a charming story. Babel's remarks about

Kipling are very much to the point, and the discrimination he makes between Kipling and Maupassant, and the choice implied in it, has the same kind of force that, in an earlier generation, Joseph Conrad's decision to write in English rather than French had. But there is something wonderfully ironic and apt about the entire incident. That Kipling, the arch-imperialist and reactionary, should wind up in the hands of a Russian-Jewish revolutionary writer is curious and paradoxical, though not unprecedented: Literary influence, fortunately, is not bound in by politics. But that the values of Kipling's prose style—and the moral values which that style embodies and implies—should be precisely the values Babel desired for his own radical and revolutionary writing cannot fail to be a surprise. But, when one thinks about it for a while, there is something very right about it all.

Glossary

Bargee: Slang for low or vulgar character, from bargeman, of the then numerous canal boats.

Blub: Weep.

Bob: A shilling, at that time equivalent to twenty-five cents.

B.O.P.: Boys' Own Paper. Weekly magazine for boys of school age, which ran adventure serials, stories of school life.

Bounds: Boundaries or limits set by the school. A boy going beyond these territorial limits would be breaking bounds, or out of bounds.

Brake: Horse-drawn open wagonette, or carriage.

Brew: v., To prepare private, or extra-institutional food.
  n., A brew—a meal of the same.

Brolly: Umbrella.

Bunk: Run for cover, bolt.

Call-over: Roll-call.

Cat: Vomit.

Cave: Look-out's call to beware, from the Latin *caveat.*

Common-Room: Dining and sitting room reserved for masters.

D.A.Q.M.G.: Deputy Assistant Quarter Master General.

Day-boy: Student living near enough to the school to attend classes and go home at night. Non-boarder.

Fag: v., To serve, run errands.
  n., Lower school boy, automatically at the orders of any senior.

First Fifteen: The school team. Rugby football has a fifteen man team.

Fives: Game played with racket and ball in an enclosed court—

netting on three sides, one solid wall, against which the ball was played, as in a squash court.

Form: Long, backless bench used in classrooms. Also, class or grade, senior or matriculating class being sixth form.

Form-room: Classroom.

Funk: n., State of fear, a coward.

v., To funk something, avoid it from fear.

Gated: Confined within school gates, i.e., within a drastically restricted set of bounds.

Gig-lamps: Spectacles.

Head of Games: Prefect in charge of sports.

Head of the School: Headmaster, or principal. Also used on the student level to describe the head prefect or head boy.

House: Pupils at boarding schools are usually divided among several houses, where they are under the direct supervision of a house-master, or senior teacher. The system of house separateness and/or competition varies in different schools but accounts for such terms as house prefect, house matches, honour of the house and so forth.

Impot: From imposition. Impot paper, ruled paper for writing lines, compositions.

Lines: Punitive task of copying a given number of Latin lines.

Lower School: The younger boys. The dividing age between the Lower and Upper School is usually fourteen, Upper School being the equivalent of High School.

Lictor: Bearer of the symbol of punitive authority. In Rome, the officials who preceeded the Consul on public occasions carrying the fasces.

Old Boys: Graduates of the school. Alumni.

Palladium: Safeguard (from Greek legend of an image of Pallas Athene on which Troy depended for safety).

Prefect: A senior boy appointed on merit to a position of considerable authority in school life, usually empowered to cane, and responsible under the masters for maintaining school discipline.

Prep: Preparation for next day's classes. Equivalent to homework.

Quod: Jail.

Side: Self-conceit.

Study: Private room shared by two or three Upper School boys, where they can spend their leisure, keep their possessions, and do their prep.

Stump: Cricket stump. One of the three upright stakes which mark the ends of the cricket pitch, guarded by the batsman.

Tertius: Third. Used to designate the third boy of the same family to attend the school, e.g., Smith Major, Smith Minor, Smith Tertius.

Tuck: Sweets, candy.

Twig: Understand.

Contents

"Let us now praise famous men"—
  Men of little showing—
For their work continueth,
And their work continueth,
  Greater than their knowing.

Western wind and open surge
  Tore us from our mothers;
Flung us on a naked shore
(Twelve bleak houses by the shore!)
Seven summers by the shore!)
  'Mid two hundred brothers.

There we met with famous men
  Set in office o'er us.
And they beat on us with rods—
Faithfully with many rods—
Daily beat us on with rods—
  For the love they bore us!

Out of Egypt unto Troy—
  Over Himalaya—
Far and sure our bands have gone—
Hy—Brasil or Babylon,
Islands of the Southern Run,
  And cities of Cathaia!

And we all praise famous men—
  Ancients of the College;
For they taught us common sense—
Tried to teach us common sense—
Truth and God's Own Common Sense
  Which is more than knowledge!

Each degree of Latitude
    Strung about Creation
Seeth one (or more) of us,
(Of one muster all of us—
Of one master all of us—)
    Keen in his vocation.

This we learned from famous men
    Knowing not its uses
When they showed in daily work
Man must finish off his work—
Right or wrong, his daily work—
    And without excuses.

Servants of the staff and chain,
    Mine and fuse and grapnel—
Some before the face of Kings,
Stand before the face of Kings;
Bearing gifts to divers Kings—
    Gifts of Case and Shrapnel.

This we learned from famous men
    Teaching in our borders.
Who declarèd it was best,
Safest, easiest, and best—
Expeditious, wise, and best—
    To obey your orders.

Some beneath the further stars
    Bear the greater burden.
Set to serve the lands they rule
(Save he serve no man may rule),

Serve and love the lands they rule,
   Seeking praise nor guerdon.

This we learned from famous men
   Knowing not we learned it.
Only, as the years went by—
Lonely, as the years went by—
Far from help as years went by
   Plainer we discerned it.

Wherefore praise we famous men
   From whose bays we borrow—
They that put aside To-day—
All the joys of their To-day—
And with toil of their To-day
   Bought for us To-morrow!

Bless and praise we famous men—
   Men of little showing!
For their work continueth
And their work continueth
Broad and deep continueth
   Great beyond their knowing!

"In Ambush"

IN SUMMER all right-minded boys built huts in the furze-hill behind the College—little lairs whittled out of the heart of the prickly bushes, full of stumps, odd root-ends, and spikes, but, since they were stricty forbidden, palaces of delight. And for the fifth summer in succession, Stalky, McTurk, and Beetle (this was before they reached the dignity of a study) had built like beavers a place of retreat and meditation, where they smoked.

Now, there was nothing in their characters as known to Mr. Prout, their house-master, at all commanding respect; nor did Foxy, the subtle red-haired school Sergeant, trust them. His business was to wear tennis-shoes, carry binoculars, and swoop hawk-like upon evil boys. Had he taken the field alone, that hut would have been raided, for Foxy knew the manners of his quarry; but Providence moved Mr. Prout, whose schoolname, derived from the size of his feet, was Hoofer, to investigate on his own account; and it was the cautious Stalky who found the track of his pugs on the very floor of their lair one peaceful afternoon when Stalky would fain have forgotten Prout and his works in a volume of Surtees and a new brierwood pipe. Crusoe, at sight of the footprint, did not act more swiftly than Stalky. He removed the pipes, swept up all loose match-ends, and departed to warn Beetle and McTurk.

But it was characteristic of the boy that he did not approach his allies till he had met and conferred with little Hartopp, President of the Natural History Society, an institution which Stalky held in contempt. Hartopp was more than surprised when the boy meekly, as he knew how, begged to propose himself, Beetle, and McTurk as candidates; confessed to a long-smothered interest in first-flowerings, and new arrivals, and volunteered, if Mr. Hartopp saw fit, to enter on the new life at once. Being a master, Hartopp was suspicious; but he was also an enthusiast, and his gentle little soul had been galled by chance-heard remarks from the three, and specially Beetle. So he was gracious to that repentant sinner, and entered the three names in his book.

Then, and not till then, did Stalky seek Beetle and McTurk in their house form-room. They were stowing away books for a quiet afternoon in the furze, which they called the "wuzzy."

"All up," said Stalky, serenely. "I spotted Heffy's fairy feet round our hut after dinner. 'Blessing they're so big."

"Con-found! Did you hide our pipes?" said Beetle.

"Oh, no. Left 'em in the middle of the hut, of course. What a blind ass you are, Beetle! D'you think nobody thinks but yourself? Well, we can't use the hut any more. Hoofer will be watchin' it."

" 'Bother! Likewise blow!' " said McTurk, thoughtfully, unpacking the volumes with which his chest was cased. The boys carried their libraries between their belt and their collar. "Nice job! This means we're under suspicion for the rest of the term."

"Why? All that Heffy has found is *a* hut. He and Foxy will watch it. It's nothing to do with us; only we mustn't be seen that way for a bit."

"Yes, and where else are we to go?" said Beetle. "You chose that place, too—an'—an' I wanted to read this afternoon."

Stalky sat on a desk drumming his heels on the form.

"You're a despondin' brute, Beetle. Sometimes I think I shall have to drop you altogether. Did you ever know your Uncle Stalky forget you yet? *His rebus infectis*—after I'd seen Heffy's mantracks marchin' round our hut, I found little Hartopp—*districto ense*—wavin' a butterfly-net. I conciliated Hartopp. 'Told him that you'd read papers to the Bug-hunters if he'd let you join, Beetle. 'Told him you liked butterflies, Turkey. Anyhow, I soothed the Hartoffles, and we're Bug-hunters now."

"What's the good of that?" said Beetle.

"Oh, Turkey, kick him!"

In the interest of science bounds were largely relaxed

for the members of the Natural History Society. They could wander, if they kept clear of all houses, practically where they chose; Mr. Hartopp holding himself responsible for their good conduct.

Beetle began to see this as McTurk began the kicking.

"I'm an ass, Stalky!" he said, guarding the afflicted part. *"Pax,* Turkey. I'm an ass."

"Don't stop, Turkey. Isn't your Uncle Stalky a great man?"

"Great man," said Beetle.

"All the same bug-huntin's a filthy business." said McTurk. "How the deuce does one begin?"

"This way," said Stalky, turning to some fags' lockers behind him. "Fags are dabs at Natural History. Here's young Braybrooke's botany-case." He flung out a tangle of decayed roots and adjusted the slide. " 'Gives one no end of a professional air, I think. Here's Clay Minor's geological hammer. Beetle can carry that. Turkey, you'd better covet a butterfly-net from somewhere."

"I'm blowed if I do," said McTurk, simply, with immense feeling. "Beetle, give me the hammer."

"All right. *I'm* not proud. Chuck us down that net on top of the lockers, Stalky."

"That's all right. It's a collapsible jamboree, too. Beastly luxurious dogs these fags are. Built like a fishin'-rod. 'Pon my sainted Sam, but we look the complete Bug-hunters! Now, listen to your Uncle Stalky! We're goin' along the cliffs after butterflies. Very few chaps come there. We're goin' to leg it, too. You'd better leave your book behind."

"Not much!" said Beetle, firmly. "I'm not goin' to be done out of my fun for a lot of filthy butterflies."

"Then you'll sweat horrid. You'd better carry my Jorrocks. 'Twon't make you any hotter."

They all sweated; for Stalky led them at a smart trot west away along the cliffs under the furze-hills, crossing combe after gorsy combe. They took no heed to flying rabbits or fluttering fritillaries, and all that Turkey said of geology was utterly unquotable.

"Are we going to Clovelly?" he puffed at last, and they

flung themselves down on the short, springy turf between the drone of the sea below and the light summer wind among the inland trees. They were looking into a combe half full of old, high furze in gay bloom that ran up to a fringe of brambles and a dense wood of mixed timber and hollies. It was as though one-half the combe were filled with golden fire to the cliff's edge. The side nearest to them was open grass, and fairly bristled with notice-boards.

"Fee-rocious old cove, this," said Stalky, reading the nearest. " 'Prosecuted with the utmost rigour of the law. G. M. Dabney, Col., J. P.,' an' all the rest of it. 'Don't seem to me that any chap in his senses would trespass here, does it?"

"You've got to prove damage 'fore you can prosecute for anything! 'Can't prosecute for trespass," said McTurk, whose father held many acres in Ireland. "That's all rot!"

"Glad of that, 'cause this looks like what we wanted. Not straight across, Beetle, you blind lunatic! Any one could spot us half a mile off. This way; and furl up your beastly butter-fly-net."

Beetle disconnected the ring, thrust the net into a pocket, shut up the handle to a two-foot stave, and slid the cane-ring round his waist. Stalky led inland to the wood, which was, perhaps, a quarter of a mile from the sea, and reached the fringe of the brambles.

"Now we can get straight down through the furze, and never show up at all," said the tactician. "Beetle, go ahead and explore. Snf! Snf! Beastly stink of fox somewhere!"

On all fours, save when he clung to his spectacles, Beetle wormed into the gorse, and presently announced between grunts of pain that he had found a very fair fox-track. This was well for Beetle, since Stalky pinched him a tergo. Down that tunnel they crawled. It was evidently a highway for the inhabitants of the combe; and to their inexpressible joy, ended, at the very edge of the cliff, in a few square feet of dry turf walled and roofed with impenetrable gorse.

"By gum! There isn't a single thing to do except lie down," said Stalky, returning a knife to his pocket. "Look here!"

He parted the tough stems before him, and it was as a

window opened on a far view of Lundy, and the deep sea sluggishly nosing the pebbles a couple of hundred feet below. They could hear young jackdaws squawking on the ledges, the hiss and jabber of a nest of hawks somewhere out of sight; and, with great deliberation, Stalky spat on to the back of a young rabbit sunning himself far down where only a cliff-rabbit could have found foothold. Great grey and black gulls screamed against the jackdaws; the heavy-scented acres of bloom round them were alive with low-nesting birds, singing or silent as the shadow of the wheeling hawks passed and returned; and on the naked turf across the combe rabbits thumped and frolicked.

"Whew! What a place! Talk of Natural History; this is it," said Stalky, filling himself a pipe. "Isn't it scrumptious? Good old sea!" He spat again approvingly, and was silent.

McTurk and Beetle had taken out their books and were lying on their stomachs, chin in hand. The sea snored and gurgled; the birds, scattered for the moment by these new animals, returned to their businesses, and the boys read on in the rich, warm, sleepy silence.

"Hullo, here's a keeper," said Stalky, shutting "Handley Cross" cautiously, and peering through the jungle. A man with a gun appeared on the sky-line to the east. "Confound him, he's going to sit down."

"He'd swear we were poachin', too," said Beetle. "What's the good of pheasants' eggs? They're always addled, too."

"Might as well get up to the wood, *I* think," said Stalky. "We don't want G. M. Dabney, Col., J. P., to be bothered about us so soon. Up the wuzzy and keep quiet! He may have followed us, you know."

Beetle was already far up the tunnel. They heard him gasp indescribably: there was the crash of a heavy body leaping through the furze.

"Aie! yeou little red rascal. I see yeou!" The keeper threw the gun to his shoulder, and fired both barrels in their direction. The pellets dusted the dry stems round them as a big fox plunged between Stalky's legs and ran over the cliff-edge.

They said nothing till they reached the wood, torn, dishevelled, hot, but unseen.

"Narrow squeak," said Stalky. "I'll swear some of the pellets went through my hair."

"Did you see him?" said Beetle. "I almost put my hand on him. Wasn't he a whopper! Didn't he stink! Hullo, Turkey, what's the matter? Are you hit?"

McTurk's lean face had turned pearly white; his mouth, generally half open, was tight shut, and his eyes blazed. They had never seen him like this save once in a sad time of civil war.

"Do you know that that was just as bad as murder?" he said, in a grating voice, as he brushed prickles from his head.

"Well, he didn't hit us," said Stalky. "I think it was rather a lark. Here, where are you going?"

"I'm going up to the house, if there is one," said McTurk, pushing through the hollies. "I am going to tell this Colonel Dabney."

"Are you crazy? He'll swear it served us jolly well right. He'll report us. It'll be a public lickin'. Oh, Turkey, don't be an ass! Think of us!"

"You fool!" said McTurk, turning savagely. "D'you suppose I'm thinkin' of *us*? It's the keeper."

"He's cracked," said Beetle, miserably, as they followed. Indeed, this was a new Turkey—a haughty, angular, nose-lifted Turkey—whom they accompanied through a shrubbery on to a lawn, where a white-whiskered old gentleman with a cleek was alternately putting and blaspheming vigorously.

"Are you Colonel Dabney?" McTurk began in this new creaking voice of his.

"I—I am, and—" his eyes travelled up and down the boy —"who—what the devil d'you want? Ye've been disturbing my pheasants. Don't attempt to deny it. Ye needn't laugh at it." (McTurk's not too lovely features had twisted themselves into a horrible sneer at the word pheasant.) "You've been bird's-nesting. You needn't hide your hat. I can see that you belong to the College. Don't attempt to deny it. Ye do! Your name and number at once, sir. Ye want to speak to me—

Eh? You saw my notice-boards? Must have. Don't attempt to deny it. Ye did! Damnable! Oh, damnable!"

He choked with emotion. McTurk's heel tapped the lawn and he stuttered a little—two sure signs that he was losing his temper. But why should he, the offender, be angry?

"Lo-look here, sir. Do—do you shoot foxes? Because, if you don't, your keeper does. We've seen him! I do-don't care what you call us—but it's an awful thing. It's the ruin of good feelin' among neighbours. A ma-man ought to say once and for all how he stands about preservin'. It's worse than murder, because there's no legal remedy." McTurk was quoting confusedly from his father, while the old gentleman made noises in his throat.

"Do you know who I am?" he gurgled at last; Stalky and Beetle quaking.

"No, sorr, nor do I care if ye belonged to the Castle itself. Answer me now, as one gentleman to another. Do ye shoot foxes or do ye not?"

And four years before Stalky and Beetle had carefully kicked McTurk out of his Irish dialect! Assuredly he had gone mad or taken a sunstroke, and as assuredly he would be slain—once by the old gentleman and once by the Head. A public licking for the three was the least they could expect. Yet—if their eyes and ears were to be trusted—the old gentleman had collapsed. It might be a lull before the storm, but—

"I do not." He was still gurgling.

"Then you must sack your keeper. He's not fit to live in the same county with a God-fearin' fox. An' a vixen, too—at this time o' year!"

"Did ye come up on purpose to tell me this?"

"Of course I did, ye silly man," with a stamp of the foot. "Would you not have done as much for me if you'd seen that thing happen on my land, now?"

Forgotten—forgotten was the College and the decency due to elders! McTurk was treading again the barren purple mountains of the rainy West coast, where in his holidays he was viceroy of four thousand naked acres, only son of a three-hundred-year-old house, lord of a crazy fishing-boat, and the idol of his father's shiftless tenantry. It was the landed man speaking to his equal—deep calling to deep—and the old gentleman acknowledged the cry.

"I apologise," said he. "I apologise unreservedly—to you, and to the Old Country. Now, will you be good enough to tell me your story?"

"We were in your combe," McTurk began, and he told his tale alternately as a schoolboy and, when the iniquity of the thing overcame him, as an indignant squire; concluding: "So you see he must be in the habit of it. I—we—one never wants to accuse a neighbour's man; but I took the liberty in this case—"

"I see. Quite so. For a reason ye had. Infamous—oh, infamous!" The two had fallen into step beside each other on the lawn, and Colonel Dabney was talking as one man to another. "This comes of promoting a fisherman—a fisherman —from his lobster-pots. It's enough to ruin the reputation of an archangel. Don't attempt to deny it. It is! Your father has brought you up well. He has. I'd much like the pleasure of his acquaintance. Very much, indeed. And these young gentlemen? English they are. Don't attempt to deny it. They came up with you, too? Extraordinary! Extraordinary, now! In the present state of education I shouldn't have thought any three boys would be well enough grounded. . . . But out of the mouths of—No—no! Not that by any odds. Don't attempt to deny it. Ye're not! Sherry always catches me under the liver, but—beer, now? Eh? What d'you say to beer, and something to eat? It's long since I was a boy—abominable nuisances; but exceptions prove the rule. And a vixen, too!"

They were fed on the terrace by a grey-haired housekeeper. Stalky and Beetle merely ate, but McTurk with bright eyes continued a free and lofty discourse; and ever the old gentleman treated him as a brother.

"My dear man, of *course* ye can come again. Did I not say exceptions prove the rule? The lower combe? Man, dear, anywhere ye please, so long as you do not disturb my pheasants. The two are not incompatible. Don't attempt to deny it.

They're not! I'll never allow another gun, though. Come and go as ye please. I'll not see you, and ye needn't see me. Ye've been well brought up. Another glass of beer, now? I tell you a fisherman he was a fisherman he shall be to-night again. He shall! Wish I could drown him. I'll convoy you to the Lodge. My people are not precisely—ah—broke to boy, but they'll know *you* again."

He dismissed them with many compliments by the high Lodge-gate in the split-oak park palings, and they stood still; even Stalky, who had played second, not to say a dumb, fiddle, regarding McTurk as one from another world. The two glasses of strong home-brewed had brought a melancholy upon the boy, for, slowly strolling with his hands in his pockets, he crooned:—"Oh, Paddy dear, and did ye hear the news that's goin' round?"

Under other circumstances Stalky and Beetle would have fallen upon him, for that song was barred utterly—anathema —the sin of witchcraft. But seeing what he had wrought, they danced round him in silence, waiting till it pleased him to touch earth.

The tea-bell rang when they were still half a mile from College. McTurk shivered and came out of dreams. The glory of his holiday estate had left him. He was a Colleger of the College, speaking English once more.

"Turkey, it was immense!" said Stalky, generously. "I didn't know you had it in you. You've got us a hut for the rest of the term, where we simply *can't* be collared. Fids! Fids! Oh, Fids! I gloat! Hear me gloat!"

They spun wildly on their heels, jodelling after the accepted manner of a "gloat," which is not unremotely allied to the primitive man's song of triumph, and dropped down the hill by the path from the gasometer just in time to meet their housemaster, who had spent the afternoon watching their abandoned hut in the "wuzzy."

Unluckily, all Mr. Prout's imagination leaned to the darker side of life, and he looked on those young-eyed cherubims most sourly. Boys that he understood attended housematches and could be accounted for at any moment. But he had heard McTurk openly deride cricket—even house-matches; Beetle's views on the honour of the house he knew were incendiary; and he could never tell when the soft and smiling Stalky was laughing at him. Consequently—since human nature is what it is—those boys had been doing wrong somewhere. He hoped it was nothing very serious, but . . .

"*Ti-ra-la-la-i-tu!* I gloat! Hear me!" Stalky, still on his heels, whirled like a dancing dervish to the dining-hall.

"*Ti-ra-la-la-i-tu!* I gloat! Hear me!" Beetle spun behind him with outstretched arms.

"*Ti-ra-la-la-i-tu!* I gloat! Hear me!" McTurk's voice cracked.

Now was there or was there not a distinct flavour of beer as they shot past Mr. Prout?

He was unlucky in that his conscience as a house-master impelled him to consult his associates. Had he taken his pipe and his troubles to little Hartopp's rooms he would, perhaps, have been saved confusion, for Hartopp believed in boys, and knew something about them. His fate led him to King, a fellow house-master, no friend of his, but a zealous hater of Stalky & Co.

"Ah-haa!" said King, rubbing his hands when the tale was told. "Curious! Now *my* house never dreamed of doing these things."

"But you see I've no proof, exactly."

"Proof? With the egregious Beetle! As if one wanted it! I suppose it is not impossible for the Sergeant to supply it? Foxy is considered at least a match for any evasive boy in my house. Of course they were smoking and drinking somewhere. That type of boy always does. They think it manly."

"But they've no following in the school, and they are distinctly—er—brutal to their juniors," said Prout, who had from a distance seen Beetle return, with interest, his butterfly-net to a tearful fag.

"Ah! They consider themselves superior to ordinary delights. Self-sufficient little animals! There's something in Mc-Turk's Hibernian sneer that would make *me* a little annoyed. And they are so careful to avoid all overt acts, too. It's sheer calculated insolence. I am strongly opposed, as you know, to interfering with another man's house; but they need a lesson, Prout. They need a sharp lesson, if only to bring down their overweening self-conceit. Were I you, I should devote myself for a week to their little performancs. Boys of that order—and I may flatter myself, but I think I know boys—don't join the Bug-hunters for love. Tell the Sergeant to keep his eye open; and, of course, in my peregrinations I may casually keep mine open, too."

"*Ti-ra-la-la-i-tu!* I gloat! Hear me!" far down the corridor.

"Disgusting!" said King. "Where do they pick up these obscene noises? One sharp lesson is what they want."

The boys did not concern themselves with lessons for the next few days. They had all Colonel Dabney's estate to play with, and they explored it with the stealth of Red Indians and the accuracy of burglars. They could enter either by the Lodge-gates on the upper road—they were careful to ingratiate themselves with the Lodge-keeper and his wife—drop down into the combe, and return along the cliffs; or they could begin at the combe, and climb up into the road.

They were careful not to cross the Colonel's path—he had served his turn, and they would not outwear their welcome—nor did they show up on the sky-line when they could move in cover. The shelter of the gorse by the cliff-edge was their chosen retreat. Beetle christened it the Pleasant Isle of Aves, for the peace and the shelter of it; and here, the pipes and tobacco once cachéd in a convenient ledge an arm's length down the cliff, their position was legally unassailable.

For, observe, Colonel Dabney had not invited them to enter his house. Therefore, they did not need to ask specific leave to go visiting; and school rules were strict on that point. He had merely thrown open his grounds to them; and, since they were lawful Bug-hunters, their extended bounds ran up to his notice-boards in the combe and his Lodge-gates on the hill.

They were amazed at their own virtue.

"And even if it wasn't," said Stalky, flat on his back, staring into the blue. "Even suppose we were miles out of bounds, no one could get at us through this wuzzy, unless he knew the tunnel. Isn't this better than lyin' up just behind the Coll—in a blue funk every time we had a smoke? Isn't your Uncle Stalky—"

"No," said Beetle—he was stretched at the edge of the cliff spitting thoughtfully. "We've got to thank Turkey for this. Turkey is the Great Man. Turkey, dear, you're distressing Heffles."

"Gloomy old ass!" said McTurk, deep in a book.

"They've got us under suspicion," said Stalky. "Hoophats *is* so suspicious somehow; and Foxy always makes every stalk he does a sort of—sort of—"

"Scalp," said Beetle. "Foxy's a giddy Chingangook."

"Poor Foxy," said Stalky. "He's goin' to catch us one of these days. 'Said to me in the Gym last night, 'I've got my eye on you, Mister Corkran. I'm only warning you for your good.' Then I said: 'Well, you jolly well take it off again, or you'll get into trouble. I'm only warnin' you for your good.' Foxy was wrath."

"Yes, but it's only fair sport for Foxy," said Beetle. "It's Hefflelinga that has the evil mind. 'Shouldn't wonder if he thought we got tight."

"I never got squiffy but once—that was in the holidays," said Stalky, reflectively; "an' it made me horrid sick. 'Pon my sacred Sam, though, it's enough to drive a man to drink, havin' an animal like Hoof for house-master."

"If we attended the matches an' yelled, 'Well hit, sir,' an' stood on one leg an' grinned every time Heffy said, 'So ho, my sons. Is it thus?' an' said, 'Yes, sir,' an' 'No, sir,' an' 'O, sir,' an' 'Please, sir,' like a lot o' filthy fa-ags, Heffy 'ud think no end of us," said McTurk, with a sneer.

"Too late to begin that."

"It's all right. The Hefflelinga means well. *But* he is an ass. *And* we show him that we think he's an ass. An' *so* Heffy don't love us. 'Told me last night after prayers that he was *in loco parentis*," Beetle grunted.

"The deuce he did!" cried Stalky. "That means he's ma-turin' something unusual dam' mean. Last time he told me that he gave me three hundred lines for dancin' the cachucha in Number Ten dormitory. *Loco parentis,* by gum! But what's the odds as long as you're 'appy? *We're* all right."

They were, and their very rightness puzzled Prout, King, and the Sergeant. Boys with bad consciences show it. They slink out past the Fives Court in haste, and smile nervously when questioned. They return, disordered, in bare time to save a call-over. They nod and wink and giggle one to the other, scattering at the approach of a master. But Stalky and his allies had long outlived these manifestations of youth. They strolled forth unconcernedly, and returned in excellent shape after a light refreshment of strawberries and cream at the Lodge.

The Lodge-keeper had been promoted to keeper, *vice* the murderous fisherman, and his wife made much of the boys. The man, too, gave them a squirrel, which they presented to the Natural History Society; thereby checkmating little Hartopp, who wished to know what they were doing for Science. Foxy faithfully worked some deep Devon lanes behind a lonely cross-roads inn; and it was curious that Prout and King, members of Common-room seldom friendly, walked together in the same direction—that is to say, north-east. Now, the Pleasant Isle of Aves lay due southwest.

"They're deep—day-vilish deep," said Stalky. "Why are they drawin' those covers?"

"Me," said Beetle, sweetly. "I asked Foxy if he had ever tasted the beer there. That was enough for Foxy, and it cheered him up a little. He and Heffy were sniffin' round our old hut so long I thought they'd like a change."

"Well, it can't last for ever," said Stalky. "Heffy's bankin' up like a thunder-cloud, an' King goes rubbin' his beastly hands, an' grinnin' like a hyena. It's shockin' demoralisin' for King. He'll burst some day."

That day came a little sooner than they expected—came when the Sergeant, whose duty it was to collect defaulters, did not attend an afternoon call-over.

"Tired of pubs, eh? He's gone up to the top of the hill with his binoculars to spot us," said Stalky. "Wonder he didn't think of that before. Did you see old Heffy cock his eye at us when we answered our names? Heffy's in it, too. *Ti-ra-la-la-i-tu!* I gloat! Hear me! Come on!"

"Aves?" said Beetle.

"Of course, but I'm not smokin' *aujourd'hui*. *Parce que je* jolly well *pense* that we'll be *suivi*. We'll go along the cliffs, slow, an' give Foxy lots of time to parallel us up above."

They strolled towards the swimming-baths, and presently overtook King.

"Oh, don't let *me* interrupt you," he said. "Engaged in scientific pursuits, of course? I trust you will enjoy yourselves, my young friends."

"You see!" said Stalky, when they were out of ear-shot. "He *can't* keep a secret. He's followin' to cut off our line of retreat. He'll wait at the baths till Heffy comes along. They've tried every blessed place except along the cliffs, and now they think they've bottled us. No need to hurry."

They walked leisurely over the combes till they reached the line of notice-boards.

"Listen a shake. Foxy's up wind comin' downhill like beans. When you hear him move in the bushes, go straight across to Aves. They want to catch us *flagrante delicto*."

They dived into the gorse at right angles to the tunnel, openly crossing the grass, and lay still in Aves.

"What did I tell you?" Stalky carefully put away the pipes and tobacco. The Sergeant, out of breath, was leaning against the fence, raking the furze with his binoculars, but he might as well have tried to see through a sand-bag. Anon, Prout and King appeared behind him. They conferred.

"Aha! Foxy don't like the notice-boards, and he don't like the prickles either. Now we'll cut up the tunnel and go to the Lodge. Hullo! They've sent Foxy into cover."

The Sergeant was waist-deep in crackling, swaying furze, his ears filled with the noise of his own progress. The boys reached the shelter of the wood, and looked down through a belt of hollies.

"Hellish noise!" said Stalky, critically. " 'Don't think Colonel Dabney will like it. I move we go into the Lodge and get something to eat. We might as well see the fun out."

Suddenly the keeper passed them at a trot.

"Who'm they to combe-bottom for Lard's sake? Master'll be crazy," he said.

"Poachers simly," Stalky replied in the broad Devon that was the boy's *langue de guerre.*

"I'll poach 'em to raights!" He dropped into the funnel-like combe, which presently began to fill with noises, notably King's voice crying: "Go on, Sergeant! Leave him alone, you, sir. He is executing *my* orders."

"Who'm yeou to give arders here, gingy whiskers? Yeou come up to the master. Come out o' that wuzzy! [This is to the Sergeant.] Yiss, I reckon us knows the boys yeou'm after. They've tu long ears an' vuzzy bellies, an' you nippies they in yeour pockets when they'm dead. Come on up to master! He'll boy yeou all yeou'm a mind to. Yeou other folk bide your side fence."

"Explain to the proprietor. You can explain, Sergeant," shouted King. Evidently the Sergeant had surrendered to the major force.

Beetle lay at full length on the turf behind the Lodge, literally biting the earth in spasms of joy.

Stalky kicked him upright. There was nothing of levity about Stalky or McTurk save a stray muscle twitching on the cheek.

They tapped at the Lodge-door, where they were always welcome.

"Come yeou right in an' set down, my little dearrs," said the woman. "They'll niver touch my man. He'll poach 'em to rights. Iss fai! Fresh berries an' cream. Us Dartymoor folk niver forgit their friends. But them Bidevor poachers, they've no hem to their garments. Sugar? My man he've digged a badger for yeou, my dearrs. 'Tis in the linhay in a box."

"Us'll take un with us when we'm finished here. I reckon yeou'm busy. We'll bide here an'—'tis washin' day with yeou, simly," said Stalky. "We'm no company to make all vitty for. Never yeou mind us. Yiss. There's plenty cream."

The woman withdrew, wiping her pink hands on her apron, and left them in the parlor. There was a scuffle of feet on

the gravel outside the heavily leaded diamond panes, and
then the voice of Colonel Dabney, something clearer than
a bugle.

"Ye can read? You've eyes in your head? Don't attempt
to deny it. Ye have!"

Beetle snatched a crochet-work antimacassar from the
shiny horsehair sofa, stuffed it into his mouth, and rolled
out of sight.

"You saw my notice-boards. Your duty? Curse your impudence, sir. Your duty was to keep off my grounds. Talk
of duty to *me!* Why—why—why, ye misbegotten poacher,
ye'll be teachin' me my A B C next! Roarin' like a bull in
the bushes down there! Boys? Boys? Boys? Keep your boys
at home, then! *I'm* not responsible for your boys! But I don't
believe it—I don't believe a word of it. Ye've a furtive look
in your eye—a furtive, sneakin', poachin' look in your eye,
that 'ud ruin the reputation of an archangel! Don't attempt
to deny it! Ye have! A sergeant? More shame to you, then,
an' the worst bargain Her Majesty ever made! A sergeant, to
run about the country poachin'—on your pension! Damnable!
Oh, damnable! But I'll be considerate. I'll be merciful! By gad,
I'll be the very essence o' humanity! Did ye, or did ye not,
see my notice-boards? Don't attempt to deny it! Ye did. Silence,
Sergeant!"

Twenty-one years in the army had left their mark on Foxy.
He obeyed.

"Now. March!"

The high Lodge-gate shut with a clang. "My duty! A
sergeant to tell me my duty!" puffed Colonel Dabney. "Good
Lard! more sergeants!"

"It's King! It's King!" gulped Stalky, his head on the
horsehair pillow. McTurk was eating the rag-carpet before
the speckless hearth, and the sofa heaved to the emotions of
Beetle. Through the thick glass the figures without showed
blue, distorted, and menacing.

"I—I protest against this outrage." King had evidently
been running uphill. "The man was entirely within his duty.
Let—let me give you my card."

"He's in flannels!" Stalky buried his head again.

"Unfortunately—*most* unfortunately—I have not one with me, but my name is King, sir, a house-master of the College, and you will find me prepared—fully prepared—to answer for this man's action. We've seen three—"

"*Did* ye see my notice-boards?"

"I admit we did; but under the circumstances—"

"I stand *in loco parentis.*" Prout's deep voice was added to the discussion. They could hear him pant.

"F'what?" Colonel Dabney was growing more and more Irish.

"I'm responsible for the boys under my charge."

"Ye are, are ye? Then all I can say is that ye set them a very bad example—a dam' bad example, if I may say so. I do not own your boys. I've not seen your boys, an' I tell you that if there was a boy grinnin' in every bush on the place, *still* ye've no shadow of a right here, comin' up from the combe that way, an' frightenin' everything in it. Don't attempt to deny it. Ye did. Ye should have come to the Lodge an' seen me like Christians, instead of chasin' your dam' boys through the length and breadth of my covers. *In loco parentis* ye are? Well, I've not forgotten my Latin either, an' I'll say to you: '*Quis custodiet ipsos custodes.*' If the masters trespass, how can we blame the boys?"

"But if I could speak to you privately," said Prout.

"I'll have nothing private with you! Ye can be as private as ye please on the other side o' that gate an'—I wish ye a very good afternoon."

A second time the gate clanged. They waited till Colonel Dabney had returned to the house, and fell into one another's arms, crowing for breath.

"Oh, my Soul! Oh, my King! Oh, my Heffy! Oh, my Foxy! Zeal, all zeal, Mr. Simple." Stalky wiped his eyes. "Oh! Oh! Oh!—'I *did* boil the exciseman!' We must get out of this or we'll be late for tea."

"Ge-ge-get the badger and make little Hartopp happy. Ma-ma-make 'em all happy," sobbed McTurk, groping for the door and kicking the prostrate Beetle before him.

They found the beast in an evil-smelling box, left two half-crowns for payment, and staggered home. Only the badger grunted most marvellous like Colonel Dabney, and they dropped him twice or thrice with shrieks of helpless laughter. They were but imperfectly recovered when Foxy met them by the Fives Court with word that they were to go up to their dormitory and wait till sent for.

"Well, take this box to Mr. Hartopp's rooms, then. We've done something for the Natural History Society, at any rate," said Beetle.

"'Fraid that won't save you, young gen'elmen," Foxy answered, in an awful voice. He was sorely ruffled in his mind.

"All sereno, Foxibus." Stalky had reached the extreme stage of hiccups. "We—we'll never desert you, Foxy. Hounds choppin' foxes in cover is more a proof of vice, ain't it? . . . No, you're right. I'm—I'm not quite well."

"They've gone a bit too far this time," Foxy thought to himself. "Very far gone, *I'd* say, excep' there was no smell of liquor. An' yet it isn't like 'em—somehow. King and Prout they 'ad their dressin'-down same as me. That's one comfort."

"Now, we must pull up," said Stalky, rising from the bed on which he had thrown himself. "We're injured innocence —as usual. *We* don't know what we've been sent up here for, do we?"

"No explanation. Deprived of tea. Public disgrace before the house," said McTurk, whose eyes were running over. "It's dam' serious."

"Well, hold on, till King loses his temper," said Beetle. "He's a libellous old rip, an' he'll be in a ravin' paddywhack. Prout's too beastly cautious. Keep your eye on King, and, if he gives us a chance, appeal to the Head. That always makes 'em sick."

They were summoned to their house-master's study, King and Foxy supporting Prout, and Foxy had three canes under his arm. King leered triumphantly, for there were tears, undried tears of mirth, on the boys' cheeks. Then the examination began.

Yes, they had walked along the cliffs. Yes, they had entered Colonel Dabney's grounds. Yes, they had seen the notice-boards (at this point Beetle sputtered hysterically). For what purpose had they entered Colonel Dabney's grounds? "Well, sir, there was a badger."

Here King, who loathed the Natural History Society because he did not like Hartopp, could no longer be restrained. He begged them not to add mendacity to open insolence. But the badger was in Mr. Hartopp's rooms, sir. The Sergeant had kindly taken it up for them. That disposed of the badger, and the temporary check brought King's temper to boiling-point. They could hear his foot on the floor while Prout prepared his lumbering inquiries. They had settled into their stride now. Their eyes ceased to sparkle; their faces were blank; their hands hung beside them without a twitch. They were learning, at the expense of a fellow-countryman, the lesson of their race, which is to put away all emotion and entrap the alien at the proper time.

So far good. King was importing himself more freely into the trial, being vengeful where Prout was grieved. They knew the penalties of trespassing? With a fine show of irresolution, Stalky admitted that he had gathered some information vaguely bearing on this head, but he thought—The sentence was dragged out to the uttermost: Stalky did not wish to play his trump with such an opponent. Mr. King desired no buts, nor was he interested in Stalky's evasions. They, on the other hand, might be interested in his poor views. Boys who crept—who sneaked—who lurked—out of bounds, even the generous bounds of the Natural History Society, which they had falsely joined as a cloak for their misdeeds—their vices—their villainies—their immoralities—

"He'll break cover in a minute," said Stalky to himself. "Then we'll run into him before he gets away."

Such boys, scabrous boys, moral lepers—the current of his words was carrying King off his feet—evil-speakers, liars, slow-bellies—yea, incipient drunkards . . .

He was merely working up to a peroration, and the boys knew it; but McTurk cut through the frothing sentence, the others echoing:

"I appeal to the Head, sir."

"I appeal to the Head, sir."

"I appeal to the Head, sir."

It was their unquestioned right. Drunkenness meant expulsion after a public flogging. They had been accused of it. The case was the Head's, and the Head's alone.

"Thou hast appealed unto Cæsar: unto Cæsar shalt thou go." They had heard that sentence once or twice before in their careers. "None the less," said King, uneasily, "you would be better advised to abide by our decision, my young friends."

"Are we allowed to associate with the rest of the school till we see the Head, sir?" said McTurk to his house-master, disregarding King. This at once lifted the situation to its loftiest plane. Moreover, it meant no word, for moral leprosy was strictly quarantined, and the Head never executed judgment till twenty-four cold hours later.

"Well—er—if you persist in your defiant attitude," said King, with a loving look at the canes under Foxy's arm. "There is no alternative."

Ten minutes later the news was over the whole school. Stalky & Co. had fallen at last—fallen by drink. They had been drinking. They had returned blind-drunk from a hut. They were even now lying hopelessly intoxicated on the dormitory floor. A few bold spirits crept up to look, and received boots about the head from the criminals.

"We've got him—got him on the Caudine Toasting-Fork!" said Stalky, after those hints were taken. "King'll have to prove his charges up to the giddy hilt."

"Too much ticklee, him bust," Beetle quoted from a book of his reading. "Didn't I say he'd go pop if we lat un bide?"

"No prep., either, O ye incipient drunkards," said McTurk, "and it's trig night, too. Hullo! Here's our dear friend Foxy. More tortures, Foxibus?"

"I've brought you something to eat, young gentlemen," said the Sergeant from behind a crowded tray. Their wars had ever been waged without malice, and a suspicion floated in Foxy's mind that boys who allowed themselves to be tracked so easily might, perhaps, hold something in reserve. Foxy had served through the Mutiny, when early and accurate information was worth much.

"I—I noticed you 'adn't 'ad anything to eat, an' I spoke to Gumbly, an' he said you wasn't exactly cut off from supplies. So I brought up this. It's your potted 'am tin, ain't it, Mr. Corkran?"

"Why, Foxibus, you're a brick," said Stalky. "I didn't think you had this much—what's the word, Beetle?"

"Bowels," Beetle replied promptly. "Thank you, Sergeant. That's young Carter's potted ham, though."

"There was a C on it. I thought it was Mr. Corkran's. This is a very serious business, young gentlemen. That's what it is. I didn't know, perhaps, but there might be something on your side which you hadn't said to Mr. King or Mr. Prout, maybe."

"There is. Heaps, Foxibus." This from Stalky through a full mouth.

"Then you see, if that was the case, it seemed to me I might represent it, quiet so to say, to the 'Ead when he asks me about it. I've got to take 'im the charges to-night, an'—it looks bad on the face of it."

" 'Trocious bad, Foxy. Twenty-seven cuts in the Gym before all the school, and public expulsion. 'Wine is a mocker, strong drink is ragin',' " quoth Beetle.

"It's nothin' to make fun of, young gentlemen. I 'ave to go to the 'Ead with the charges. An'—an' you mayn't be aware, per'aps, that I was followin' you this afternoon; havin my suspicions."

"Did ye see the notice-boards?" croaked McTurk, in the very brogue of Colonel Dabney.

"Ye've eyes in your head. Don't attempt to deny it. Ye did!" said Beetle.

" A sergeant! To run about poachin' on your pension! Damnable! Oh, damnable!" said Stalky, without pity.

"Good Lord!" said the Sergeant, sitting heavily upon a bed. "Where—where the devil *was* you? I might ha' known it was a do—somewhere."

"Oh, you clever maniac!" Stalky resumed. "We mayn't be aware you were followin' us this afternoon, mayn't we? 'Thought you were stalkin' us, eh? Why, we led you bung into it, of course. Colonel Dabney—don't you think he's a nice man, Foxy?—Colonel Dabney's our pet particular friend. We've been goin' there for weeks and weeks. He invited us. You and your duty! Curse your duty, sir! Your duty was to keep off his covers."

"You'll never be able to hold up your head again, Foxy. The fags'll hoot at you," said Beetle. "Think of your giddy prestige!"

The Sergeant was thinking—hard.

"Look 'ere, young gentlemen," he said earnestly. "You aren't surely ever goin' to tell, are you? Wasn't Mr. Prout and Mr. King in—in it too?"

"Foxibusculus, they *was*. They was—singular horrid. Caught it worse than you. We heard every word of it. You got off easy, considerin'. If I'd been Dabney I swear I'd ha' quodded you. I think I'll suggest it to him to-morrow."

"An' it's all goin' up to the 'Ead. Oh, Good Lord!"

"Every giddy word of it, my Chingangook," said Beetle, dancing. "Why shouldn't it? *We've* done nothing wrong. *We* ain't poachers. *We* didn't cut about blastin' the characters of poor, innocent boys—sayin' they were drunk."

"That I didn't," said Foxy. "I—I only said that you be-'aved uncommon odd when you come back with that badger. Mr. King may have taken the wrong hint from that."

" 'Course he did; an' he'll jolly well shove all the blame on you when he finds out he's wrong. We know King, if you don't. I'm ashamed of you. You ain't fit to be a sergeant," said McTurk.

"Not with three thorough-goin' young devils like you, I ain't. I've been had. I've been ambuscaded. Horse, foot, an' guns, I've been had, an'—an' there'll be no holdin' the junior forms after this. M'r'over, the 'Ead will send me with a note to Colonel Dabney to ask if what you say about bein' invited was true."

"Then you'd better go in by the Lodge-gates this time,

instead of chasin' your dam' boys—oh that was the Epistle
to King—so it was. We-el, Foxy? Stalky put his chin on his
hands and regarded the victim with deep delight.

"*Ti-ra-la-la-i-tu!* I gloat! Hear me!" said McTurk. "Foxy
brought us tea when we were moral lepers. Foxy has a heart.
Foxy has been in the Army, too."

"I wish I'd ha' had you in my company, young gentlemen,"
said the Sergeant from the depths of his heart; "I'd ha' given
you something."

"Silence at drum-head court-martial," McTurk went on.
"I'm advocate for the prisoner; and, besides, this is much too
good to tell all the other brutes in the Coll. They'd *never*
understand. They play cricket, and say: 'Yes, sir,' and 'O,
sir,' and 'No, sir.' "

"Never mind that. Go ahead," said Stalky.

"Well, Foxy's a good little chap when he does not esteem
himself so as to be clever."

" 'Take not out your 'ounds on a werry windy day,' "
Stalky struck in. "*I* don't care if you let him off."

"Nor me," said Beetle. "Heffy is my only joy—Heffy and
King."

"I 'ad to do it," said the Sergeant, plaintively.

"Right, O! Led away by bad companions in the execution
of his duty or—or words to that effect. You're dismissed with
a reprimand, Foxy. *We* won't tell about *you*. I swear we
won't," McTurk concluded. "Bad for the discipline of the
school. Horrid bad."

"Well," said the Sergeant, gathering up the tea-things,
"knowin' what I know o' the young dev—gentlemen of the
College, I'm very glad to 'ear it. But what am I to tell the
'Ead?"

"Anything you jolly well please, Foxy. *We* aren't the
criminals."

To say that the Head was annoyed when the Sergeant appeared after dinner with the day's crime-sheet would be
putting it mildly.

"Corkran, McTurk & Co., I see. Bounds as usual. Hullo!

What the deuce is this? Suspicion of drinking. Whose charge?"

"Mr. King's, sir. I caught 'em out of bounds, sir; at least that was 'ow it looked. But there's a lot be'ind, sir." The Sergeant was evidently troubled.

"Go on," said the Head. "Let us have your version.

He and the Sergeant had dealt with one another for some seven years; and the Head knew that Mr. King's statements depended very largely on Mr. King's temper.

"I thought they were out of bounds along the cliffs. But it come out they wasn't, sir. I saw them go into Colonel Dabney's woods, and—Mr. King and Mr. Prout come along —and—the fact was, sir, we was mistook for poachers by Colonel Dabney's people—Mr. King and Mr. Prout and me. There was some words, sir, on both sides. The young gentlemen slipped 'ome somehow, and they seemed 'ighly humorous, sir. Mr. King was mistook by Colonel Dabney himself—Colonel Dabney bein' strict. Then they preferred to come straight to you, sir, on account of what—what Mr. King may 'ave said about their 'abits afterwards in Mr. Prout's study. I only said they was 'ighly humorous, laughin' and gigglin,' an' a bit above 'emselves. They've since told me, sir, in a humorous way, that they was invited by Colonel Dabney to go into 'is woods."

"I see. They didn't tell their house-master that, of course."

"They took up Mr. King on appeal just as soon as he spoke about their—'abits. Put in the appeal at once, sir, an' asked to be sent to the dormitory waitin' for you. I've since gathered, sir, in their humorous way, sir, that some'ow or other they've 'eard about every word Colonel Dabney said to Mr. King and Mr. Prout when he mistook 'em for poachers. I—I might ha' known when they led me on so that they 'eld the inner line of communications. It's—it's a plain do, sir, if you ask me; an' they're gloatin' over it in the dormitory."

The Head saw—saw even to the uttermost farthing—and his mouth twitched a little under his moustache.

"Send them to me at once, Sergeant. This case needn't wait over."

"Good evening," said he when the three appeared under escort. "I want your undivided attention for a few minutes. You've known me for five years, and I've known you for— twenty-five. I think we understand one another perfectly. I am now going to pay you a tremendous compliment (the brown one, please, Sergeant. Thanks. You needn't wait). I'm going to execute you without rhyme, Beetle, or reason. I know you went to Colonel Dabney's covers because you were invited. I'm not even going to send the Sergeant with a note to ask if your statement is true; because I am convinced that on this occasion you have adhered strictly to the truth. I know, too, that you were not drinking. (You can take off that virtuous expression, McTurk, or I shall begin to fear you don't understand me.) There is not a flaw in any of your characters. And that is why I am going to perpetrate a howling injustice. Your reputations have been injured, haven't they? You have been disgraced before the house, haven't you? You have a peculiarly keen regard for the honour of your house, haven't you? Well, *now* I am going to lick you."

Six apiece was their portion upon that word.

"And this I think"—the Head replaced the cane, and flung the written charge into the wastepaper basket—"covers the situation. When you find a variation from the normal—this will be useful to you in later life—always meet him in an abnormal way. And that reminds me. There are a pile of paper-backs on that shelf. You can borrow them if you put them back. I don't think they'll take any harm from being read in the open. They smell of tobacco rather. You will go to prep. this evening as usual. Good night," said that amazing man.

"Good night, and thank you, sir."

"I swear I'll pray for the Head to-night," said Beetle. "Those last two cuts were just flicks on my collar. There's a 'Monte Cristo' in that lower shelf. I saw it. Bags I, next time we go to Aves!"

"Dearr man!" said McTurk. "No gating. No imports. No beastly questions. All settled. Hullo! what's King goin' in to him for—King and Prout?"

Whatever the nature of that interview, it did not improve either King's or Prout's ruffled plumes, for when they came out of the Head's house, six eyes noted that the one was red and blue with emotion as to his nose, and that the other was sweating profusely. That sight compensated them amply for the Imperial Jaw with which they were favoured by the two. It seems—and who so astonished as they?—that they had held back material facts; that they were guilty both of *suppressio veri* and *suggestio falsi* (well-known gods against whom they often offended); further, that they were malignant in their dispositions, untrustworthy in their characters, pernicious and revolutionary in their influences, abandoned to the devils of wilfulness, pride, and a most intolerable conceit. Ninthly, and lastly, they were to have a care and to be very careful.

They were careful, as only boys can be when there is a hurt to be inflicted. They waited through one suffocating week till Prout and King were their royal selves again; waited till there was a house-match—their own house, too—in which Prout was taking part; waited, further, till he had buckled on his pads in the pavilion and stood ready to go forth. King was scoring at the window, and the three sat on a bench without.

Said Stalky to Beetle: "I say, Beetle, *quis custodiet ipsos custodes?*"

"Don't ask me," said Beetle. "I'll have nothin' private with you. Ye can be as private as ye please the other end of the bench; and I wish ye a very good afternoon."

McTurk yawned.

"Well, ye should ha' come up to the Lodge like Christians instead o' chasin' your—a-hem—boys through the length an' breadth of my covers. *I* think these house-matches are all rot. Let's go over to Colonel Dabney's an' see if he's collared any more poachers."

That afternoon there was joy in Aves.

Slaves of the Lamp—Part I

THE MUSIC-ROOM on the top floor of Number Five was filled with the "Aladdin" company at rehearsal. Dickson Quartus, commonly known as Dick Four, was Aladdin, stage-manager, ballet-master, half the orchestra, and largely librettist, for the "book" had been rewritten and filled with local allusions. The pantomime was to be given next week, in the downstairs study occupied by Aladdin, Abanazar, and the Emperor of China. The Slave of the Lamp, with the Princess Badroulboudour and the Widow Twankay, owned Number Five study across the same landing, so that the company could be easily assembled. The floor shook to the stamp-and-go of the ballet, while Aladdin, in pink cotton tights, a blue and tinsel jacket, and a plumed hat, banged alternately on the piano and his banjo. He was the moving spirit of the game, as befitted a senior who had passed his Army Preliminary and hoped to enter Sandhurst next spring.

Aladdin came to his own at last, Abanazar lay poisoned on the floor, the Widow Twankay danced her dance, and the company decided it would "come all right on the night."

"What about the last song, though?" said the Emperor, a tallish, fair-headed boy with a ghost of a moustache, at which he pulled manfully. "We need a rousing old tune."

"'John Peel'? 'Drink, Puppy, Drink'?" suggested Abanazar, smoothing his baggy lilac pajamas. "Pussy" Abanazar never looked more than one-half awake, but he owned a soft, slow smile which well suited the part of the Wicked Uncle.

"Stale," said Aladdin. "Might as well have 'Grandfather's Clock.' What's that thing you were humming at prep. last night, Stalky?"

Stalky, The Slave of the Lamp, in black tights and doublet, a black silk half-mask on his forehead, whistled lazily where he lay on the top of the piano. It was a catchy music-hall tune.

Dick Four cocked his head critically, and squinted down a large red nose.

"Once more, and I can pick it up," he said, strumming. "Sing the words."

"Arrah, Patsy, mind the baby! Arrah, Patsy, mind the child!
Wrap him in an overcoat, he's surely going wild!
Arrah, Patsy, mind the baby! just you mind the child awhile!
He'll kick and bite and cry all night! Arrah, Patsy, mind
    the child!"

"Rippin'! Oh, rippin'!" said Dick Four. "Only we sha'n't have any piano on the night. We must work it with the banjoes—play an' dance at the same time. You try, Tertius."

The Emperor pushed aside his pea-green sleeves of state, and followed Dick Four on a heavy nickel-plated banjo.

"Yes, but I'm dead all this time. Bung in the middle of the stage, too," said Abanazar.

"Oh, that's Beetle's biznai," said Dick Four. "Vamp it up, Beetle. Don't keep us waiting all night. You've got to get Pussy out of the light somehow, and bring us all in dancin' at the end."

"All right. You two play it again," said Beetle, who, in a grey skirt and a wig of chestnut sausage-curls, set slantwise above a pair of spectacles mended with an old boot-lace, represented the Widow Twankay. He waved one leg in time to the hammered refrain, and the banjoes grew louder.

"Um! Ah! Er—'Aladdin now has won his wife,'" he sang, and Dick Four repeated it.

"'Your Emperor is appeased.'" Tertius flung out his chest as he delivered his line.

"Now jump up, Pussy! Say, 'I think I'd better come to life!' Then we all take hands and come forward: 'We hope you've all been pleased.' *Twiggez-vous?*"

"*Nous Twiggons.* Good enough. What's the chorus for the final ballet? It's four kicks and a turn," said Dick Four.

"Oh! Er!

"John Short will ring the curtain down,
And ring the prompter's bell;
We hope you know before you go
That we all wish you well."

"Rippin'! Rippin'! Now for the Widow's scene with the Princess. Hurry up, Turkey."

McTurk, in a violet silk skirt and a coquettish blue turban, slouched forward as one thoroughly ashamed of himself. The Slave of the Lamp climbed down from the piano, and dispassionately kicked him. "Play up, Turkey," he said; "this is serious." But there fell on the door the knock of authority. It happened to be King, in gown and mortar-board, enjoying a Saturday evening prowl before dinner.

"Locked doors! Locked doors!" he snapped with a scowl. "What's the meaning of this; and what, may I ask, is the intention of this—this epicene attire?"

"Pantomime, sir. The Head gave us leave," said Abanazar, as the only member of the Sixth concerned. Dick Four stood firm in the confidence born of well-fitting tights, but Beetle strove to efface himself behind the piano. A grey princess-skirt borrowed from a day-boy's mother and a spotted cotton bodice unsystematically padded with imposition-paper make one ridiculous. And in other regards Beetle had a bad conscience.

"As usual!" sneered King. "Futile foolery just when your careers, such as they may be, are hanging in the balance. I see! Ah, I see! The old gang of criminals—allied forces of disorder—Corkran"—The Slave of the Lamp smiled politely —"McTurk"—the Irishman scowled—"and, of course, the unspeakable Beetle, our friend Gigadibs." Abanazar, the Emperor, and Aladdin had more or less of characters, and King passed them over. "Come forth, my inky buffoon, from behind yonder instrument of music! You supply, I presume, the doggerel for this entertainment. Esteem yourself to be, as it were, a poet?"

"He's found one of 'em," thought Beetle, noting the flush on King's cheek-bone.

"I have just had the pleasure of reading an effusion of yours to my address, I believe—an effusion intended to rhyme. So—so you despise me, Master Gigadibs, do you? I am quite aware—you need not explain—that it was ostensibly *not* intended for my edification. I read it with laughter—yes, with laughter. These paper pellets of inky boys—still a boy we are, Master Gigadibs—do not disturb my equanimity."

"Wonder which it was," thought Beetle. He had launched many lampoons on an appreciative public ever since he discovered that it was possible to convey reproof in rhyme.

In sign of his unruffled calm, King proceeded to tear Beetle, whom he called Gigadibs, slowly asunder. From his untied shoe-strings to his mended spectacles (the life of a poet at a big school is hard) he held him up to the derision of his associates—with the usual result. His wild flowers of speech— King had an unpleasant tongue—restored him to good humour at the last. He drew a lurid picture of Beetle's latter end as a scurrilous pamphleteer dying in an attic, scattered a few compliments over McTurk and Corkran, and, reminding Beetle that he must come up for judgment when called upon, went to Common-room, where he triumphed anew over his victims.

"And the worst of it," he explained in a loud voice over his soup, "is that I waste such gems of sarcasm on their thick heads. It's miles above them, I'm certain."

"We-ell," said the school chaplain, slowly, "I don't know what Corkran's appreciation of your style may be, but young McTurk reads Ruskin for his amusement."

"Nonsense! He does it to show off. I mistrust the dark Celt."

"He does nothing of the kind. I went into their study the other night, unofficially, and McTurk was gluing up the back of four odd numbers of 'Fors Clavigera.'"

"I don't know anything about their private lives," said a mathematical master, hotly, "but I've learned by bitter experience that Number Five study are best left alone. They are utterly soulless young devils." He blushed as the others laughed.

But in the music-room there were wrath and bad language.

Only Stalky, Slave of the Lamp, lay on the piano unmoved.

"That little swine Manders minor must have shown him your stuff. He's always suckin' up to King. Go and kill him," he drawled. "Which one was it, Beetle?"

"Dunno," said Beetle, struggling out of the skirt. "There was one about his hunting for popularity with the small boys, and the other one was one about him in hell, tellin' the Devil he was a Balliol man. I swear both of 'em rhymed all right. By gum! P'r'aps Manders minor showed him both! *I'll* correct his cæsuras for him."

He disappeared down two flights of stairs, flushed a small pink-and-white boy in a form-room next door to King's study, which, again, was immediately below his own, and chased him up the corridor into a form-room sacred to the revels of the Lower Third. Thence he came back, greatly disordered, to find McTurk, Stalky, and the others of the company, in his study enjoying an unlimited "brew"—coffee, cocoa, buns, new bread hot and steaming, sardine, sausage, ham-and-tongue paste, pilchards, three jams, and at least as many pounds of Devonshire cream.

"My Hat!" said he, throwing himself upon the banquet. "Who stumped up for this, Stalky?" It was within a month of term-end, and blank starvation had reigned in the studies for weeks.

"You," said Stalky, serenely.

"Confound you! You haven't been popping my Sunday bags, then?"

"Keep your hair on. It's only your watch."

"Watch! I lost it—weeks ago. Out on the Burrows, when we tried to shoot the old ram—the day our pistol burst."

"It dropped out of your pocket (you're so beastly careless, Beetle), and McTurk and I kept it for you. I've been wearing it for a week, and you never noticed. Took it into Bideford after dinner to-day. Got thirteen and sevenpence. Here's the ticket."

"Well, that's pretty average cool," said Abanazar behind a slab of cream and jam, as Beetle, reassured upon the safety of his Sunday trousers, showed not even surprise, much less resentment. Indeed, it was McTurk who grew angry, saying:

"You gave him the ticket, Stalky? You *pawned* it? You unmitigated beast! Why, last month you and Beetle sold mine! 'Never got a sniff of any ticket."

"Ah, that was because you locked your trunk, and we wasted half the afternoon hammering it open. We might have pawned it if you'd behaved like a Christian, Turkey."

"My Aunt!" said Abanazar, "you chaps *are* communists. Vote of thanks to Beetle, though."

"That's beastly unfair," said Stalky, "when I took all the trouble to pawn it. Beetle never knew he had a watch. Oh, I say, Rabbits-Eggs gave me a lift into Bideford this afternoon."

Rabbits-Eggs was the local carrier—an outcrop of the early Devonian formation. It was Stalky who had invented his unlovely name. "He was pretty average drunk, or he wouldn't have done it. Rabbits-Eggs is a little shy of me, somehow. But I swore it was *pax* between us, and gave him a bob. He stopped at two pubs on the way in, so he'll be howling drunk to-night. Oh, don't begin reading, Beetle; there's a council of war on. What the deuce is the matter with your collar?"

" 'Chivied Manders minor into the Lower Third box-room. 'Had all his beastly little friends on top of me," said Beetle from behind a jar of pilchards and a book.

"You ass! Any fool could have told you where Manders would bunk to," said McTurk.

"I didn't think," said Beetle, meekly, scooping out pilchards with a spoon.

" 'Course you didn't. You never do." McTurk adjusted Beetle's collar with a savage tug. "Don't drop oil all over my 'Fors,' or I'll scrag you!"

"Shut up, you—you Irish Biddy! 'Tisn't your beastly 'Fors.' It's one of mine."

The book was a fat, brown-backed volume of the later Sixties, which King had once thrown at Beetle's head that Beetle might see whence the name Gigadibs came. Beetle had quietly annexed the book, and had seen—several things. The quarter-comprehended verses lived and ate with him, as the bedropped pages showed. He removed himself from all that world, drifting at large with wondrous Men and Women, till McTurk hammered the pilchard spoon on his head and he snarled.

"Beetle! You're oppressed and insulted and bullied by King. Don't you feel it?"

"Let me alone! I can write some more poetry about him if I am, I suppose."

"Mad! Quite mad!" said Stalky to the visitors, as one exhibiting strange beasts. "Beetle reads an ass called Brownin', and McTurk reads an ass called Ruskin; and—"

"Ruskin isn't an ass," said McTurk. "He's almost as good as the Opium Eater. He says 'we're children of noble races trained by surrounding art.' That means *me,* and the way I decorated the study when you two badgers would have stuck up brackets and Christmas cards. Child of a noble race, trained by surrounding art, stop reading, or I'll shove a pilchard down your neck!"

"It's two to one," said Stalky, warningly, and Beetle closed the book, in obedience to the law under which he and his companions had lived for six checkered years.

The visitors looked on delighted. Number Five study had a reputation for more variegated insanity than the rest of the school put together; and so far as its code allowed friendship with outsiders it was polite and open-hearted to its neighbours on the same landing.

"What rot do you want now?" said Beetle.

"King! War!" said McTurk, jerking his head towards the wall, where hung a small wooden West-African war-drum, a gift to McTurk from a naval uncle.

"Then we shall be turned out of the study again," said Beetle, who loved his flesh-pots. "Mason turned us out for— just warbling on it." Mason was the mathematical master who had testified in Common-room.

"Warbling?—O Lord!" said Abanazar. "We couldn't hear ourselves speak in our study when you played the infernal thing. What's the good of getting turned out of your study, anyhow?"

"We lived in the form-rooms for a week, too," said Beetle, tragically. "And it was beastly cold."

"Ye-es, but Mason's rooms were filled with rats every day we were out. It took him a week to draw the inference," said McTurk. "He loathes rats. 'Minute he let us go back the rats stopped. Mason's a little shy of us now, but there was no evidence."

"Jolly well there wasn't," said Stalky, "when I got out on the roof and dropped the beastly things down his chimney. But, look here—question is, are our characters good enough just now to stand a study row?"

"Never mind mine," said Beetle. "King swears I haven't any."

"I'm not thinking of you," Stalky returned scornfully. "You aren't going up for the Army, you old bat. I don't want to be expelled—and the Head's getting rather shy of us, too."

"Rot!" said McTurk. "The Head never expels except for beastliness or stealing. But I forgot; you and Beetle *are* thieves —regular burglars."

The visitors gasped, but Stalky interpreted the parable with large grins.

"Well, you know, that little beast Manders minor saw Beetle and me hammerin' McTurk's trunk open in the dormitory when we took his watch last month. Of course Manders sneaked to Mason, and Mason solemnly took it up as a case of theft, to get even with us about the rats."

"That just put Mason into our giddy hands," said McTurk, blandly. "We were nice to him, 'cause he was a new master and wanted to win the confidence of the boys. 'Pity he draws inferences, though. Stalky went to his study and pretended to blub, and told Mason he'd lead a new life if Mason would let him off this time, but Mason wouldn't. 'Said it was his duty to report him to the Head."

"Vindictive swine!" said Beetle. "It was all those rats! Then *I* blubbed, too, and Stalky confessed that he'd been a thief in regular practice for six years, ever since he came to the school; and that I'd taught him—*à la* Fagin. Mason turned white with joy. He thought he had us on toast."

"Gorgeous! Gorgeous!" said Dick Four. "We never heard of this."

" 'Course not. Mason kept it jolly quiet. He wrote down all our statements on impot-paper. There wasn't anything he wouldn't believe," said Stalky.

"And handed it all up to the Head, *with* an extempore prayer. It took about forty pages," said Beetle. "I helped him a lot."

"And then, you crazy idiots?" said Abanazar.

"Oh, we were sent for; and Stalky asked to have the 'depositions' read out, and the Head knocked him spinning into a waste-paper basket. Then he gave us eight cuts apiece—welters—for—for—takin' unheard-of liberties with a new master. I saw his shoulders shaking when we went out. Do you know," said Beetle, pensively, "that Mason can't look at us now in second lesson without blushing? We three stare at him sometimes till he regularly trickles. He's an awfully sensitive beast."

"He read 'Eric, or Little by Little,' " said McTurk; "so we gave him 'St. Winifred's, *or* the World of School.' They spent all their spare time stealing at St. Winifred's, when they weren't praying or getting drunk at pubs. Well, that was only a week ago, and the Head's a little bit shy of us. He called it constructive deviltry. Stalky invented it all."

"Not the least good having a row with a master unless you can make an ass of him," said Stalky, extended at ease on the hearth-rug. "If Mason didn't know Number Five—well, he's learned, that's all. Now, my dearly beloved 'earers"—Stalky curled his legs under him and addressed the company—"we've got that strong, perseverin' man King on our hands. He went miles out of his way to provoke a conflict." (Here Stalky snapped down the black silk domino and assumed the air of a judge.) "He has oppressed Beetle, McTurk, and me, *privatim et seriatim*, one by one, as he could catch us. But *now* he has insulted Number Five up in the music-room, and in the presence of these—these ossifers of the Ninety-third, wot look like hair-dressers. Binjimin, we must make him cry 'Capivi!' "

Stalky's reading did *not* include Browning or Ruskin.

"And, besides," said McTurk, "he's a Philistine, a basket-hanger. He wears a tartan tie. Ruskin says that any man who wears a tartan tie will, without doubt, be damned everlastingly."

"Bravo, McTurk," said Tertius; "I thought he was only a beast."

"He's that, too, of course, but he's worse. He has a china basket with blue ribbons and a pink kitten on it, hung up in his window to grow musk in. You know when I got all that old oak carvin' out of Bideford Church, when they were restoring it (Ruskin says that any man who'll restore a church is an unmitigated sweep), and stuck it up here with glue? Well, King came in and wanted to know whether we'd done it with a fret-saw! Yah! He is the King of basket-hangers!"

Down went McTurk's inky thumb over an imaginary arena full of bleeding Kings. "*Placetne*, child of a generous race!" he cried to Beetle.

"Well," began Beetle, doubtfully, "he comes from Balliol, but I'm going to give the beast a chance. You see I can always make him hop with some more poetry. He can't report me to the Head, because it makes him ridiculous. (Stalky's quite right.) But he shall have his chance."

Beetle opened the book on the table, ran his finger down a page, and began at random:

> "*Or who in Moscow towards the Czar*
> *With the demurest of footfalls,*
> *Over the Kremlin's pavement white*
> *With serpentine and syenite,*
> *Steps with five other generals—*"

"That's no good. Try another," said Stalky.

"Hold on a shake; I know what's coming." McTurk was reading over Beetle's shoulder.

> "*That simultaneously take snuff,*
> *For each to have pretext enough*

> *And kerchiefwise unfold his sash,*
> *Which—softness' self—is yet the stuff*

(Gummy! What a sentence!)

> *To hold fast where a steel chain snaps*
> *And leave the grand white neck no gash.*

(Full stop.)"

" 'Don't understand a word of it," said Stalky.

"More fool you! Construe," said McTurk. "Those six bargees scragged the Czar, and left no evidence. *Actum est* with King."

"He gave me that book, too," said Beetle, licking his lips:

> *"There's a great text in Galatians,*
> *Once you trip on it entails*
> *Twenty-nine distinct damnations,*
> *One sure if another fails."*

Then irrelevantly:

> *"Setebos! Setebos! and Setebos!*
> *Thinketh he liveth in the cold of the moon."*

"He's just come in from dinner," said Dick Four, looking through the window. "Manders minor is with him."

" 'Safest place for Manders minor just now," said Beetle.

"Then you chaps had better clear out," said Stalky politely to the visitors. " 'Tisn't fair to mix you up in a study row. Besides, we can't afford to have evidence."

"Are you going to begin at once?" said Aladdin.

"Immediately, if not sooner," said Stalky, and turned out the gas. "Strong, perseverin' man—King. Make him cry 'Capivi!' G'way, Binjimin."

The company retreated to their own neat and spacious study with expectant souls.

"When Stalky blows out his nostrils like a horse," said Aladdin to the Emperor of China, "he's on the war-path. 'Wonder what King will get."

"Beans," said the Emperor. "Number Five generally pays in full."

"Wonder if I ought to take any notice of it officially," said Abanazar, who had just remembered he was a prefect.

"It's none of your business, Pussy. Besides, if you did, we'd have them hostile to *us;* and we shouldn't be able to do any work," said Aladdin. "They've begun already."

Now that West-African war-drum had been made to signal across estuaries and deltas. Number Five was forbidden to wake the engine within ear-shot of the school. But a deep, devastating drone filled the passages as McTurk and Beetle scientifically rubbed its top. Anon it changed to the blare of trumpets—of savage pursuing trumpets. Then, as McTurk slapped one side, smooth with the blood of ancient sacrifice, the roar broke into short coughing howls such as the wounded gorilla throws in his native forest. These were followed by the wrath of King—three steps at a time, up the staircase, with a dry whir of the gown. Aladdin and company, listening, squeaked with excitement as the door crashed open. King stumbled into the darkness, and cursed those performers by the gods of Balliol and quiet repose.

"Turned out for a week," said Aladdin, holding the study door on the crack. "Key to be brought down to his study in five minutes. 'Brutes! Barbarians! Savages! Children!' He's rather agitated. 'Arrah, Patsy, mind the baby,' " he sang in a whisper as he clung to the door-knob, dancing a noiseless war-dance.

King went down-stairs again, and Beetle and McTurk lit the gas to confer with Stalky. But Stalky had vanished.

"Looks like no end of a mess," said Beetle, collecting his books and mathematical instrument case. "A week in the form-rooms isn't any advantage to us."

"Yes, but don't you see that Stalky isn't here, you owl!" said McTurk. "Take down the key, and look sorrowful. King'll only jaw you for half an hour. I'm going to read in the lower form-room."

"But it's always me," mourned Beetle.

"Wait till we see," said McTurk, hopefully. "I don't know any more than you do what Stalky means, but it's something. Go down and draw King's fire. You're used to it."

No sooner had the key turned in the door than the lid of the coal-box, which was also the window-seat, lifted cautiously. It had been a tight fit, even for the lithe Stalky, his head between his knees, and his stomach under his right ear. From a drawer in the table he took a well-worn catapult, a handful of buckshot, and a duplicate key of the study; noiselessly he raised the window and kneeled by it, his face turned to the road, the wind-sloped trees, the dark levels of the Burrows, and the white line of breakers falling nine-deep along the Pebbleridge. Far down the steep-banked Devonshire lane he heard the husky hoot of the carrier's horn. There was a ghost of melody in it, as it might have been the wind in a gin-bottle essaying to sing, "It's a way we have in the Army."

Stalky smiled a tight-lipped smile, and at extreme range opened fire: the old horse half wheeled in the shafts.

"Where he gwaine tu?" hiccoughed Rabbits-Eggs. Another buckshot tore through the rotten canvas tilt with a vicious zipp.

"*Habet!*" murmured Stalky, as Rabbits-Eggs swore into the patient night, protesting that he saw the "dommed colleger" who was assaulting him.

*　　*　　*　　*　　*

"And so," King was saying in a high head voice to Beetle, whom he had kept to play with before Manders minor, well knowing that it hurts a Fifth-form boy to be held up to a fag's derision, "and so, Master Beetle, in spite of all our verses, which we are so proud of, when we presume to come into direct conflict with even so humble a representative of authority as myself, for instance, we are turned out of our studies, are we not?"

"Yes, sir," said Beetle, with a sheepish grin on his lips and murder in his heart. Hope had nearly left him, but he clung to a well-established faith that never was Stalky so dangerous as when he was invisible.

"You are *not* required to criticise, thank you. Turned out of our studies, we are, just as if we were no better than little Manders minor. Only inky schoolboys we are, and must be treated as such."

Beetle pricked up his ears, for Rabbits-Eggs was swearing savagely on the road, and some of the language entered at the upper sash. King believed in ventilation. He strode to the window, gowned and majestic, very visible in the gaslight.

"I zee 'un! I zee 'un!" roared Rabbits-Eggs, now that he had found a visible foe—another shot from the darkness above. "Yiss, yeou, yeou long-nosed, fower-eyed, gingy-whiskered beggar! Yeou'm tu old for such goin's on. Aie! Poultice yeour nose, I tall 'ee! Poultice yeour long nose!"

Beetle's heart leaped up within him. Somewhere, somehow, he knew, Stalky moved behind these manifestations. There were hope and the prospect of revenge. He would embody the suggestion about the nose in deathless verse. King threw up the window, and sternly rebuked Rabbits-Eggs. But the carrier was beyond fear or fawning. He had descended from the cart, and was stooping by the roadside.

It all fell swiftly as a dream. Manders minor raised his hand to his head with a cry, as a jagged flint cannoned on to some rich tree-calf bindings in the book-shelf. Another quoited along the writing-table. Beetle made zealous feint to stop it, and in that endeavour overturned a student's lamp, which dripped, *via* King's papers and some choice books, greasily on to a Persian rug. There was much broken glass on the window-seat; the china basket—McTurk's aversion—cracked to flinders, had dropped her musk plant and its earth over the red rep cushions; Manders minor was bleeding profusely from a cut on the cheek-bone; and King, using strange words, every one of which Beetle treasured, ran forth to find the school-sergeant, that Rabbits-Eggs might be instantly cast into jail.

"Poor chap!" said Beetle, with a false, feigned sympathy.

"Let it bleed a little. That'll prevent apoplexy," and he held the blind head skilfully over the table, and the papers on the table, as he guided the howling Manders to the door.

Then did Beetle, alone with the wreckage, return good for evil. How, in that office, a complete set of "Gibbon" was scarred all along the back as by a flint; how so much black and copying ink came to be mingled with Manders's gore on the table-cloth; why the big gum-bottle, unstoppered, had rolled semicircularly across the floor; and in what manner the white china door-knob grew to be painted with yet more of Manders's young blood, were matters which Beetle did not explain when the rabid King returned to find him standing politely over the reeking hearth-rug.

"You never told me to go, sir," he said, with the air of Casabianca, and King consigned him to the outer darkness.

But it was to a boot-cupboard under the staircase on the ground floor that he hastened, to loose the mirth that was destroying him. He had not drawn breath for a first whoop of triumph when two hands choked him dumb.

"Go to the dormitory and get me my things. Bring 'em to Number Five lavatory. I'm still in tights," hissed Stalky, sitting on his head. "Don't run. Walk."

But Beetle staggered into the form-room next door, and delegated his duty to the yet unenlighened McTurk, with an hysterical précis of the campaign thus far. So it was McTurk, of the wooden visage, who brought the clothes from the dormitory while Beetle panted on a form. Then the three buried themselves in Number Five lavatory, turned on all the taps, filled the place with steam, and dropped weeping into the baths, where they pieced out the war.

"*Moi! Je! Ich! Ego!*" gasped Stalky. "I waited till I couldn't hear myself think, while you played the drum! Hid in the coal-locker—and tweaked Rabbits-Eggs—and Rabbits-Eggs rocked King. Wasn't it beautiful? Did you hear the glass?"

"Why, he—he—he," shrieked McTurk, one trembling finger pointed at Beetle.

"Why, I—I—I was through it all," Beetle howled; "in his study, being jawed."

"Oh, my soul" said Stalky, with a yell, disappearing under water.

"The—the glass was nothing. Manders minor's head's cut open. La-la-lamp upset all over the rug. Blood on the books and papers. The gum! The gum! The gum! The ink! The ink! The ink! O Lord!"

Then Stalky leaped out, all pink as he was, and shook Beetle into some sort of coherence; but his tale prostrated them afresh.

"I bunked for the boot-cupboard the second I heard King go down-stairs. Beetle tumbled in on top of me. The spare key's hid behind the loose board. There isn't a shadow of evidence," said Stalky. They were all chanting together.

"And he turned us out himself—himself—him*self!*" This from McTurk. "He can't begin to suspect us. Oh, Stalky, it's the loveliest thing we've ever done."

"Gum! Gum! Dollops of gum!" shouted Beetle, his spectacles gleaming through a sea of lather. "Ink and blood all mixed. I beheld the little beast's head all over the Latin proses for Monday. Golly, how the oil stunk! And Rabbits-Eggs told King to poultice his nose! Did you hit Rabbits-Eggs, Stalky?"

"Did I jolly well not? Tweaked him all over. Did you hear him curse? Oh, I shall be sick in a minute if I don't stop."

But dressing was a slow process, because McTurk was obliged to dance when he heard that the musk basket was broken, and, moreover, Beetle retailed all King's language with emendations and purple insets.

"Shockin'!" said Stalky, collapsing in a helpless welter of half-hitched trousers. "So dam' bad, too, for innocent boys Lower Third one for assaultin' Beetle when he chivied Manders minor. Come on! It's an alibi, Samivel; and, besides, if we let 'em off they'll be worse next time."

The Lower Third had set a guard upon their form-room for the space of a full hour, which to a boy is a lifetime. Now they were busy with their Saturday evening businesses—like us! Wonder what they'd say at 'St. Winifred's, *or* the World of School.'" By gum! That reminds me we owe the cooking sparrows over the gas with rusty nibs; brewing un-holy drinks in gallipots; skinning moles with pocket-knives; attending to paper trays full of silkworms, or discussing the iniquities of their elders with a freedom, fluency, and point that would have amazed their parents. The blow fell without warning. Stalky upset a form crowded with small boys among their own cooking utensils, McTurk raided the untidy lockers as a terrier digs at a rabbit-hole, while Beetle poured ink upon such heads as he could not appeal to with a Smith's Classical Dictionary. Three brisk minutes accounted for many silk-worms, pet larvæ, French exercises, school caps, half-prepared bones and skulls, and a dozen pots of home-made sloe jam. It was a great wreckage, and the form-room looked as though three conflicting tempests had smitten it.

"Phew!" said Stalky, drawing breath outside the door (amid groans of "Oh, you beastly ca-ads! You think your-selves awful funny," and so forth). *"That's* all right. Never let the sun go down upon your wrath. Rummy little devils, fags. Got no notion o' combinin'."

"Six of 'em sat on my head when I went in after Manders minor," said Beetle. "I warned 'em what they'd get, though."

"Everybody paid in full—beautiful feelin'," said McTurk, absently, as they strolled along the corridor. "Don't think we'd better say much about King, though, do you, Stalky?"

"Not *much.* Our line is injured innocence, of course—same as when the Sergeant reported us on suspicion of smoking in the bunkers. If I hadn't thought of buyin' the pepper and spillin' it all over our clothes, he'd have smelt us. King was gha-astly facetious about that. 'Called us bird-stuffers in form for a week."

"Ah, King hates the Natural History Society because little Hartopp is president. Mustn't do anything in the Coll without glorifyin' King," said McTurk. "But he must be a putrid ass, you know, to suppose at our time o' life we'd go out and stuff birds like fags."

"Poor old King!" said Beetle. "He's awf'ly unpopular in Common-room, and they'll chaff his head off about Rabbits-

Eggs. Golly! How lovely! How beautiful! How holy! But you should have seen his face when the first rock came in! *And* the earth from the basket!"

So they were all stricken helpless for five minutes.

They repaired at last to Abanazar's study, and were received reverently.

"What's the matter?" said Stalky, quick to realise new atmospheres.

"You know jolly well," said Abanazar. "You'll be expelled if you get caught. King is a gibbering maniac."

"Who? Which? What? Expelled for how? We only played the war-drum. We've got turned out for that already."

"Do you chaps mean to say you didn't make Rabbits-Eggs drunk and bribe him to rock King's rooms?"

"Bribe him? No, that I'll swear we didn't," said Stalky, with a relieved heart, for he loved not to tell lies. "What a low mind you've got, Pussy! We've been down having a bath. Did Rabbits-Eggs rock King? Strong, perseverin' man King? Shockin'!"

"Awf'ly. King's frothing at the mouth. There's bell for prayers. Come on."

"Wait a sec," said Stalky, continuing the conversation in a loud and cheerful voice, as they descended the stairs. "What did Rabbits-Eggs rock King for?"

"I know," said Beetle, as they passed King's open door. "I was in his study."

"Hush, you ass!" hissed the Emperor of China.

"Oh, he's gone down to prayers," said Beetle, watching the shadow of the house-master on the wall. "Rabbits-Eggs was only a bit drunk, swearin' at his horse, and King jawed him through the window, and then, of course, he rocked King."

"Do you mean to say," said Stalky, "that King began it?"

King was behind them, and every well-weighed word went up the staircase like an arrow.

"I can only swear," said Beetle, "that King cursed like a bargee. Simply disgustin'. I'm goin' to write to my father about it."

"Better report it to Mason," suggested Stalky. "He knows

our tender consciences. Hold on a shake. I've got to tie my boot-lace."

The other study hurried forward. They did not wish to be dragged into stage asides of this nature. So it was left to McTurk to sum up the situation beneath the guns of the enemy.

"You see," said the Irishman, hanging on the banister, "he begins by bullying little chaps; then he bullies the big chaps; then he bullies some one who isn't connected with the College, and then he catches it. Serves him jolly well right. . . . I beg your pardon, sir. I didn't see you were coming down the staircase."

The black gown tore past like a thunder-storm, and in its wake, three abreast, arms linked, the Aladdin company rolled up the big corridor to prayers, singing with most innocent intention:

"Arrah, Patsy, mind the baby! Arrah, Patsy, mind the child!
Wrap him in an overcoat, he's surely going wild!
Arrah, Patsy, mind the baby! Just you mind the child awhile!
He'll kick and bite and cry all night! Arrah, Patsy, mind
the child!"

An Unsavoury Interlude

It was a maiden aunt of Stalky who sent him both books, with the inscription, "To dearest Artie, on his sixteenth birthday"; it was McTurk who ordered their hypothecation; and it was Beetle, returned from Bideford, who flung them on the window-sill of Number Five study with news that Bastable would advance but ninepence on the two; "Eric, or Little by Little," being almost as great a drug as "St. Winifred's." "An' I don't think much of your aunt. We're nearly out of cartridges, too—Artie, dear."

Whereupon Stalky rose up to grapple with him, but McTurk sat on Stalky's head, calling him a "pure-minded boy" till peace was declared. As they were grievously in arrears with a Latin prose, as it was a blazing July afternoon, and as they ought to have been at a house cricket-match, they began to renew their acquaintance, intimate and unholy, with the volumes.

"Here we are!" said McTurk. " 'Corporal punishment produced on Eric the worst effects. He burned *not* with remorse or regret'—make a note o' that, Beetle—'but with shame and violent indignation. He glared'—oh, naughty Eric! Let's get to where he goes in for drink."

"Hold on half a shake. Here's another sample. 'The Sixth,' he says, 'is the palladium of all public schools.' " But this lot"— Stalky rapped the gilded book—"can't prevent fellows drinkin' and stealin', an' lettin' fags out of window at night, an'—an' doin' what they please. Golly, what we've missed—not goin' to St. Winifred's! . . ."

"I'm sorry to see any boys of my house taking so little interest in their matches."

Mr. Prout could move very silently if he pleased, though that is no merit in a boy's eyes. He had flung open the study door without knocking—another sin—and looked at them suspiciously. "Very sorry, indeed, I am to see you frowsting in your studies."

"We've been out ever since dinner, sir," said McTurk, wearily. One house-match is just like another, and their "ploy" of that week happened to be rabbit-shooting with saloon-pistols.

"I can't see a ball when it's coming, sir," said Beetle. "I've had my gig-lamps smashed at the Nets till I got excused. I wasn't any good even as a fag, then, sir."

"Tuck is probably your form. Tuck and brewing. Why can't you three take any interest in the honour of your house?"

They had heard that phrase till they were wearied. The "honour of the house" was Prout's weak point, and they knew well how to flick him on the raw.

"If you order us to go down, sir, of course we'll go," said Stalky, with maddening politeness. But Prout knew better than that. He had tried the experiment once at a big match, when the three, self-isolated, stood to attention for half an hour in full view of all the visitors, to whom fags, subsidised for that end, pointed them out as victims of Prout's tyranny. And Prout was a sensitive man.

In the infinitely petty confederacies of the Common-room, King and Macrea, fellow house-masters, had borne it in upon him that by games, and games alone, was salvation wrought. Boys neglected were boys lost. They must be disciplined. Left to himself, Prout would have made a sympathetic house-master; but he was never so left, and with the devilish insight of youth, the boys knew to whom they were indebted for his zeal.

"Must we go down, sir?" said McTurk.

"I don't want to order you to do what a right-thinking boy should do gladly. I'm sorry." And he lurched out with some hazy impression that he had sown good seed on poor ground.

"Now what does he suppose is the use of that?" said Beetle.

"Oh, he's cracked. King jaws him in Common-room about not keepin' us up to the mark, an' Macrea burbles about 'dithcipline,' an' old Heffy sits between 'em sweatin' big drops. I heard Oke [the Common-room butler] talking to Richards [Prout's house-servant] about it down in the basement the other day when I went down to bag some bread," said Stalky.

"What did Oke say?" demanded McTurk, throwing "Eric" into a corner.

"Oh, he said, 'They make more n'ise nor a nest full o' jack-daws, an' half of it like we'd no ears to our heads that waited on 'em. They talks over old Prout—what he've done an' left undone about his boys. An' how their boys be fine boys, an' hisn be dom bad.' Well, Oke talked like that, you know, and Richards got awf'ly wrathy. He has a down on King for something or other. Wonder why?"

"Why, King talks about Prout in form-room—makes allusions, an' all that—only half the chaps are such asses they can't see what he's drivin' at. And d'you remember what he said about the 'Casual House' last Tuesday? He meant us. They say he says perfectly beastly things to his own house, making fun of Prout's," said Beetle.

"Well, we didn't come here to mix up in their rows," McTurk said wrathfully. "Who'll bathe after call-over? King's takin' it in the cricket-field. Come on." Turkey seized his straw and led the way.

They reached the sun-blistered pavilion over against the grey Pebbleridge just before roll-call, and, asking no questions, gathered from King's voice and manner that his house was on the road to victory.

"A, ha!" said he, turning to show the light of his countenance. "Here we have the ornaments of the Casual House at last. You consider cricket beneath you, I believe"—the crowd, flannelled, sniggered—"and from what I have seen this afternoon, I fancy many others of your house hold the same view. And may I ask what you purpose to do with your noble selves till tea-time?"

"Going down to bathe, sir," said Stalky.

"And whence this sudden zeal for cleanliness? There is nothing about you that particularly suggests it. Indeed, so far as I remember—I may be at fault—but a short time ago—"

"Five years, sir," said Beetle, hotly.

King scowled. "One of you was that thing called a water-funk. Yes, a water-funk. So now you wish to wash? It is well. Cleanliness never injured a boy or—a house. We will proceed to business," and he addressed himself to the call-over board.

"What the deuce did you say anything to him for, Beetle?" said McTurk, angrily, as they strolled towards the big, open sea-baths.

" 'Twasn't fair—remindin' one of bein' a water-funk. My first term, too. Heaps of chaps are—when they can't swim."

"Yes, you ass; but he saw he'd fetched you. You ought never to answer King."

"But it wasn't fair, Stalky."

"My Hat! You've been her six years, and you expect fairness. Well, you *are* a dithering idiot."

A knot of King's boys, also bound for the baths, hailed them, beseeching them to wash—for the honour of their house.

"That's what comes of King's jawin' and messin'. Those young animals wouldn't have thought of it unless he'd put it into their heads. Now they'll be funny about it for weeks," said Stalky. "Don't take any notice."

The boys came nearer, shouting an opprobrious word. At last they moved to windward, ostentatiously holding their noses.

"That's pretty," said Beetle. "They'll be sayin' our house stinks next."

When they returned from the baths, damp-headed, languid, at peace with the world. Beetle's forecast came only too true. They were met in the corridor by a fag—a common, Low-Second fag—who at arm's length handed them a carefully wrapped piece of soap "with the compliments of King's house."

"Hold on," said Stalky, checking immediate attack. "Who put you up to this, Nixon? Rattray and White? [Those were two leaders in King's house.] Thank you. There's no answer."

"Oh, it's too sickening to have this kind o' rot shoved on to a chap. What's the sense of it? What's the fun of it?" said McTurk.

"It will go on to the end of the term, though." Beetle wagged his head sorrowfully. He had worn many jests threadbare on his own account.

In a few days it became an established legend of the school that Prout's house did not wash and were therefore noisome. Mr. King was pleased to smile succulently in form when one of his boys drew aside from Beetle with certain gestures.

"There seems to be some disability attaching to you, my Beetle, or else why should Burton major withdraw, so to speak, the hem of his garments? I confess I am still in the dark. Will some one be good enough to enlighten me?"

Naturally, he was enlightened by half the form.

"Extraordinary! Most extraordinary! However, each house has its traditions, with which I would not for the world interfere. *We* have a prejudice in favour of washing. Go on, Beetle —from '*jugurtha tamen*'—and, if you can, avoid the more flagrant forms of guessing."

Prout's house was furious because Macrea's and Hartopp's houses joined King's to insult them. They called a house-meeting after dinner—an excited and angry meeting of all save the prefects, whose dignity, though they sympathised, did not allow them to attend. They read ungrammatical resolutions, and made speeches beginning, "Gentlemen, we have met on this occasion," and ending with, "It's a beastly shame," precisely as houses have done since time and schools began.

Number Five study attended, with its usual air of bland patronage. At last McTurk, of the lanthorn jaws, delivered himself:

"You jabber and jaw and burble, and that's about all you can do. What's the good of it? King's house'll only gloat because they've drawn you, and King will gloat, too. Besides, that resolution of Orrin's is chock-full of bad grammar, and King'll gloat over *that*."

"I thought you an' Beetle would put it right, an'—an' we'd post it in the corridor," said the composer, meekly.

"*Par si je le connai.* I'm not goin' to meddle with the biznai," said Beetle. "It's a gloat for King's house. Turkey's quite right."

"Well, won't Stalky, then?"

But Stalky puffed out his cheeks and squinted down his

nose in the style of Panurge, and all he said was, "Oh, you abject burblers!"

"You're three beastly scabs!" was the instant retort of the democracy, and they went out amid execrations.

"This is piffling," said McTurk. "Let's get our sallies, and go and shoot bunnies."

Three saloon-pistols, with a supply of bulleted breech-caps, were stored in Stalky's trunk, and this trunk was in their dormitory, and their dormitory was a three-bed attic one, opening out of a ten-bed establishment, which, in turn, communicated with the great range of dormitories that ran practically from one end of the College to the other. Macrea's house lay next to Prout's, King's next to Macrea's, and Hartopp's beyond that again. Carefully locked doors divided house from house, but each house, in its internal arrangements—the College had originally been a terrace of twelve large houses—was a replica of the next; one straight roof covering all.

They found Stalky's bed drawn out from the wall to the left of the dormer-window, and the latter end of Richards protruding from a two-foot-square cupboard in the wall.

"What's all this? I've never noticed it before. What are you tryin' to do, Fatty?"

"Fillin' basins, Muster Corkran." Richards's voice was hollow and muffled. "They've been savin' me trouble. Yiss."

" 'Looks like it," said McTurk. "Hi! You'll stick if you don't take care."

Richards backed puffing.

"I can't rache 'un. Yiss, 'tess a turncock, Muster McTurk. They've took an' runned all the watter-pipes a story higher in the houses—runned 'em all along under the 'ang of the heaves, like. Runned 'em in last holidays. *I* can't rache the turncock."

"Let me try," said Stalky, diving into the aperture.

"Slip 'ee to the left, then, Muster Corkran. Slip 'ee to the left, an' feel in the dark."

To the left Stalky wriggled, and saw a long line of lead pipe disappearing up a triangular tunnel, whose roof was the rafters and boarding of the college roof, whose floor was sharp-edged joists, and whose side was the rough studding of the lath-and-plaster wall under the dormer.

"Rummy show. How far does it go?"

"Right along, Muster Corkran—right along from end to end. Her runs under the 'ang of the heaves. Have 'ee rached the stopcock yet? Mr. King got 'un put in to save us carryin' watter from down-stairs to fill the basins. No place for a lusty man like old Richards. I'm tu thickabout to go ferritin'. Thank 'ee, Muster Corkran."

The water squirted through the tap just inside the cupboard, and, having filled the basins, the grateful Richards waddled away.

The boys sat round-eyed on their beds considering the possibilities of this trove. Two floors below them they could hear the hum of the angry house; for nothing is so still as a dormitory in mid-afternoon of a midsummer term.

"It has been papered over till now." McTurk examined the little door. "If we'd only known before!"

"I vote we go down and explore. No one will come up this time o' day. We needn't keep *cavé*."

They crawled in, Stalky leading, drew the door behind them, and on all fours embarked on a dark and dirty road full of plaster, odd shavings, and all the raffle that builders leave in the waste room of a house. The passage was perhaps three feet wide, and, except for the struggling light round the edges of the cupboards (there was one to each dormer), almost pitchy dark.

"Here's Macrea's house," said Stalky, his eye at the crack of the third cupboard. "I can see Barnes's name on his trunk. Don't make such a row, Beetle! We can get right to the end of the Coll. Come on! . . . We're in King's house now—I can see a bit of Rattray's trunk. How these beastly boards hurt one's knees!" They heard his nails scraping on plaster.

"That's the ceiling below. Look out! If we smashed that the plaster 'ud fall down in the lower dormitory," said Beetle.

"Let's," whispered McTurk.

"An' be collared first thing? Not much. Why, I can shove my hand ever so far up between these boards."

Stalky thrust an arm to the elbow between the joists.

"No good stayin' here. I vote we go back and talk it over. It's a crummy place. 'Must say I'm grateful to King for his water-works."

They crawled out, brushed one another clean, slid the saloon-pistols down a trouser-leg, and hurried forth to a deep and solitary Devonshire lane in whose flanks a boy might sometimes slay a young rabbit. They threw themselves down under the rank elder-bushes, and began to think aloud.

"You know," said Stalky at last, sighting at a distant sparrow, "we could hide our sallies in there like anything."

"Huh!" Beetle snorted, choked, and gurgled. He had been silent since they left the dormitory. "Did you ever read a book called 'The History of a House' or something? I got it out of the library the other day. A Frenchwoman wrote it—Violet somebody. But it's translated, you know; and it's very interestin'. Tells you how a house is built."

"Well, if you're in a sweat to find out *that,* you can go down to the new cottages they're building for the coast-guard."

"My Hat! I will." He felt in his pockets. "Give me tuppence, some one."

"Rot! Stay here, and don't mess about in the sun."

"Gi' me tuppence."

"I say, Beetle, you aren't stuffy about anything, are you?" said McTurk, handing over the coppers. His tone was serious, for though Stalky often, and McTurk occasionally, manœuvred on his own account, Beetle had never been known to do so in all the history of the confederacy.

"No, I'm not. I'm thinking."

"Well, we'll come, too," said Stalky, with a general's suspicion of his aides.

"Don't want you."

"Oh, leave him alone. He's been taken worse with a poem," said McTurk. "He'll go burbling down to the Pebbleridge and spit it all up in the study when he comes back."

"Then why did he want the tuppence, Turkey? He's gettin' too beastly independent. Hi! There's a bunny. No, it ain't. It's a cat, by Jove! You plug first."

Twenty minutes later a boy with a straw hat at the back of his head, and his hands in his pockets, was staring at workmen as they moved about a half-finished cottage. He produced some ferocious tobacco, and was passed from the forecourt into the interior, where he asked many questions.

"Well, let's have your beastly epic," said Turkey, as they burst into the study, to find Beetle deep in Viollet-le-Duc and some drawings. "We've had no end of a lark."

"Epic? What epic? I've been down to the coast-guard."

"No epic? Then we will slay you, O Beetle," said Stalky, moving to the attack. "You've got something up your sleeve, *I* know, when you talk in that tone!"

"Your Uncle Beetle"—with an attempt to imitate Stalky's war-voice—"is a great man."

"Oh, no; he jolly well isn't anything of the kind. You deceive yourself, Beetle. Scrag him, Turkey!"

"A great man," Beetle gurgled from the floor. "*You* are futile—look out for my tie!—futile burblers. I am the Great Man. I gloat. Ouch! Hear me!"

"Beetle, de-ah"—Stalky dropped unreservedly on Beetle's chest—"we love you, an' you're a poet. If I ever said you were a doggaroo, I apologise; but you know as well as we do that you can't do anything by yourself without mucking it."

"I've got a notion."

"And you'll spoil the whole show if you don't tell your Uncle Stalky. Cough it up, ducky, and we'll see what we can do. Notion, you fat impostor—I knew you had a notion when you went away! Turkey said it was a poem."

"I've found out how houses are built. Le' me get up. The floor-joists of one room are the ceiling-joists of the room below."

"Don't be so filthy technical."

"Well, the man told me. The floor is laid on top of those joists—those boards on edge that we crawled over—but the floor stops at a partition. Well, if you get behind a partition, same as you did in the attic, don't you see that you can shove anything you please under the floor between the floor-boards and the lath and plaster of the ceiling below? Look here. I've drawn it."

He produced a rude sketch, sufficient to enlighten the allies. There is no part of the modern school curriculum that deals with architecture, and none of them had yet reflected whether floors and ceilings were hollow or solid. Outside his own immediate interests the boy is as ignorant as the savage he so admires but he has also the savage's resource.

"I see," said Stalky. "I shoved my hand there. An' then?"

"An' then . . . They've been calling us stinkers, you know. We might shove somethin' under—sulphur, or something that stunk pretty bad—an' stink 'em out. I know it can be done somehow." Beetle's eyes turned to Stalky handling the diagrams.

"Stinks?" said Stalky, interrogatively. Then his face grew luminous with delight. "By gum! I've got it. Horrid stinks! Turkey!" He leaped at the Irishman. "This afternoon—just after Beetle went away! *She's* the very thing!"

"Come to my arms, my beamish boy," carolled McTurk, and they fell into each other's arms dancing. "Oh, frabjous day! Calloo, callay! She will! She will!"

"Hold on," said Beetle. "I don't understand."

"Dearr man! It shall, though. Oh, Artie, my pure-souled youth, let us tell our darling Reggie about Pestiferous Stinkadores."

"Not until after call-over. Come on!"

"I say," said Orrin, stiffly, as they fell into their places along the walls of the gymnasium. "The house are goin' to hold another meeting."

"Hold away, then." Stalky's mind was elsewhere.

"It's about you three this time."

"All right, give 'em my love . . . *Here, sir*," and he tore down the corridor.

Gambolling like kids at play, with bounds and side-starts, with caperings and curvetings, they led the almost bursting Beetle to the rabbit-lane, and from under a pile of stones drew forth the new-slain corpse of a cat. Then did Beetle see the inner meaning of what had gone before, and lifted up his voice in thanksgiving for that the world held warriors so wise as Stalky and McTurk.

"Well-nourished old lady, ain't she?" said Stalky. "How long d'you suppose it'll take her to get a bit whiff in a confined space?"

"Bit whiff! What a coarse brute you are!" said McTurk. "Can't a poor pussy-cat get under King's dormitory floor to die without your pursuin' her with your foul innuendoes?"

"What did she die under the floor for?" said Beetle, looking to the future.

"Oh, they won't worry about *that* when they find her," said Stalky.

"A cat may look at a king." McTurk rolled down the bank at his own jest. "Pussy, you don't know how useful you're goin' to be to three pure-souled, high-minded boys."

"They'll have to take up the floor for her, same as they did in Number Nine when the rat croaked. Big medicine—heap big medicine! Phew! O Lord, I wish I could stop laughin'," said Beetle.

"Stinks! Hi, stinks! Clammy ones!" McTurk gasped as he regained his place. "And"—the exquisite humour of it brought them sliding down together in a tangle—"it's all for the honour of the house, too!"

"An' they're holdin another meetin'—on us," Stalky panted, his knees in the ditch and his face in the long grass. "Well, let's get the bullet out of her and hurry up. The sooner she's bedded out the better."

Between them they did some grisly work with a penknife; between them (ask not who buttoned her to his bosom) they took up the corpse and hastened back, Stalky arranging their plan of action at the full trot.

The afternoon sun, lying in broad patches on the bed-rugs, saw three boys and an umbrella disappear into a dormitory wall. In five minutes they emerged, brushed themselves all over, washed their hands, combed their hair, and descended.

"Are you sure you shoved her far enough under?" said McTurk, suddenly.

"Hang it, man, I shoved her the full length of my arm and Beetle's brolly. That must be about six feet. She's bung in the middle of King's big upper ten-bedder. Eligible central situation, *I* call it. She'll stink out his chaps, and Hartopp's and Macrea's, when she really begins to fume. I swear your Uncle Stalky is a great man. Do you realise what a great man he is, Beetle?"

"Well, I had the notion first, hadn't I—? only—"

"You couldn't do it without your Uncle Stalky could you?"

"They've been calling us stinkers for a week now," said McTurk. "Oh, *won't* they catch it!"

"Stinker! Yah! Stink-ah!" rang down the corridor.

"And she's there," said Stalky, a hand on either boy's shoulder. "She—is—there, gettin' ready to surprise 'em. Presently she'll begin to whisper to 'em in their dreams. Then she'll whiff. Golly, how she'll whiff! Oblige me by thinkin' of it for two minutes."

They went to their study in more or less of silence. There they began to laugh—laugh as only boys can. They laughed with their foreheads on the tables, or on the floor; laughed at length, curled over the backs of chairs or clinging to a bookshelf; laughed themselves limp.

And in the middle of it Orrin entered on behalf of the house.

"Don't mind us, Orrin; sit down. You don't know how we respect and admire you. There's something about your pure, high young forehead, full of the dreams of innocent boyhood, that's no end fetchin'. It is, indeed."

"The house sent me to give you this." He laid a folded sheet of paper on the table and retired with an awful front.

"It's the Resolution! Oh, read it, some one. I'm too silly-sick with laughin' to see," said Beetle.

Stalky jerked it open with a precautionary sniff.

"Phew! Phew! Listen. *'The house notices with pain and contempt the attitude of indifference'*— how many *f*'s in 'indifference,' Beetle?"

"Two for choice."

"Only one here—'adopted by the occupants of Number Five study in relation to the insults offered to Mr. Prout's house at the recent meeting in Number Twelve form-room, and the house hereby pass a vote of censure on the said study.' That's all."

"And she bled all down my shirt, too!" said Beetle.

"An' I'm catty all over," said McTurk, "though I washed twice."

"An' I nearly broke Beetle's brolly plantin' her where she would blossom!"

The situation was beyond speech, but not laughter. There was some attempt that night to demonstrate against the three in their dormitory; so they came forth.

"You see," Beetle began suavely as he loosened his braces, "the trouble with you is that you're a set of unthinkin' asses. You've no more brains than spidgers. We've told you that heaps of times, haven't we?"

"We'll give all three of you a dormitory lickin'. You always jaw at us as if you were prefects," cried one.

"Oh, no, you won't," saaid Stalky, "because you know that if you did you'd get the worst of it sooner or later. *We* aren't in any hurry. *We* can afford to wait for our little revenges. You've made howlin' asses of yourselves, and just as soon as King gets hold of your precious resolutions tomorrow you'll find that out. If you aren't sick an' sorry by tomorrow night, I'll—I'll eat my hat."

But, or ever the dinner-bell rang the next day, Prout's were sadly aware of their error. King received stray members of that house with an exaggerated attitude of fear. Did they purpose to cause him to be dismissed from the College by unanimous resolution? What were their views concerning the government of the school, that he might hasten to give effect to them? He would not offend them for worlds; but he feared —he sadly feared—that his own house, who did not pass resolutions (but washed), might somewhat deride.

King was a happy man, and his house, basking in the favour of his smile, made that afternoon a long penance to the misled Prouts. And Prout himself, with a dull and lowering visage, tried to think out the rights and wrongs of it all, only plunging deeper into bewilderment. Why should his house be called "Stinkers"? Truly, it was a small thing, but he had been trained to believe that straws show which way the wind blows, and that there is no smoke without fire. He approached King in Common-room with a sense of injustice, but King was pleased to be full of airy persiflage that tide, and brilliantly danced dialectical rings round Prout.

"Now," said Stalky at bedtime, making pilgrimage through the dormitories before the prefects came up, "*now* what have you got to say for yourselves? Foster, Carton, Finch, Longbridge, Marlin, Brett! I heard you chaps catchin' it from King —he made hay of you—an' all you could do was to wriggle an' grin' an' say, 'Yes, sir,' an' 'No, sir,' an' 'O, sir,' an' 'Please, sir'! You an' your resolution! Urh!"

"Oh, shut up, Stalky."

"Not a bit of it. You're a gaudy lot of resolutionists, you are! You've made a sweet mess of it. Perhaps you'll have the decency to leave us alone next time."

Here the house grew angry, and in many voices pointed out how this blunder would never have come to pass if Number Five study had helped them from the first.

"But you chaps are so beastly conceited, an'— an' you swaggered into the meetin' as if we were a lot of idiots," growled Orrin of the Resolution.

"That's precisely what you *are!* That's what we've been tryin' to hammer into your thick heads all this time," said Stalky. "Never mind, we'll forgive you. Cheer up. You can't help bein' asses, you know," and, the enemy's flank deftly turned, Stalky hopped into bed.

That night was the first of sorrow among the jubilant Kings. By some accident of under-floor draughts the cat did not vex the dormitory beneath which she lay, but the next one to the right; stealing on the air rather as a pale-blue sensation than as any poignant offence. But the mere adumbration of an odour is enough for the sensitive nose and clean tongue of youth. Decency demands that we draw several carbolised sheets over what the dormitory said to Mr. King and what Mr. King replied. He was genuinely proud of his house and fastidious in all that concerned their well-being. He came; he sniffed; he said things. Next morning a boy in that dormitory confided to his bosom friend, a fag of Macrea's, that there was trouble in their midst which King would fain keep secret.

But Macrea's boy had also a bosom friend in Prout's, a shock-headed fag of malignant disposition, who, when he had wormed out the secret, told—told it in a high-pitched treble that rang along the corridor like a bat's squeak.

"An'—an' they've been calling us 'stinkers' all this week. Why, Harland minor says they simply can't sleep in his dormitory for the stink. Come on!"

"With one shout and with one cry" Prout's juniors hurled themselves into the war, and through the interval between first and second lesson some fifty twelve-year-olds were embroiled on the gravel outside King's windows to a tune whose *Leit-motif* was the word "stinker."

"Hark to the minute-gun at sea!" said Stalky. They were in their study collecting books for second lesson—Latin, with King. "I thought his azure brow was a bit cloudy at prayers. 'She is comin', sister Mary. She is—'"

"If they make such a row now, what *will* they do when she really begins to look up an' take notice?"

"Well, no vulgar repartee, Beetle. All we want is to keep out of this row like gentlemen."

"'Tis but a little faded flower.' Where's my Horace? Look here, I don't understand what she means by stinkin' out Rattray's dormitory first. We holed in under White's, didn't we?" asked McTurk, with a wrinkled brow.

"Skittish little thing. She's rompin' about all over the place, I suppose."

"My Aunt! King'll be a cheerful customer at second lesson. I haven't prepared my Horace one little bit, either," said Beetle. "Come on!"

They were outside the form-room door now. It was within five minutes of the bell, and King might arrive at any moment.

Turkey elbowed into a cohort of scuffling fags, cut out

Thornton tertius (he that had been Harland's bosom friend), and bade him tell his tale.

It was a simple one, interrupted by tears. Many of King's house had already battered him for libel.

"Oh, it's nothing," McTurk cried. "He says that King's house stinks. That's all."

"Stale!" Stalky shouted. "We knew that years ago, only we didn't choose to run about shoutin' 'Stinker!' We've got some manners, if they haven't. Catch a fag, Turkey, and make sure of it."

Turkey's long arm closed on a harried and anxious ornament of the Lower Second.

"Oh, McTurk, please let me go. I don't stink—I swear I don't!"

"Guilty conscience!" cried Beetle! "Who said you did?"

"What d'you make of it?" Stalky punted the small boy into Beetle's arms.

"Snf! Snf! He does, though. I think it's leprosy—or thrush. P'r'aps it's both. Take it away."

"Indeed, Master Beetle"—King generally came to the house door for a minute or two as the bell rang—"we are vastly indebted to you for your diagnosis, which seems to reflect almost as much credit on the natural unwholesomeness of your mind as it does upon your pitiful ignorance of the diseases of which you discourse so glibly. We will, however, test your knowledge in other directions."

That was a merry lesson, but, in his haste to scarify Beetle, King clean neglected to give him an imposition, and since at the same time he supplied him with many priceless adjectives for later use, Beetle was well content, and applied himself most seriously throughout third lesson (algebra with little Hartopp) to composing a poem entitled "The Lazar-house."

After dinner King took his house to bathe in the sea off the Pebbleridge. It was an old promise; but he wished he could have evaded it, for all Prout's lined up by the Fives Court and cheered with intention. In his absence not less than half the school invaded the infected dormitory to draw their own conclusions. The cat had gained in the last twelve hours, but a battle-field of the fifth day could not have been so flamboyant as the spies reported.

"My word, she *is* doin' herself proud," said Stalky. "Did you ever smell anything like it? Ah, an' she isn't under White's dormitory at all yet."

"But she will be. Give her time," said Beetle. "She'll twine like a giddy honeysuckle. What howlin' Lazarites they are! No house is justified in makin' itself a stench in the nostrils of decent—"

"High-minded, pure-souled boys. *Do* you burn with remorse and regret?" said McTurk, as they hastened to meet the house coming up from the sea. King had deserted it, so speech was unfettered. Round its front played a crowd of skirmishers—all houses mixed—flying, reforming, shrieking insults. On its tortured flanks marched the Hoplites, seniors hurling jests one after another—simple and primitive jests of the Stone Age. To these the three added themselves, dispassionately, with an air of aloofness, almost sadly.

"And they look all right, too," said Stalky. "It can't be Rattray, can it? Rattray?"

No answer.

"Rattray, dear? He seems stuffy about something or other. Look here, old man, *we* don't bear any malice about your sending that soap to us last week, do we? Be cheerful, Rat. You can live this down all right. I dare say it's only a few fags. Your house is so beastly slack, though."

"You aren't going back to the house, are you?" said McTurk. The victims desired nothing better. "You've simply no conception of the reek up there. Of course, frowzin' as you do, you wouldn't notice it; but after this nice wash and the clean, fresh air, even *you'd* be upset. 'Much better camp on the Burrows. We'll get you some straw. Shall we?" The house hurried in to the tune of "John Brown's body," sung by loving schoolmates, and barricaded themselves in their form-room. Straightway Stalky chalked a large cross, with "Lord, have mercy upon us," on the door, and left King to find it.

The wind shifted that night and wafted a carrion-reek into Macrea's dormitories; so that boys in nightgowns pounded on the locked door between the houses, entreating King's to wash. Number Five study went to second lesson with not more than half a pound of camphor apiece in their clothing; and King, too wary to ask for explanations, gibbered awhile and hurled them forth. So Beetle finished yet another poem at peace in the study.

"They're usin' carbolic now. Malpas told me," said Stalky. "King thinks it's the drains."

She'll need a lot o' carbolic," said McTurk. "No harm tryin', I suppose. It keeps King out of mischief."

"I swear I thought he was goin' to kill me when I sniffed just now. He didn't mind Burton major sniffin' at me the other day, though. He never stopped Alexander howlin' 'Stinker!' into our form-room before—before we doctored 'em. He just grinned," said Stalky. "What was he frothing over you for, Beetle?"

"Aha! That was my subtle jape. I had him on toast. You know he always jaws about the learned Lipsius."

" 'Who at the age of four'—*that* chap?" said McTurk.

"Yes. Whenever he hears I've written a poem. Well, just as I was sittin' down, I whispered, 'How is our learned Lipsius?' to Burton major. Old Butt grinned like an owl. *He* didn't know what I was drivin' at; but King jolly well did. That was really why he hove us out. Ain't you grateful? Now shut up. I'm goin' to write the 'Ballad of the Learned Lipsius.' "

"Keep clear of anything coarse, then," said Stalky. "I shouldn't like to be coarse on this happy occasion."

"Not for wo-orlds. What rhymes to 'stenches,' some one?"

In Common-room at lunch King discoursed acridly to Prout of boys with prurient minds, who perverted their few and baleful talents to sap discipline and corrupt their equals, to deal in foul imagery and destroy reverence.

"But you didn't seem to consider this when your house called us—ah—stinkers. If you hadn't assured me that you never interfere with another man's house, I should almost believe that it was a few casual remarks of yours that started all this nonsense."

Prout had endured much, for King always took his temper to meals.

"You spoke to Beetle yourself, didn't you? Something about not bathing, and being a water-funk?" the school chaplain put in. "I was scoring in the pavilion that day."

"I may have—jestingly. I really don't pretend to remember every remark I let fall among small boys; and full well I know the Beetle has no feelings to be hurt."

"May be; but he, or they—it comes to the same thing—have the fiend's own knack of discovering a man's weak place. I confess I rather go out of my way to conciliate Number Five study. It may be soft, but so far, I believe, I am the only man here whom they haven't maddened by their—well—attentions."

"That is all beside the point. I flatter myself I can deal with them alone as occasion arises. But if they feel themselves morally supported by those who should wield an absolute and open-handed justice, then I say that my lot is indeed a hard one. Of all things I detest, I admit that anything verging on disloyalty among ourselves is the first."

The Common-room looked at one another out of the corners of their eyes, and Prout blushed.

"I deny it absolutely," he said. "Er—in fact, I own that I personally object to all three of them. It is not fair, therefore, to—"

"How long do you propose to allow it?" said King.

"But surely," said Macrea, deserting his usual ally, "the blame, if any, rests with you, King. You can't hold them responsible for the—you prefer the good old Anglo-Saxon, I believe—stink in your house. My boys are complaining of it now."

"What can you expect? You know what boys are. Naturally they take advantage of what to them is a heaven-sent opportunity," said little Hartopp. "What *is* the trouble in your dormitories, King?"

Mr. King explained that as he had made it the one rule of his life never to interfere with another man's house, so he expected not to be too patently interfered with. They might

be interested to learn—here the chaplain heaved a weary sigh
—that he had taken all steps that, in his poor judgment,
would meet the needs of the case. Nay, further, he had himself expended, with no thought of reimbursement, sums, the
amount of which he would not specify, on disinfectants. This
he had done because he knew by bitter—by most bitter—
experience that the management of the College was slack,
dilatory, and inefficient. He might even add, almost as slack
as the administration of certain houses which now thought fit
to sit in judgment of his actions. With a short summary of his
scholastic career, and a précis of his qualifications, including
his degrees, he withdrew, slamming the door.

"Heigh-ho!" said the chaplain. "Ours is a dwarfing life—
a belittling life, my brethren. God help all schoolmasters!
They need it."

"I don't like the boys, I own"—Prout dug viciously with
his fork into the table-cloth—"and I don't pretend to be a
strong man, as you know. But I confess I can't see any reason
why I should take steps against Stalky and the others because
King happens to be annoyed by—by—"

"Falling into the pit he has digged," said little Hartopp.
"Certainly not, Prout. No one accuses *you* of setting one
house against another through sheer idleness."

"A belittling life—a belittling life." The chaplain rose. "I
go to correct French exercises. By dinner King will have
scored off some unlucky child of thirteen; he will repeat to us
every word of his brilliant repartees, and all will be well."

"But about those three. Are they so prurient-minded?"

"Nonsense," said little Hartopp. "If you thought for a
minute, Prout, you would see that the 'precocious flow of
fetid imagery,' that King complains of, is borrowed whole-
sale from King. *He* 'nursed the pinion that impelled the steel.'
Naturally he does not approve. Come into the smoking-room
for a minute. It isn't fair to listen to boys; but they should
be now rubbing it into King's house outside. Little things
please little minds."

The dingy den off the Common-room was never used for
anything except gowns. Its windows were ground glass; one

could not see out of it, but one could hear almost every word on the gravel outside. A light and wary footstep came up from Number Five.

"Rattray!" in a subdued voice—Rattray's study fronted that way. "D'you know if Mr. King's anywhere about? I've got a—" McTurk discreetly left the end of the sentence open.

"No. He's gone out," said Rattray, unguardedly.

"Ah! The learned Lipsius is airing himself, is he? His Royal Highness has gone to fumigate." McTurk climbed on the railings, where he held forth like the never-wearied rook.

"Now in all the Coll there was no stink like the stink of King's house, for it stank vehemently and none knew what to make of it. Save King. And he washed the fags *privatim et seriatim*. In the fish-pools of Hesbon washed he them, with an apron about his loins."

"Shut up, you mad Irishman!" There was the sound of a golf-ball spurting up gravel.

"It's no good getting wrathy, Rattray. We've come to jape with you. Come on, Beetle. They're all at home. You can wind 'em."

"Where's the Pomposo Stinkadore? 'Tisn't safe for a pure-souled, high-minded boy to be seen round his house these days. Gone out, has he? Never mind. I'll do the best I can, Rattray. I'm *in loco parentis* just now."

("One for you, Prout," whispered Macrea, for this was Mr. Prout's pet phrase.)

"I have a few words to impart to you, my young friend. We will discourse together awhile."

Here the listening Prout sputtered: Beetle, in a strained voice, had chosen a favourite gambit of King's.

"I repeat, Master Rattray, we will confer, and the matter of our discourse shall not be stinks, for that is a loathsome and obscene word. We will, with your good leave—granted, I trust, Master Rattray, granted, I trust—study this—this scabrous upheaval of latent demoralisation. What impresses me most is not so much the blatant indecency with which you swagger abroad under your load of putrescence" (you must imagine this discourse punctuated with golf-balls, but old

Rattray was ever a bad shot) "as the cynical immorality with which you revel in your abhorrent aromas. Far be it from me to interfere with another's house—"

("Good Lord!" said Prout, "but this *is* King."

"Line for line, letter for letter; listen," said little Hartopp.)

"But to say that you stink, as certain lewd fellows of the baser sort aver, is to say nothing—less than nothing. In the absence of your beloved house-master, for whom no one has a higher regard than myself, I will, if you will allow me, explain the grossness—the unparalleled enormity—the appalling fetor of the stenches (I believe in the good old Anglo-Saxon word), stenches, sir, with which you have seen fit to infect your house. . . . Oh, bother! I've forgotten the rest, but it was very beautiful. Aren't you grateful to us for labourin' with you this way, Rattray? Lots of chaps 'ud never have taken the trouble, but we're grateful, Rattray."

"Yes, we're horrid grateful," grunted McTurk. "We don't forget that soap. *We're* polite. Why ain't you polite, Rat?"

"Hallo!" Stalky cantered up, his cap over one eye. "Exhortin' the Whiffers, eh? I'm afraid they're too far gone to repent. Rattray! White! Perowne! Malpas! No answer. This is distressin'. This is truly distressin'. Bring out your dead, you glandered lepers!" *fantastic !!!*

"You think yourself funny, don't you?" said Rattray, stung from his dignity by this last. "It's only a rat or something under the floor. We're going to have it up to-morrow."

"Don't try to shuffle it off on a poor dumb animal, and dead, too. I loathe prevarication. 'Pon my soul, Rattray—"

"Hold on. The Hartoffles never said ' 'Pon my soul' in all his little life," said Beetle, critically.

("Ah!" said Prout to little Hartopp.)

"Upon my word, sir, upon my word, sir, I expected better things of you, Rattray. Why can you not own up to your misdeeds like a man? Have *I* ever shown any lack of confidence in *you?*"

("It's not brutality," murmured little Hartopp, as though answering a question no one had asked. "It's boy; only boy.")

"And this was the house"—Stalky changed from a pecking,

fluttering voice to tragic earnestness—"this was the—the—open cesspit that dared to call us 'stinkers.' And now—and now, it tries to shelter itself behind a dead rat. You annoy me, Rattray. You disgust me! You irritate me unspeakably! Thank Heaven, I am a man of equable temper—"

("This is to your address, Macrea," said Prout.

"I fear so, I fear so.")

"Or I should scarcely be able to contain myself before your mocking visage."

"Cavé!" in an undertone. Beetle had spied King sailing down the corridor.

"And what may you be doing here, my little friends?" the house-master began. "I had a fleeting notion—correct me if I am wrong" (the listeners with one accord choked)—"that if I found you outside my house I should visit you with dire pains and penalties."

"We were just goin' for a walk, sir," said Beetle.

"And you stopped to speak to Rattray *en route?*"

"Yes, sir. We've been throwing golf-balls," said Rattray, coming out of the study.

("Old Rat is more of a diplomat that I thought. So far he is strictly within the truth," said little Hartopp. "Observe the ethics of it, Prout.")

"Oh, you were sporting with them, were you? I must say I do not envy you your choice of associates. I fancied they might have been engaged in some of the prurient discourse with which they have been so disgustingly free of late. I should strongly advise you to direct your steps most carefully in the future. Pick up those golf-balls." He passed on.

*   *   *   *   *

Next day Richards, who had been a carpenter in the Navy, and to whom odd jobs were confided, was ordered to take up a dormitory floor; for Mr. King held that something must have died there.

"We need not neglect all our work for a trumpery incident of this nature; though I am quite aware that little things please little minds. Yes, I have decreed the boards to be taken up after lunch under Richards's auspices. I have no doubt it will be vastly interesting to a certain type of so-called intellect; but any boy of my house or another's found on the dormitory stairs will *ipso facto* render himself liable to three hundred lines."

The boys did not collect on the stairs, but most of them waited outside King's. Richards had been bound to cry the news from the attic window, and, if possible, to exhibit the corpse.

" 'Tis a cat, a dead cat!" Richard's face showed purple at the window. He had been in the chamber of death and on his knees for some time.

"Cat be blowed!" cried McTurk. "It's a dead fag left over from last term. Three cheers for King's dead fag!"

They cheered lustily.

"Show it, show it! Let's have a squint at it!" yelled the juniors. "Give her to the Bug-hunters." (This was the Natural History Society.) "The cat looked at the King—and died of it! Hoosh! Yai! Yaow! Maiow! Ftzz!" were some of the cries that followed.

Again Richards appeared.

"She've been"—he checked himself suddenly—"dead a long taime."

The school roared.

"Well, come on out for a walk," said Stalky in a well-chosen pause. "It's all very disgustin', and I do hope the Lazar-house won't do it again."

"Do what?" a King's boy cried furiously.

"Kill a poor innocent cat every time you want to get off washing. It's awfully hard to distinguish between you as it is. I prefer the cat, I must say. She isn't quite so whiff. What are you goin' to do, Beetle?"

"Je vais gloater. Je vais gloater tout le blessed afternoon. Jamais j'ai gloaté comme je gloaterai aujourd'hui. Nous bunkerons aux bunkers."

And it seemed good to them so to do.

* * * * *

Down in the basement, where the gas flickers and the boots stand in racks, Richards, amid his blacking-brushes, held forth to Oke of the Common-room, Gumbly of the dining-halls, and fair Lena of the laundry.

"Yiss. Her were in a shockin' staate an' condition. Her nigh made me sick, I tal 'ee. But I rowted 'un out, an' I rowted 'un out, an' I made all shipshape, though her smelt like to bilges."

"Her died mousin', I rackon, poor thing," said Lena.

"Then her moused different to any made cat o' God's world, Lena. I up with the top-board, an' she were lyin' on her back, an' I turned 'un ovver with the brume-handle, an' 'twas her back was all covered with the plaster from 'twixt the lathin'. Yiss, I tal 'ee. An' under her head there lay, like, so's to say, a little pillow o' plaster druv up in front of her by raison of her slidin' along on her back. No cat niver went mousin' on her back, Lena. Some one had shoved her along right underneath, so far as they could shove 'un. Cats don't make theyselves pillows for to die on. Shoved along, she were, when she was settin' for to be cold, laike."

"Oh, yeou'm too clever to live, Fatty. Yeou go get wed an' taught some sense," said Lena, the affianced of Gumbly.

"'Larned a little 'fore iver some maidens was born. Sarved in the Queen's Navy, I have, where yeou'm taught to use your eyes. Yeou go 'tend your own business, Lena."

"Do 'ee mean what yeou'm been tellin' us?" said Oke.

"Ask me no questions, I'll give 'ee no lies. Bullet-hole clane thru from side to side, an' tu heart-ribs broke like withies. I seed 'un when I turned 'un ovver. They'm clever, oh, they'm clever, but they'm not too clever for old Richards! 'Twas on the born tip o' my tongue to tell, tu, but . . . he said us niver washed, he hid. Let his dom boys call us 'stinkers,' he did. Sarve 'un dom well raight, I say!"

Richards spat on a fresh boot and fell to his work, chuckling.

The Impressionists

THEY HAD DROPPED into the chaplain's study for a Saturday night smoke—all four housemasters—and the three briers and the one cigar reeking in amity proved the Reverend John Gillett's good generalship. Since the discovery of the cat, King had been too ready to see affront where none was meant, and the Reverend John, buffer-state and general confidant, had worked for a week to bring about a good understanding. He was fat, clean-shaven, except for a big moustache, of an imperturbable good temper, and, those who loved him least said, a guileful Jesuit. He smiled benignantly upon his handiwork—four sorely tried men talking without very much malice.

"Now remember," he said, when the conversation turned that way, "I impute nothing. But every time that any one has taken direct steps against Number Five study, the issue has been more or less humiliating to the taker."

"I can't admit that. I pulverise the egregious Beetle daily for his soul's good; and the others with him," said King.

"Well, take your own case, King, and go back a couple of years. Do you remember when Prout and you were on their track—for hutting and trespass, wasn't it? Have you forgotten Colonel Dabney?"

The others laughed. King did not care to be reminded of his career as a poacher.

"That was one instance. Again, when you had rooms below them—I always said that that was entering the lion's den—you turned them out."

"For making disgusting noises. Surely, Gillett, you don't excuse—"

"All I say is that you turned them out. That same evening your study was wrecked."

"By Rabbits-Eggs—most beastly drunk—from the road," said King. "What has that—?"

The Reverend John went on.

"Lastly, they conceive that aspersions are cast upon their personal cleanliness—a most delicate matter with all boys. Ve-ry good. Observe how, in each case, the punishment fits the crime. A week after your house calls them 'stinkers,' King, your house is, not to put too fine a point on it, stunk out by a dead cat who chooses to die in the one spot where she can annoy you most. Again the long arm of coincidence! *Summa.* You accuse them of trespass. Through some absurd chain of circumstances—they may or may not be at the other end of it—you and Prout are made to appear as trespassers. You evict them. For a time your study is made untenable. I have drawn the parallel in the last case. Well?"

"She was under the centre of White's dormitory," said King. "There are double floor-boards there to deaden noise. No boy, even in my own house, could possibly have pried up the boards without leaving some trace—and Rabbits-Eggs was phenomenally drunk that other night."

"They are singularly favoured by fortune. That is all I ever said. Personally, I like them immensely, and I believe I have a little of their confidence. I confess I like being called 'Padre.' They are at peace with me; consequently I am not treated to bogus confessions of theft."

"You mean Mason's case?" said Prout, heavily. "That always struck me as peculiarly scandalous. I thought the Head should have taken up the matter more thoroughly. Mason may be misguided, but at least he is thoroughly sincere and means well."

"I confess I cannot agree with you, Prout," said the Reverend John. "He jumped at some silly tale of theft on their part; accepted another boy's evidence without, so far as I can see, any inquiry; and—frankly, I think he deserved all he got."

"They deliberately outraged Mason's best feelings," said Prout. "A word to me on their part would have saved the whole thing. But they preferred to lure him on; to play on his ignorance of their characters—"

"That may be," said King, "but I don't like Mason. I dislike him for the very reason that Prout advances to his credit. He means well."

"Our criminal tradition is not theft—among ourselves, at least," said little Hartopp.

"For the head of a house that raided seven head of cattle from the innocent pot-wallopers of Northam, isn't that rather a sweeping statement?" said Macrea.

"Precisely so," said Hartopp, unabashed. "That, with gate-lifting, and a little poaching and hawk-hunting on the cliffs, is our salvation."

"It does us far more harm as a school—" Prout began.

"Than any hushed-up scandal could? Quite so. Our reputation among the farmers is most unsavoury. But I would much sooner deal with any amount of ingenious crime of that nature than—some other offences."

"They may be all right, but they are unboy-like, abnormal, and, in my opinion, unsound," Prout insisted. "The moral effect of their performances must pave the way for greater harm. It makes me doubtful how to deal with them. I might separate them."

"You might, of course; but they have gone up the school together for six years. *I* shouldn't care to do it," said Macrea.

"They use the editorial 'we,'" said King, irrelevantly. "It annoys me. 'Where's your prose, Corkran?' 'Well, sir, we haven't quite done it yet.' 'We'll bring it in a minute,' and so on. And the same with the others."

"There's great virtue in that 'we,'" said little Hartopp. "You know I take them for trig. McTurk may have some conception of the meaning of it; but Beetle is as the brutes that perish about sines and cosines. He copies serenely from Stalky, who positively rejoices in mathematics."

"Why don't you stop it?" said Prout.

"It rights itself at the exams. Then Beetle shows up blank sheets, and trusts to his 'English' to save him from a fall. I fancy he spends most of his time with me in writing verse."

"I wish to Heaven he would transfer a little of his energy in that direction to Elegiacs." King jerked himself upright.

"He is, with the single exception of Stalky, the very vilest manufacturer of 'barbarous hexameters' that I have ever dealt with."

"The work is combined in that study," said the chaplain. "Stalky does the mathematics, McTurk the Latin, and Beetle attends to their English and French. At least, when he was in the sick-house last month—"

"Malingering," Prout interjected.

"Quite possibly. I found a very distinct falling off in their 'Roman d'un Jeune Homme Pauvre' translations."

"I think it is profoundly immoral," said Prout. "I've always been opposed to the study system."

"It would be hard to find any study where the boys don't help each other; but in Number Five the thing has probably been reduced to a system," said little Hartopp. "They have a system in most things."

"They confess as much," said the Reverend John. "I've seen McTurk being hounded up the stairs to elegise the 'Elegy in a Churchyard,' while Beetle and Stalky went to punt-about."

"It amounts to systematic cribbing," said Prout, his voice growing deeper and deeper.

"No such thing," little Hartopp returned. "You can't teach a cow the violin."

"In intention it is cribbing."

"But we spoke under the seal of the confessional, didn't we?" said the Reverend John.

"You say you've heard them arranging their work in this way, Gillett," Prout persisted.

"Good Heavens! Don't make *me* Queen's evidence, my dear fellow. Hartopp is equally incriminated. If they ever found out that I had sneaked, our relations would suffer—and I value them."

"I think your attitude in this matter is weak," said Prout, looking round for support. "It would be really better to break up the study—for a while—wouldn't it?"

"Oh, break it up by all means," said Macrea. "We shall see them if Gillett's theory holds water."

"Be wise, Prout. Leave them alone, or calamity will overtake you; and what is much more important, they will be annoyed with me. I am too fat, alas! to be worried by bad boys. Where are you going?"

"Nonsense! They would not dare—but I am going to think this out," said Prout. "It needs thought. In intention they cribbed, and I must think out my duty."

"He's perfectly capable of putting the boys on their honour. It's *I* that am a fool." The Reverend John looked round remorsefully. "Never again will I forget that a master is not a man. Mark my words," said the Reverend John. "There will be trouble."

* * * * *

But by the yellow Tiber
Was tumult and affright.

Out of the blue sky (they were still rejoicing over the cat war) Mr. Prout had dropped into Number Five, read them a lecture on the enormity of cribbing, and bidden them return to the form-rooms on Monday. They had raged, solo and chorus, all through the peaceful Sabbath, for their sin was more or less the daily practice of all the studies.

"What's the good of cursing?" said Stalky at last. "We're all in the same boat. We've got to go back and consort with the house. A locker in the form-room, and a seat at prep. in Number Twelve." (He looked regretfully round the cosey study which McTurk, their leader in matters of Art, had decorated with a dado, a stencil, and cretonne hangings.)

"Yes! Heffy lurchin' into the form-rooms like a frowzy old retriever, to see if we aren't up to something. You know he never leaves his house alone, these days," said McTurk. "Oh, it will be giddy!"

"Why aren't you down watchin' cricket? I like a robust healthy boy. You musn't frowzt in a form-room. Why don't you take an interest in your house? Yah!" quoted Beetle.

"Yes, why don't we? Let's! We'll take an interest in the house. We'll take no end of interest in the house! He hasn't had us in the form-rooms for a year. We've learned a lot since then. Oh, we'll make it a be-autiful house before we've done! 'Member that chap in 'Eric' or 'St. Winifred's'—Belial somebody? I'm goin' to be Belial," said Stalky, with an ensnaring grin.

"Right O," said Beetle, "and I'll be Mammon. I'll lend money at usury—that's what they do at all schools accordin' to the B.O.P. Penny a week on a shillin'. That'll startle Heffy's weak intellect. You can be Lucifer, Turkey."

"What have I got to do?" McTurk also smiled.

"Head conspiracies—and cabals—and boycotts. Go in for that 'stealthy intrigue' that Heffy is always talkin' about. Come on!"

The house received them on their fall with the mixture of jest and sympathy always extended to boys turned out of their study. The known aloofness of the three made them more interesting.

"Quite like old times, ain't it?" Stalky selected a locker and flung in his books. "We've come to sport with you, my young friends, for a while, because our beloved house-master has hove us out of our diggin's."

" 'Serve you jolly well right," said Orrin, "you cribbers!"

"This will never do," said Stalky. "We can't maintain our giddy prestige, Orrin, de-ah, if you make these remarks."

They wrapped themselves lovingly about the boy, thrust him to the opened window, and drew down the sash to the nape of his neck. With an equal swiftness they tied his thumbs together behind his back with a piece of twine, and then, because he kicked furiously, removed his shoes.

There Mr. Prout happened to find him a few minutes later, guillotined and helpless, surrounded by a convulsed crowd who would not assist.

Stalky, in an upper form-room, had gathered himself allies against vengeance. Orrin presently tore up at the head of a boarding party, and the form-room grew one fog of dust through which boys wrestled, stamped, shouted, and yelled. A desk was carried away in the tumult, a knot of warriors reeled into and split a door-panel, a window was broken, and a gas-jet fell. Under cover of the confusion the three escaped to the corridor, whence they called in and sent up passers-by to the fray.

"Rescue, Kings! Kings! Kings! Number Twelve form-room! Rescue, Prouts—Prouts! Rescue, Macreas! Rescue, Hartopps!"

The juniors hurried out like bees aswarm, asking no questions, clattered up the staircase, and added themselves to the embroilment.

"Not bad for the first evening's work," said Stalky, rear-ranging his collar. "I fancy Prout'll be somewhat annoyed. We'd better establish an *alibi*." So they sat on Mr. King's railings till prep.

"You see," quoth Stalky, as they strolled up to prep. with the ignoble herd, "if you get the houses well mixed up an' scufflin', it's even bettin' that some ass will start a real row. Hullo, Orrin, you look rather metagrobolised."

"It was all your fault, you beast! You started it. We've got two hundred lines apiece, and Heffy's lookin' for you. Just see what that swine Malpas did to my eye!"

"I like your saying *we* started it. Who called us cribbers? Can't your infant mind connect cause and effect yet? Some day you'll find out that it don't pay to jest with Number Five."

"Where's that shillin' you owe me?" said Beetle, suddenly. Stalky could not see Prout behind him, but returned the lead without a quaver.

"I only owed you ninepence, you old usurer."

"You've forgotten the interest," said McTurk. "A halfpenny a week per bob is Beetle's charge. You must be beastly rich, Beetle."

"Well, Beetle lent me sixpence." Stalky came to a full stop and made as to work it out on his fingers. "Sixpence on the nineteenth, didn't he?"

"Yes; but you've forgotten you paid no interest on the other bob—the one I lent you before."

"But you took my watch as security." The game was developing itself almost automatically.

"Never mind. Pay me my interest, or I'll charge you interest on interest. Remember, I've got your note-of-hand!" shouted Beetle.

"You are a cold-blooded Jew," Stalky groaned.

"Hush!" said McTurk, very loudly indeed, and started as Prout came upon them.

"I didn't see you in that disgraceful affair in the form-room just now," said he.

"What, sir? We're just come up from Mr. King's," said Stalky. "Please, sir, what am I to do about prep.? They've broken the desk you told me to sit at, and the form's just swimming with ink."

"Find another seat—find another seat. D'you expect me to dry-nurse you? I wish to know whether you are in the habit of advancing money to your associates, Beetle?"

"No, sir; not as a general rule, sir."

"It is a most reprehensible habit. I thought that my house, at least, would be free from it. Even with my opinion of you, I hardly thought it was one of your vices."

"There's no harm in lending money, sir, is there?"

"I am not going to bandy words with you on your notions of morality. How much have you lent Corkran?"

"I—I don't quite know," said Beetle. It is difficult to improvise a going concern on the spur of the minute.

"You seemed certain enough just now."

"I think it's two and fourpence," said McTurk, with a glance of cold scorn at Beetle.

In the hopelessly involved finances of the study there was just that sum to which both McTurk and Beetle laid claim, as their share in the pledging of Stalky's second-best Sunday trousers. But Stalky had maintained for two terms that the money was his "commission" for effecting the pawn; and had, of course, spent it on a study "brew."

"Understand this, then. You are not to continue your operations as a money-lender. Two and fourpence, you said, Corkran?"

Stalky had said nothing, and continued so to do.

"Your influence for evil is quite strong enough without buying a hold over your companions." He felt in his pockets, and (oh joy!) produced a florin and fourpence. "Bring me what you call Corkran's note-of-hand, and be thankful that I do not carry the matter any further. The money is stopped from your pocket-money, Corkran. The receipt to my study, at once."

Little they cared! Two and fourpence in a lump is worth six weekly sixpences any hungry day of the week.

"But what the dooce *is* a note-of-hand?" said Beetle. "I only read about it in a book."

"Now you've jolly well got to make one," said Stalky.

"Yes—but our ink don't turn black till the next day. S'pose he'll spot that?"

"Not him. He's too worried," said McTurk. "Sign your name on a bit of impot-paper, Stalky, and write, 'I O U two and fourpence.' Aren't you grateful to me for getting that out of Prout? Stalky'd never have paid. . . . Why, you ass!"

Mechanically Beetle had handed over the money to Stalky as treasurer of the study. The custom of years is not lightly broken.

In return for the document, Prout expounded to Beetle the enormity of money-lending, which, like everything except compulsory cricket, corrupted houses and destroyed good feeling among boys, made youth cold and calculating, and opened the door to all evil. Finally, did Beetle know of any other cases? If so, it was his duty as proof of repentance to let his house-master know. No names need be mentioned.

Beetle did not know—at least, he was not quite sure, sir. How could he give evidence against his friends? The house might, of course—here be feigned an anguished delicacy—be full of it. He was not in a position to say. He had not met with any open competition in his trade; but if Mr. Prout considered it was a matter that affected the honour of the house (Mr. Prout did consider it precisely that), perhaps the house-prefects would be better . . .

He spun it out till half-way through prep.

"And," said the amateur Shylock, returning to the form-room and dropping at Stalky's side, "if he don't think the house is putrid with it, I'm several Dutchmen—that's all. . . . I've been to Mr. Prout's study, sir." This to the prep.-master. "He said I could sit where I liked, sir. . . . Oh, he is just tricklin' with emotion. . . . Yes, sir, I'm only askin' Corkran to let me have a dip in his ink."

After prayers, on the road to the dormitories, Harrison and Craye, senior house-prefects, zealous in their office, waylaid them with great anger.

"What have you been doing to Heffy this time, Beetle? He's been jawin' us all the evening."

"What has His Serene Transparency been vexin' you for?" said McTurk.

"About Beetle lendin' money to Stalky," began Harrison; "and then Beetle went and told him that there was any amount of money-lendin' in the house."

"No, you don't," said Beetle, sitting on a boot-basket. "That's just what I didn't tell him. I spoke the giddy truth. He asked me if there was much of it in the house; and I said I didn't know."

"He thinks you're a set of filthy Shylocks," said McTurk. "It's just as well for you he don't think you're burglars. You know he never gets a notion out of his conscientious old head."

"Well-meanin' man. Did it all for the best." Stalky curled gracefully round the stair-rail. "Head in a drain-pipe. Full confession in the left boot. Bad for the honour of the house— very."

"Shut up," said Harrison. "You chaps always behave as if you were jawin' us when we come to jaw you."

"You're a lot too cheeky," said Craye.

"I don't quite see where the cheek comes in, except on your part, in interferin' with a private matter between me an' Beetle after it has been settled by Prout." Stalky winked cheerfully at the others.

"That's the worst of clever little swots," said McTurk, addressing the gas. "They get made prefects before they have any tact, and then they annoy chaps who could really help 'em to look after the honour of the house."

"We won't trouble you to do that!" said Craye, hotly.

"Then what are you badgerin' us for?" said Beetle. "On your own showing, you've been so beastly slack, looking after the house, that Prout believes it's a nest of money-lenders.

I've told him that I've lent money to Stalky, and no one else. I don't know whether he believes me, but that finishes my case. The rest is *your* business."

"Now we find out," Stalky's voice rose, "that there is apparently an organised conspiracy throughout the house. For aught we know, the fags may be lendin' and borrowin' far beyond their means. *We* aren't responsible for it. We're only the rank and file."

"Are you surprised we don't wish to associate with the house?" said McTurk, with dignity. "We've kept ourselves to ourselves in our study till we were turned out, and now we find ourselves let in for—for this sort of thing. It's simply disgraceful."

"Then you hector and bullyrag us on the stairs," said Stalky, "about matters that are your business entirely. You know we aren't prefects."

"You threatened us with a prefect's lickin' just now," said Beetle, boldly inventing as he saw the bewilderment in the faces of the enemy.

"And if you expect you'll gain anything from us by your way of approachin' us, you're jolly well mistaken. That's all. Good night."

They clattered up-stairs, injured virtue on every inch of their backs.

"But—but what the dickens have *we* done?" said Harrison, amazedly, to Craye.

"I don't know. Only—it always happens that way when one has anything to do with them. They're so beastly plausible."

And Mr. Prout called the good boys into his study anew, and succeeded in sinking both his and their innocent minds ten fathoms deeper in blindfolded bedazement. He spoke of steps and measures, of tone and loyalty in the house and to the house, and urged them to take up the matter tactfully.

So they demanded of Beetle whether he had any connection with any other establishment. Beetle promptly went to his house-master, and wished to know by what right Harrison and Craye had reopened a matter already settled between him and his house-master. In injured innocence no boy excelled Beetle.

Then it occurred to Prout that he might have been unfair to the culprit, who had not striven to deny or palliate his offence. He sent for Harrison and Craye, reprehending them very gently for the tone they had adopted to a repentant sinner, and when they returned to their study, they used the language of despair. They then made headlong inquisition through the house, driving the fags to the edge of hysterics, and unearthing, with tremendous pomp and parade, the natural and inevitable system of small loans that prevails among small boys.

"You see, Harrison, Thornton minor lent me a penny last Saturday, because I was fined for breaking the window; and I spent it at Keyte's. I didn't know there was any harm in it. And Wray major borrowed twopence from me when my uncle sent me a post-office order—I cashed it at Keyte's—for five bob; but he'll pay me back before the holidays. We didn't know there was anything wrong in it."

They waded through hours of this kind of thing, but found no usury, or anything approaching to Beetle's gorgeous scale of interest. The seniors—for the school had no tradition of deference to prefects outside compulsory games—told them succinctly to go about their business. They would not give evidence on any terms. Harrison was one idiot, and Craye was another; but the greatest of all, they said, was their house-master.

When a house is thoroughly upset, however good its conscience, it breaks into knots and coteries—small gatherings in the twilight, box-room committees, and groups in the corridor. And when from group to group, with an immense affectation of secrecy, three wicked boys steal, crying *"Cavé!"* when there is no need of caution, and whispering "Don't tell!" on the heels of trumpery confidences that instant invented, a very fine air of plot and intrigue can be woven round such a house.

At the end of a few days, it dawned on Prout that he moved in an atmosphere of perpetual ambush. Mysteries hedged him on all sides, warnings ran before his heavy feet, and counter-signs were muttered behind his attentive back. McTurk and

Stalky invented many absurd and idle phrases—catch-words that swept through the house as fire through stubble. It was a rare jest, and the only practical outcome of the Usury Commission, that one boy should say to a friend, with awful gravity, "Do you think there's much of it going on in the house?" The other would reply, "Well, one can't be too careful, you know." The effect on a house-master of humane conscience and good intent may be imagined. Again, a man who has sincerely devoted himself to gaining the esteem of his charges does not like to hear himself described, even at a distance, as "Popularity Prout" by a dark and scowling Celt with a fluent tongue. A rumour that stories—unusual stories—are told in the form-rooms, between the lights, by a boy who does not command his confidence, agitates such a man; and even elaborate and tender politeness—for the courtesy wise-grown men offer to a bewildered child was the courtesy that Stalky wrapped round Prout—restores not his peace of mind.

"The tone of the house seems changed—changed for the worse," said Prout to Harrison and Craye. "Have you noticed it? I don't for an instant impute—"

He never imputed anything; but, on the other hand, he never did anything else, and, with the best intentions in the world, he had reduced the house-prefects to a state as nearly bordering on nervous irritation as healthy boys can know. Worst of all, they began at times to wonder whether Stalky & Co. had not some truth in their often-repeated assertions that Prout was a gloomy ass.

"As you know, I am not the kind of man who puts himself out for every little thing he hears. *I* believe in letting the house work out their own salvation—with a light guiding hand on the reins, of course. But there is a perceptible lack of reverence—a lower tone in matters that touch the honour of the house, a sort of hardness."

"Oh, Prout he is a nobleman, a nobleman, a nobleman!
Our Heffy is a nobleman—
He does an awful lot,
Because his popularity—

Oh, pop-u-pop-u-larity—
His giddy popularity
Would suffer did he not!"

The study door stood ajar; and the song, borne by twenty clear voices, came faint from a form-room. The fags rather liked the tune; the words were Beetle's.

"That's a thing no sensible man objects to," said Prout, with a lopsided smile; "but you know straws show which way the wind blows. Can you trace it to any direct influence? I am speaking to you now as heads of the house."

"There isn't the least doubt of it," said Harrison, angrily. "I know what you mean, sir. It all began when Number Five study came to the form-rooms. There's no use blinkin' it, Craye. You know that, too."

"They make things rather difficult for us, sometimes," said Craye. "It's more their manner than anything else, that Harrison means."

"Do they hamper you in the discharge of your duties, then?"

"Well, no, sir. They only look on and grin—and turn up their noses generally."

"Ah," said Prout, sympathetically.

"I think, sir," said Craye, plunging into the business boldly, "it would be a great deal better if they were sent back to their study—better for the house. They are rather old to be knocking about the form-rooms."

"They are younger than Orrin, or Flint, and a dozen others that I can think of."

"Yes, sir; but that's different, somehow. They're rather influential. They have a knack of upsettin' things in a quiet way that one can't take hold of. At least, if one does—"

"And you think they would be better in their own study again?"

Emphatically Harrison and Craye were of that opinion. As Harrison said to Craye, afterwards, "They've weakened our authority. They're too big to lick; they've made an exhibition of us over this usuary business, and we're a laughing-stock to the rest of the school. I'm going up [for Sandhurst, understood] next term. They've managed to knock me out of half my work already with their—their lunacy. If they go back to their study we may have a little peace."

"Hullo, Harrison!" McTurk ambled round the corner, with a roving eye on all possible horizons. "Bearin' up, old man? That's right. Live it down! Live it down!"

"What d'you mean?"

"You look a little pensive," said McTurk. "Exhaustin' job superintendin' the honour of the house, ain't it? By the way, how are you off for mares'-nests?"

"Look here," said Harrison, hoping for instant reward. "We've recommended Prout to let you go back to your study."

"The dooce you have! And who under the sun are *you* to interfere between us and our house-master? Upon my Sam, you two try us very hard—you do, indeed. Of course we don't know how far you abuse your position to prejudice us with Mr. Prout; but when you deliberately stop me to tell me you've been makin' arrangements behind our back—in secret —with Prout—I—I don't know really what we ought to do."

"That's beastly unfair!" cried Craye.

"It is." McTurk had adopted a ghastly solemnity that sat well on his long, lean face. "Hang it all! A prefect's one thing and an usher's another; but you seem to combine 'em. You recommend this—you recommend that! *You* say how and when we go back to our study!"

"But—but—we thought you'd like it, Turkey. We did, indeed. You know you'll be ever so much more comfortable there." Harrison's voice was almost tearful.

McTurk turned away as though to hide his emotions.

"They're broke!" He hunted up Stalky and Beetle in a box-room. "They're sick! They've been beggin' Heffy to let us go back to Number Five. Poor devils! Poor little devils!"

"It's the olive branch," was Stalky's comment. "It's the giddy white flag, by gum! Come to think of it, we *have* metagrobolised 'em."

Just after tea that day, Mr. Prout sent for them to say that if they chose to ruin their future by neglecting their work, it was entirely their own affair. He wished them, however, to understand that their presence in the form-rooms could not be tolerated one hour longer. He personally did not care to think of the time he must spend in eliminating the traces of their evil influences. How far Beetle had pandered to the baser side of youthful imagination he would ascertain later; and Beetle might be sure that if Mr. Prout came across any soul-corrupting consequences—

"Consequences of what, sir?" said Beetle, genuinely bewildered this time; and McTurk quietly kicked him on the ankle for being "fetched" by Prout.

Beetle, the house-master continued, knew very well what was intended. Evil and brief had been their careers under his eye; and as one standing *in loco parentis* to their yet uncontaminated associates, he was bound to take his precautions. The return of the study key closed the sermon.

"But what was the baser-side-of-imagination business?" said Beetle on the stairs.

"I never knew such an ass as you are for justifyin' yourself," said McTurk. "I hope I jolly well skinned your ankle. Why do you let yourself be drawn by everybody?"

"Draws be blowed! I must have tickled him up in some way I didn't know about. If I'd had a notion of that before, of course I could have rubbed it in better. It's too late now. What a pity! 'Baser side.' What *was* he drivin' at?"

"Never mind," said Stalky. "I knew we could make it a happy little house. I said so, remember—but I swear I didn't think we'd do it so soon."

* * * * *

"No," said Prout most firmly in Common-room. "I maintain that Gillett is wrong. True, I let them return to their study."

"With your known views on cribbing, too?" purred little Hartopp. "What an immoral compromise!"

"One moment," said the Reverend John. "I—we—all of us have exercised an absolutely heart-breaking discretion for the last ten days. Now we want to know. Confess—have you known a happy minute since—"

"As regards my house, I have not," said Prout. "But you are entirely wrong in your estimate of those boys. In justice to the others—in self-defence—"

"Ha! I said it would come to that," murmured the Reverend John.

"—I was forced to send them back. Their moral influence was unspeakable—simply un-unspeakable."

And bit by bit he told his tale, beginning with Beetle's usury, and ending with the house-prefects' appeal.

"Beetle in the *rôle* of Shylock is new to me," said King, with twitching lips. "I heard rumours of it—"

"Before?" said Prout.

"No, after you had dealt with them; but I was careful not to inquire. I never interfere with—"

"I myself," said Hartopp, "would cheerfully give him five shillings if he could work out one simple sum in compound interest without three gross errors."

"Why—why—why!" Mason, the mathematical master, stuttered, a fierce joy on his face, "you've been bad—precisely the same as me!"

"And so you held an inquiry?" Little Hartopp's voice drowned Mason's ere Prout caught the import of the sentence.

"The boy himself hinted at the existence of a good deal of it in the house," said Prout.

"He is passed master in that line," said the chaplain. "But, as regards the honour of the house—"

"They lowered it in a week. I have striven to build it up for years. My own house-prefects—and boys do not willingly complain of each other—besought me to get rid of them. You say you have their confidence, Gillett: they may tell you another tale. As far as I am concerned, they may go to the devil in their own way. I'm sick and tired of them," said Prout, bitterly.

But it was the Reverend John, with a smiling countenance, who went to the devil just after number Five had cleared away a very pleasant little brew (it cost them two and four-pence) and was settling down to prep.

"Come in, Padre, come in," said Stalky, thrusting forward the best chair. "We've only met you official-like these last ten days."

"You were under sentence," said the Reverend John. "I do not consort with malefactors."

"Ah, but we're restored again," said McTurk. "Mr. Prout has relented."

"Without a stain on our characters," said Beetle. "It was a painful episode, Padre, most painful."

"Now, consider for a while, and perpend, *mes enfants*. It is about your characters that I've called to-night. In the language of the schools, what the dooce *have* you been up to in Mr. Prout's house? It isn't anything to laugh over. He says that you so lowered the tone of the house he had to pack you back to your studies. Is that true?"

"Every word of it, Padre."

"Don't be flippant, Turkey. Listen to me. I've told you very often that no boys in the school have a greater influence for good or evil than you have. You know I don't talk about ethics and moral codes, because I don't believe that the young of the human animal realises what they mean for some years to come. All the same, I don't want to think you've been perverting the juniors. Don't interrupt, Beetle. Listen to me! Mr. Prout has a notion that you have been corrupting your associates somehow or other."

"Mr. Prout has so many notions, Padre," said Beetle, wearily. "Which one is this?"

"Well, he tells me that he heard you telling a story in the twilight in the form-room, in a whisper. And Orrin said, just as he opened the door, 'Shut up, Beetle; it's too beastly.' Now, then?"

"You remember Mrs. Oliphant's 'Beleaguered City' that you lent me last term?" said Beetle.

The Padre nodded.

"I got the notion out of that. Only, instead of a city, I made it the Coll in a fog—besieged by ghosts of dead boys, who hauled chaps out of their beds in the dormitory. All the names are quite real. You tell it in a whisper, you know—with the names. Orrin didn't like it one little bit. None of 'em have ever let me finish it. It gets just awful at the end part."

"But why in the world didn't you explain to Mr. Prout, instead of leaving him under the impression——?"

"Padre Sahib," said McTurk, "it isn't the least good explainin' to Mr. Prout. If he hasn't one impression, he's bound to have another."

"He'd do it with the best o' motives. He's *in loco parentis*," purred Stalky.

"You young demons!" the Reverend John replied. "And am I to understand that the—the usury business was another of your house-master's impressions?"

"Well—we helped a little in that," said Stalky. "I did owe Beetle two and fourpence—at least, Beetle says I did, but I never intended to pay him. Then we started a bit of an argument on the stairs, and—Mr. Prout dropped into it accidental. That was how it was, Padre. He paid me cash down like a giddy Dook (stopped it out of my pocket-money just the same), and Beetle gave him my note-of-hand all correct. I don't know what happened after that."

"I was too truthful," said Beetle. "I always am. You see, he was under an impression, Padre, and I suppose I ought to have corrected that impression; but of course I couldn't be *quite* certain that his house wasn't given over to money-lendin', could I? I thought the house-prefects might know more about it than I did. They ought to. They're giddy palladiums of public schools."

"They did, too—by the time they'd finished," said McTurk. "As nice a pair of conscientious, well-meanin', upright, pure-souled boys as you'd ever want to meet, Padre. They turned the house upside down—Harrison and Craye—with the best motives in the world."

"They said so. 'They said it very loud and clear. They went and shouted in our ear,'" said Stalky.

"My own private impression is that all three of you will infallibly be hanged," said the Reverend John.

"Why, *we* didn't do anything," McTurk replied. "It was all Mr. Prout. Did you ever read a book about Japanese wrestlers? My uncle—he's in the Navy—gave me a beauty once."

"Don't try to change the subject, Turkey."

"I'm not, sir. I'm givin' an illustration—same as a sermon. These wrestler-chaps have got some sort of trick that let's the other chap do all the work. Then they give a little wriggle, and he upsets himself. It's called *shibbuwichee* or *tokonoma*, or somethin'. Mr. Prout's a *shibbuwicher*. It isn't our fault."

"Did you suppose we went round corruptin' the minds of the fags?" said Beetle. "They haven't any, to begin with; and if they had, they're corrupted long ago. I've been a fag, Padre."

"Well, I fancied I knew the normal range of your iniquities; but if you take so much trouble to pile up circumstantial evidence against yourselves, you can't blame any one if—"

"We don't blame any one, Padre. We haven't said a word against Mr. Prout, have we?" Stalky looked at the others. "We love him. He hasn't a notion how we love him."

"H'm! You dissemble your love very well. Have you ever thought who got you turned out of your study in the first place?"

"It was Mr. Prout turned us out," said Stalky, with significance.

"Well, I was that man. I didn't mean it; but some words of mine, I'm afraid, gave Mr. Prout the impression—"

Number Five laughed aloud.

"You see it's just the same thing with you, Padre," said McTurk. "He *is* quick to get an impression, ain't he? But you mustn't think we don't love him, 'cause we do. There isn't an ounce of vice about him."

A double knock fell on the door.

"The Head to see Number Five study in his study at once," said the voice of Foxy, the school-sergeant.

"Whew!" said the Reverend John. "It seems to me that there is a great deal of trouble coming for some people."

"My word! Mr. Prout's gone and told the Head," said

Stalky. "He's a moral double-ender. Not fair, luggin' the Head into a house-row."

"I should recommend a copy-book on a—h'm—safe and certain part," said the Reverend John, disinterestedly.

"Huh! He licks across the shoulders, an' it would slam like a beastly barn door," said Beetle. "Good night, Padre. We're in for it."

Once more they stood in the presence of the Head—Belial, Mammon, and Lucifer. But they had to deal with a man more subtle than them all. Mr. Prout had talked to him, heavily and sadly, for half an hour; and the Head had seen all that was hidden from the house-master.

"You've been bothering Mr. Prout," he said pensively. "House-masters aren't here to be bothered by boys more than is necessary. I don't like being bothered by these things. You are bothering *me*. That is a very serious offence. You see it?"

"Yes, sir."

"Well, now, I purpose to bother you, on personal and private grounds, because you have broken into my time. You are much too big to lick, so I suppose I shall have to mark my displeasure in some other way. Say, a thousand lines apiece, a week's gating, and a few things of that kind. Much too big to lick, aren't you?"

"Oh, no, sir," said Stalky, cheerfully; for a week's gating in the summer term is serious.

"Ve-ry good. Then we will do what we can. I wish you wouldn't bother me."

It was a fair, sustained, equable stroke, with a little draw to it, but what they felt most was his unfairness in stopping to talk between executions. Thus:

"Among the—lower classes this would lay me open to a charge of—assault. You should be more grateful for your—privileges than you are. There is a limit—one finds it by experience, Beetle—beyond which it is never safe to pursue private vendettas, because—don't move—sooner or later one comes—into collision with the—higher authority, who has studied the animal. *Et ego*—McTurk, please—*in Arcadia vixi.* There's a certain flagrant injustice about this that ought to appeal to—your temperament. And that's all! You will tell your house-master that you have been formally caned by me."

"My word!" said McTurk, wriggling his shoulder-blades all down the corridor. "That was business! The Prooshan Bates has an infernal straight eye."

"Wasn't it wily of me to ask for the lickin','" said Stalky, "instead of those impots?"

"Rot! We were in for it from the first. *I* knew the cock of his old eye," said Beetle. "I was within an inch of blubbing."

"Well, I didn't exactly smile," Stalky confessed.

"Let's go down to the lavatory and have a look at the damage. One of us can hold the glass and t'others can squint."

They proceeded on these lines for some ten minutes. The wales were very red and very level. There was not a penny to choose between any of them for thoroughness, efficiency, and a certain clarity of outline that stamps the work of the artist.

"What are you doing down there?" Mr. Prout was at the head of the lavatory stairs, attracted by the noise of splashing.

"We've only been caned by the Head, sir, and we're washing off the blood. The Head said we were to tell you. We were coming to report ourselves in a minute, sir. (*Sotto voce.*) That's a score for Heffy!"

"Well, he deserves to score something, poor devil," said McTurk, putting on his shirt. "We've sweated a stone and a half off him since we began."

"But look here, why aren't we wrathy with the Head? He said it was a flagrant injustice. So it is!" said Beetle.

"Dear man," said McTurk, and vouchsafed no further answer.

It was Stalky who laughed till he had to hold on by the edge of a basin.

"You *are* a funny ass! What's that for?" said Beetle.

"I'm—I'm thinking of the flagrant injustice of it!"

The Moral Reformers

THERE WAS NO DISGUISING the defeat. Victory was to Prout, but they grudged it not. If he had broken the rules of the game by calling in the Head, they had had a good run for their money.

The Reverend John sought the earliest oportunity of talking things over. Members of a bachelor Common-room, of a school where masters' studies are designedly dotted among studies and form-rooms, can, if they choose, see a great deal of their charges. Number Five had spent some cautious years in testing the Reverend John. He was emphatically a gentleman. He knocked at a study door before entering; he comported himself as a visitor and not a strayed lictor; he never prosed, and he never carried over into official life the confidences of idle hours. Prout was ever an unmitigated nuisance; King came solely as an avenger of blood; even little Hartopp, talking natural history, seldom forgot his office; but the Reverend John was a guest desired and beloved by Number Five.

Behold him, then, in their only arm-chair, a bent brier between his teeth, chin down in three folds on his clerical collar, and blowing like an amiable whale, while Number Five discoursed of life as it appeared to them, and specially of that last interview with the Head—in the matter of usury.

"One licking once a week would do you an immense amount of good," he said, twinkling and shaking all over; "and, as you say, you were entirely in the right."

"Ra-ather, Padre! We could have proved it if he'd let us talk," said Stalky: "but he didn't. The Head's a downy bird."

"He understands you perfectly. Ho! ho! Well, you worked hard enough for it."

"But he's awfully fair. He doesn't lick a chap in the morning an' preach at him in the afternoon," said Beetle.

"He can't; he ain't in Orders, thank Goodness," said McTurk. Number Five held the very strongest views on clerical head-masters, and were ever ready to meet their pastor in argument.

"Almost all other schools have clerical Heads," said the Reverend John, gently.

"It isn't fair on the chaps," Stalky replied. "Makes 'em sulky. Of course it's different with *you*, sir. You belong to the school—same as we do. I mean ordinary clergymen."

"Well, I am a most ordinary clergyman; and Mr. Hartopp's in Orders, too."

"Ye-es, but he took 'em after he came to the Coll. We saw him go up for his exam. That's all right," said Beetle. "But just think if the Head went and got ordained!"

"What would happen, Beetle?"

"Oh, the Coll 'ud go to pieces in a year, sir. There's no doubt o' that."

"How d'you know?" The Reverend John was smiling.

"We've been here nearly six years now. There are precious few things about the Coll we don't know," Stalky replied. "Why, even you came the term after I did, sir. I remember your asking our names in form your first lesson. Mr. King, Mr. Prout, and the Head, of course, are the only masters senior to us—in that way."

"Yes, we've changed a good deal—in Common-room."

"Huh!" said Beetle, with a grunt. "They came here, an' they went away to get married. Jolly good riddance, too!"

"Doesn't our Beetle hold with matrimony?"

"No, Padre; don't make fun of me. I've met chaps in the holidays who've got married house-masters. It's perfectly awful! They have babies and teething and measles and all that sort of thing right bung *in* the school; and the masters' wives give tea-parties—tea-parties, Padre!—and ask the chaps to breakfast."

"That don't matter so much," said Stalky. "But the house-masters let their houses alone, and they leave everything to the prefects. Why, in one school, a chap told me, there were big baize doors and a passage about a mile long between the house and the master's house. They could do just what they pleased."

"Satan rebuking sin with a vengeance."

"Oh larks are right enough; but you know what we mean, Padre. After a bit it gets worse an' worse. Then there's a big bust-up and a row that gets into the papers, and a lot of chaps are expelled, you know."

"Always the wrong 'uns; don't forget that. Have a cup of cocoa, Padre?" said McTurk, with the kettle.

"No, thanks; I'm smoking. Always the wrong 'uns? Proceed, my Stalky."

"And then"—Stalky warmed to the work—"everybody says, 'Who'd ha' thought it? Shockin' boys! Wicked little kids!' It all comes of havin' married house-masters, *I* think."

"A Daniel come to judgment."

"But it does," McTurk interrupted. "I've met chaps in the holidays, an' they've told me the same thing. It looks awfully pretty for one's people to see—a nice separate house with a nice lady in charge, an' all that. But it isn't. It takes the house-masters off their work, and it gives the prefects a heap too much power, an'—an'—it rots up everything. You see, it isn't as if we were just an ordinary school. We take crammers' rejections as well as good little boys like Stalky. We've got to do that to make our name, of course, and we get 'em into Sandhurst somehow or other, don't we?"

"True, O Turk. Like a book thou talkest, Turkey."

"And so we want rather different masters, don't you think so, to other places? We aren't like the rest of the schools."

"It leads to all sorts of bullyin', too, a chap told me," said Beetle.

"Well you *do* need most of a single man's time, I must say." The Reverend John considered his hosts critically. "But do you never feel that the world—the Common-room—is too much with you sometimes?"

"Not exactly—in summer, anyhow." Stalky's eye roved contentedly to the window. "Our bounds are pretty big, too, and they leave us to ourselves a good deal."

"For example, here am I sitting in your study, very much in your way, eh?"

"Indeed you aren't Padre. Sit down. Don't go, sir. You know we're glad whenever you come."

There was doubting the sincerity of the voices. The Reverend John flushed a little with pleasure and refilled his brier.

"And we generally know where the Common-room are," said Beetle, triumphantly. "Didn't you come through our lower dormitories last night after ten, sir?"

"I went to smoke a pipe with your house-master. No, I didn't give him any impressions. I took a short cut through your dormitories."

"I sniffed a whiff of 'baccy, this mornin'. Yours is stronger than Mr. Prout's. *I* knew," said Beetle, wagging his head.

"Good heavens!" said the Reverend John, absently. It was some years before Beetle perceived that this was rather a tribute to innocence than observation. The long, light, blindless dormitories, devoid of inner doors, were crossed at all hours of the night by masters visiting one another; for bachelors sit up later than married folk. Beetle had never dreamed that there might be a purpose in this steady policing.

"Talking about bullying," the Reverend John resumed, "you all caught it pretty hot when you were fags, didn't you?"

"Well, we must have been rather awful little beasts," said Beetle, looking serenely over the gulf between eleven and sixteen. "My Hat, what bullies they were then—Fairburn, 'Gobby' Maunsell, and all that gang!"

" 'Member when 'Gobby' called us the Three Blind Mice, and we had to get up on the lockers and sing while he buzzed ink-pots at us?" said Stalky. "They *were* bullies if you like!"

"But there isn't any of it now," said McTurk, soothingly.

"That's where you make a mistake. We're all inclined to say that everything is all right as long as we aren't ourselves hurt. I sometimes wonder if it is extinct—bullying."

"Fags bully each other horrid; but the upper forms are supposed to be swottin' for exams. They've got something else to think about," said Beetle.

"Why? What do you think?" Stalky was watching the chaplain's face.

"I have my doubts." Then, explosively, "On my word, for three moderately intelligent boys you aren't very observant. I suppose you were too busy making things warm for your house-master to see what lay under your noses when you were in the form-rooms last week?"

"What, sir? I—I swear we didn't see any thing," said Beetle.

"Then I'd advise you to look. When a little chap is whimpering in a corner, and wears his clothes like rags, and never does any work, and is notoriously the dirtiest little 'corridor-caution' in the Coll, something's wrong somewhere."

"That's Clewer," said McTurk, under his breath.

"Yes, Clewer. He comes to me for his French. It's his first term, and he's almost as complete a wreck as you were, Beetle. He's not naturally clever, but he has been hammered till he's nearly an idiot."

"Oh, no. They sham silly to get off more lickings," said Beetle. "*I* know that."

"I've never actually seem him knocked about," said the Reverend John.

"The genuine article don't do that in public," said Beetle. "Fairburn never touched me when any one was looking on."

"You needn't swagger about it, Beetle," said McTurk. "We all caught it in our time."

"But I got it worse than any one," said Beetle. "If you want an authority on bullyin', Padre, come to me. Corkscrews— brush-drill — keys — head-knucklin'— arm-twistin'— rockin' —Ag Ags—and all the rest of it."

"Yes. I do want you as an authority, or rather I want your authority to stop it—all of you."

"What about Abana and Pharpar, Padre—Harrison and Craye? They are Mr. Prout's pets," said McTurk, a little bitterly. "*We* aren't even sub-prefects."

"I've considered that, but on the other hand, since most bullying is mere thoughtlessness—"

"Not one little bit of it, Padre," said McTurk. "Bullies like bullyin'. They mean it. They think it up in lesson and practise it in the quarters."

"Never mind. If the thing goes up to the prefects it may make another house-row. You've had one already. Don't laugh. Listen to me. I ask you—my own Tenth Legion—to take the thing up quietly. I want little Clewer made to look fairly clean and decent—"

"Blowed if *I* wash him!" whispered Stalky.

"—Decent and self-respecting. As for the other boy, whoever he is, you can use your influence"—a purely secular light flickered in the chaplain's eye—"in any way you please to—to dissuade him. That's all. I'll leave it to you. Good night, *mes enfants.*"

* * * * *

"Well, what are we goin' to do?" Number Five stared at each other.

"Young Clewer would give his eyes for a place to be quiet in. *I* know that," said Beetle. "If we made him a study-fag, eh?"

"No!" said McTurk, firmly. "He's a dirty little brute, and he'd mess up everything. Besides, we ain't goin' to have any beastly Erickin'. D'you want to walk about with your arm round his neck?"

"He'd clean out the jam-pots, anyhow; an' the burnt-porridge saucepan—it's filthy now."

"Not good enough," said Stalky, bringing up both heels with a crash on the table. "If we find the merry jester who's been bullyin' him an' make him happy, that'll be all right. Why didn't we spot him when we were in the form-rooms, though?"

"Maybe a lot of fags have made a dead set at Clewer. They do that sometimes."

"Then we'll have to kick the whole of the lower school in our house—on spec. Come on," said McTurk.

"Keep you hair on! We mustn't make a fuss about the biznai. Whoever it is, he's kept quiet or we'd have seen him," said Stalky. "We'll walk round and sniff about till we're sure."

They drew the house form-rooms, accounting for every junior and senior against whom they had suspicions; investigated, at Beetle's suggestion the lavatories and box-rooms, but without result. Everybody seemed to be present save Clewer.

"Rum!" said Stalky, pausing outside a study door. "Golly!"

A thin piping mixed with tears came muffled through the panels.

"*As beautiful Kitty one morning was tripping—*"

"Louder, you young devil, or I'll buzz a book at you!"

"*With a pitcher of milk—* Oh, Campbell, *please* don't! *To the fair of—*"

A book crashed on something soft and squeals arose.

"Well, I never thought it was a study-chap, anyhow. That accounts for our not spotting him," said Beetle. "Sefton and Campbell are rather hefty chaps to tackle. Besides, one can't go into their study like a form-room."

"What swine!" McTurk listened. "Where's the fun of it? I suppose Clewer's faggin' for them."

"They aren't prefects. That's one good job," said Stalky, with his war-grin. "Sefton and Campbell! Um! Campbell and Sefton! Ah! One of 'em's a crammer's pup."

The two were precocious hairy youths between seventeen and eighteen, sent to the school in despair by parents who hoped that six months' steady cram might, perhaps, jockey them into Sandhurst. Nominally they were in Mr. Prout's house; actually they were under the Head's eye; and since he was very careful never to promote strange new boys to prefectships, they considered they had a grievance against the school. Sefton had spent three months with a London crammer, and the tale of his adventures there lost nothing in the telling. Campbell, who had a fine taste in clothes and a fluent vocabulary, followed his lead in looking down loftily on the rest of the world. This was only their second term, and the school, used to what it profanely called "crammers' pups," had treated them with rather galling reserve. But their whiskers—Sefton owned a real razor—and their moustaches were beyond question impressive.

"Shall we go in an' dissuade 'em?" McTurk asked. "I've never had much to do with 'em, but I'll bet my hat Campbell's a funk."

"No-o! That's *oratio directa*," said Stalky, shaking his head. "I like *oratio obliqua*. 'Sides, where'd our moral influence be then? Think o' that!"

"Rot! What are you goin' to do?" Beetle turned into Lower Number Nine form-room, next door to the study.

"Me?" The lights of war flickered over Stalky's face. "Oh, I want to jape with 'em. Shut up a bit!"

He drove his hands into his pockets and stared out of window at the sea, whistling between his teeth. Then a foot tapped the floor; one shoulder lifted; he wheeled, and began the short quick double-shuffle—the war-dance of Stalky in meditation. Thrice he crossed the empty form-room, with compressed lips and expanded nostrils, swaying to the quick-step. Then he halted before the dumb Beetle and softly knuckled his head, Beetle bowing to the strokes. McTurk nursed one knee and rocked to and fro. They could hear Clewer howling as though his heart would break.

"Beetle is the sacrifice," Stalky said at last. "I'm sorry for you, Beetle. 'Member Galton's 'Art of Travel' [one of the forms had been studying that pleasant work] an' the kid whose bleatin' excited the tiger?"

"Oh, curse!" said Beetle, uneasily. It was not his first season as a sacrifice. "Can't you get on without me?"

" 'Fraid not, Beetle, dear. You've got to be bullied by Turkey an' me. The more you howl, o' course, the better it'll be. Turkey go an' covet a stump and a box-rope from somewhere. We'll tie him up for a kill—*à la* Galton. 'Member when 'Molly' Fairburn made us cock-fight with our shoes off, an' tied up our knees?"

"But that hurt like sin."

"Course it did. What a clever chap you are, Beetle! Turkey'll knock you all over the place. 'Member we've had a big row all round, an' I've trapped you into doin' this. Lend us your wipe."

Beetle was trussed for cock-fighting; but, in addition to the transverse stump betwen elbow and knee, his knees were bound with a box-rope. In this posture, at a push from Stalky he rolled over sideways, covering himself with dust.

"Ruffle his hair, Turkey. Now you get down, too. 'The bleatin' of the kid excites the tiger.' You two are in such a sweatin' wax with me that you only curse. 'Member that. I'll tickle you up with a stump. You'll have to blub, Beetle."

"Right O! I'll work up to it in half a shake," said Beetle.

"Now begin—and remember the bleatin' o' the kid."

"Shut up, you brutes! Let me up! You've nearly cut my knees off. Oh, you *are* beastly cads! *Do* shut up. 'Tisn't a joke!" Beetle's protest was, in tone, a work of art.

"Give it to him, Turkey! Kick him! Roll him over! Kill him! Don't funk, Beetle, you brute. Kick him again, Turkey."

"He's not blubbin' really. Roll up, Beetle, or I'll kick you into the fender," roared McTurk.

They made a hideous noise among them, and the bait allured their quarry.

"Hullo! What's the giddy jest?" Sefton and Campbell entered to find Beetle on his side, his head against the fender, weeping copiously, while McTurk prodded him in the back with his toes.

"It's only Beetle," Stalky explained. "He's shammin' hurt. I can't get Turkey to go for him properly."

Sefton promptly kicked both boys, and his face lighted. "All right, I'll attend to 'em. Get up an' cock-fight, you two. Give me the stump. I'll tickle 'em. Here's a giddy jest! Come on, Campbell. Let's cook 'em."

Then McTurk turned on Stalky and called him very evil names.

"You said you were goin' to cock-fight too, Stalky. Come on!"

"More ass you for believin' me, then!" shrieked Stalky.

"Have you chaps had a row?" said Campbell.

"Row?" said Stalky. "Huh! I'm only educatin' them. D'you know anythin' about cock-fighting, Seffy?"

"Do I know? Why, at Maclagan's, where I was crammin' in town, we used to cock-fight in his drawing-room, and little Maclagan daren't say anything. But we were just the same as men there, of course. Do I know? *I'll* show you."

"Can't I get up?" moaned Beetle, as Stalky sat on his shoulder.

"Don't jaw, you fat piffler. You're going to fight Seffy."

"He'll slay me!"

"Oh, lug 'em into our study," said Campbell. "It's nice an' quiet in there. I'll cock-fight Turkey. This is an improvement on young Clewer."

"Right O! I move it's shoes-off for them an' shoes-on for us," said Sefton, joyously, and the two were flung down on the study floor. Stalky rolled them behind an arm-chair.

"Now I'll tie you two up an' direct the bull-fight. Golly, what wrists you have, Seffy! They're too thick for a wipe; got a box-rope?" said he.

"Lots in the corner," Sefton replied. "Hurry up! Stop blubbin', you brute, Beetle. We're goin' to have a giddy campaign. Losers have to sing for the winners—sing odes in honour of the conqueror. You call yourself a beastly poet, don't you, Beetle? I'll poet you." He wriggled into position by Campbell's side.

Swiftly and scientifically the stumps were thrust through the natural crooks, and the wrists tied with well-stretched box-ropes to an accompaniment of insults from McTurk, bound, betrayed, and voluble behind the chair.

Stalky set away Campbell and Sefton, and strode over to his allies locking the door on the way.

"And that's all right," said he in a changed voice.

"What the devil—?" Sefton began. Beetle's false tears had ceased; McTurk, smiling, was on his feet. Together they bound the knees and ankles of the enemy even more straitly.

Stalky took the arm-chair and contemplated the scene with his blandest smile. A man trussed for cock-fighting is, perhaps, the most helpless thing in the world.

" 'The bleatin' of the kid excites the tiger.' Oh, you frabjous asses!" He lay back and laughed till he could no more. The victims took in the situation but slowly.

"We'll give you the finest lickin' you ever had in your young lives when we get up!" thundered Sefton from the floor. "You'll laugh the other side of your mouth before you've done. What the deuce d'you mean by this?"

"You'll see in two shakes," said McTurk. "Don't swear like that. What we want to know is, why you two hulkin' swine have been bullyin' Clewer?"

"It's none of your business."

"What did you bully Clewer for?" The question was repeated with maddening iteration by each in turn. They knew their work.

"Because we jolly well chose!" was the answer at last. "Let's get up." Even then they could not realise the game.

"Well, now we're goin' to bully you because we jolly well choose. We're goin' to be just as fair to you as you were to Clewer. He couldn't do anything against you. You can't do anything to us. Odd, ain't it?"

"Can't we? You wait an' see."

"Ah," said Beetle, reflectively, "that shows you've never been properly jested with. A public lickin' ain't in it with a gentle jape. Bet a bob you'll weep an' promise anything."

"Look here, young Beetle, we'll half kill you when we get up. I'll promise you that, at any rate."

"You're going to be half killed first, though. Did you give Clewer Head-knuckles?"

"Did you give Clewer Head-knuckles?" McTurk echoed. At the twentieth repetition—no boy can stand the torture of one unvarying query, which is the essence of bullying—came confession.

"We did, confound you!"

"Then you'll be knuckled"; and knuckled they were, according to ancient experience. Head-knuckling is no trifle; "Molly" Fairburn of the old days could not have done better.

"Did you give Clewer Brush-drill?"

This time the question was answered sooner, and Brush-drill was dealt out for the space of five minutes by Stalky's watch. They could not even writhe in their bonds. No brush is employed in Brush-drill.

"Did you give Clewer the Key?"

"No; we didn't. I swear we didn't!" from Campbell, rolling in agony.

"Then we'll give it to you, so you can see what it would be like if you had."

The torture of the Key—which has no key at all—hurts excessively. They endured several minutes of it, and their language necessitated the gag.

"Did you give Clewer Corkscrews?"

"Yes. Oh, curse your silly souls! Let us alone, you cads."

They were corkscrewed, and the torture of the Corkscrew —this has nothing to do with corkscrews—is keener than the torture of the Key.

The method and silence of the attacks was breaking their nerves. Between each new torture came the pitiless, dazing rain of questions, and when they did not answer to the point, Isabella-coloured handkerchiefs were thrust into their mouths.

"Now are those all the things you did to Clewer? Take out the gag, Turkey, and let 'em answer."

"Yes, I swear that was all. Oh, you're killing us, Stalky!" cried Campbell.

"Pre-cisely what Clewer said to you. I heard him. Now we're goin' to show you what real bullyin' is. What I don't like about you, Sefton, is, you come to the Coll with your stick-up collars an' patent-leather boots, an' you think you can teach us something about bullyin'. *Do* you think you can teach us anything about bullyin'? Take out the gag and let him answer."

"No!"—ferociously.

"He says no. Rock him to sleep. Campbell can watch."

It needs three boys and two boxing-gloves to rock a boy to sleep. Again the operation has nothing to do with its name. Sefton was "rocked" till his eyes set in his head and he gasped and crowed for breath sick and dizzy.

"My Aunt!" said Campbell, appalled, from his corner, and turned white.

"Put him away," said Stalky. "Bring on Campbell. Now this *is* bullyin'. Oh, I forgot! I say, Campbell, what did you bully Clewer for? Take out his gag and let him answer."

"I—I don't know. Oh, let me off! I swear I'll make it *pax*. Don't 'rock' me!"

" 'The bleatin' of the kid excites the tiger.' He says he don't know. Set him up, Beetle. Give me the glove an' put in the gag."

In silence Campbell was "rocked" sixty-four times.

"I believe I'm goin' to die!" he gasped.

"He says he is goin' to die.. Put him away. Now, Sefton!
Oh, I forgot! Sefton, what did you bully Clewer for?"

The answer is unprintable; but it brought not the faintest
flush to Stalky's downy cheek.

"Make him an Ag Ag, Turkey!"

And an Ag Ag was he made, forthwith. The hard-bought
experience of nearly eighteen years was at his disposal, but he
did not seem to appreciate it.

"He says we are sweeps. Put him away! Now, Campbell!
Oh, I forgot! I say, Campbell, what did you bully Clewer
for?"

Then came the tears—scalding tears; appeals for mercy and
abject promises of peace. Let them cease the tortures and
Campbell would never lift hand against them. The questions
began again—to an accompaniment of small persuasions.

"You seem hurt Campbell. Are you hurt?"

"Yes. Awfully!"

"He says he is hurt. Are you broke?"

"Yes, yes! I swear I am. Oh, stop!"

"He says he is broke. Are you humble?"

"Yes!"

"He says he is humble. Are you devilish humble?"

"Yes!"

"He says he is devilish humble. Will you bully Clewer any
more?"

"No. No-ooh!"

"He says he won't bully Clewer. Or any one else?"

"No. I swear I won't."

"Or any one else. What about that lickin' you and Sefton
were goin' to give us?"

"I won't! I won't! I swear I won't!"

"He says he won't lick us. Do you esteem yourself to know
anything about bullyin'?"

"No, I don't!"

"He says he doesn't know anything about bullyin'. Haven't
we taught you a lot?"

"Yes—yes!"

"He says we've taught him a lot. Aren't you grateful?"

"Yes!"

"He says he is grateful. Put him away. Oh, I forgot! I say, Campbell, what did you bully Clewer for?"

He wept anew; his nerves being raw. "Because I was a bully. I suppose that's what you want me to say?"

"He says he is a bully. Right he is. Put him in the corner. No more japes for Campbell. Now, Sefton!"

"You devils! You young devils!" This and much more as Sefton was punted across the carpet by skilful knees.

" 'The bleatin' of the kid excites the tiger.' We're goin' to make you beautiful. Where does he keep his shaving things? [Campbell told.] Beetle, get some water. Turkey, make the lather. We're goin' to shave you. Seffy, so you'd better lie jolly still, or you'll get cut. I've never shaved any one before."

"Don't! Oh, don't! Please don't!"

"Gettin' polite, eh? I'm only goin' to take off one ducky little whisker—"

"I'll—I'll make it *pax*, if you don't. I swear I'll let you off your lickin' when I get up!"

"—*And* half that moustache we're so proud of. He says he'll let us off our lickin'. Isn't he kind?"

McTurk laughed into the nickel-plated shaving-cup, and settled Sefton's head between Stalky's vice-like knees.

"Hold on a shake," said Beetle, "you can't shave long hairs. You've got to cut all that moustache short first, an' then scrope him."

"Well, I'm not goin' to hunt about for scissors. Won't a match do? Chuck us the match-box. He *is* a hog, you know; we might as well singe him. Lie still!"

He lit a vesta, but checked his hand. "I only want to take off half, though."

"That's all right." Beetle waved the brush. "I'll lather up to the middle—see? and you can burn off the rest."

The thin-haired first moustache of youth fluffed off in flame to the lather-line in the centre of the lip, and Stalky rubbed away the burnt stumpage with his thumb. It was not a very gentle shave, but it abundantly accomplished its purpose.

"Now the whisker on the other side. Turn him over!" Between match and razor this, too, was removed. "Give him his shaving-glass. Take the gag out. I want to hear what he'll say."

But there were no words. Sefton gazed at the lopsided wreck in horror and despair. Two fat tears rolled down his cheek.

"Oh, I forgot! I say, Sefton, what did you bully Clewer for?"

"Leave me alone! Oh, you infernal bullies, leave me alone! Haven't I had enough?"

"He says we must leave him alone," said McTurk.

"He says we are bullies, an' we haven't even begun yet," said Beetle. "You're ungrateful, Seffy. Golly! You *do* look an atrocity and a half!"

"He says he has had enough," said Stalky. "He errs!"

"Well, to work, to work!" chanted McTurk, waving a stump. "Come on, my giddy Narcissus. Don't fall in love with your own reflection!"

"Oh, let him off," said Campbell from his corner; "he's blubbing, too."

Sefton cried like a twelve-year-old with pain, shame, wounded vanity, and utter helplessness

"You'll make it *pax*, Sefton, won't you? You can't stand up to those young devils—"

"Don't be rude, Campbell, de-ah," said McTurk, "or you'll catch it again!"

"You *are* devils, you know," said Campbell.

"What? for a little bullyin'—same as you've been givin' Clewer! How long have you been jestin' with him?" said Stalky. "All this term?"

"We didn't always knock him about, though!"

"You did when you could catch him," said Beetle, cross-legged on the floor, dropping a stump from time to time across Sefton's instep. "Don't I know it!"

"I—perhaps we did."

"And you went out of your way to catch him? Don't I know it! Because he was an awful little beast, eh? Don't I know it! Now, you see, *you're* awful beasts, and you're gettin' what he got—for bein' a beast. Just because we choose."

"We never really bullied him—like you've done us."

"Yah!" said Beetle. "They never really bully—'Molly' Fairburn didn't. Only knock 'em about a little bit. That's what they say. Only kick their souls out of 'em, and they go and blub in the box-rooms. Shove their heads into the ulsters an' blub. Write home three times a day—yes, you brute, I've done that—askin' to be taken away. You've never been bullied properly, Campbell. I'm sorry you made *pax*."

"I'm not!" said Campbell, who was a humourist in a way. "Look out, you're slaying Sefton!"

In his excitement Beetle had used the stump unreflectingly, and Sefton was now shouting for mercy.

"An' you!" he cried, wheeling where he sat. "You've never been bullied, either. Where were you before you came here?"

"I—I had a tutor."

"Yah! You would. You never blubbed in your life. But you're blubbin' now, by gum. Aren't you blubbin'?"

"Can't you see, you blind beast?" Sefton fell over sideways, tear-tracks furrowing the dried lather. Crack came the cricket-stump on the curved latter-end of him.

"Blind, am I," said Beetle, "and a beast? Shut up, Stalky. I'm goin' to jape a bit with our friend, *à la* 'Molly' Fairburn. *I* think I can see. Can't I see, Sefton?"

"The point is well taken," said McTurk, watching the stump at work. "You'd better say that he sees, Seffy"

"You do—you can! I swear you do!" yelled Sefton, for strong arguments were coercing him.

"Aren't my eyes lovely?" The stump rose and fell steadily throughout this catechism.

"Yes."

"A gentle hazel, aren't they?"

"Yes—oh, yes!"

"What a liar you are! They're sky-blue. Ain't they sky-blue?"

"Yes—oh, yes!"

"You don't know your mind from one minute to another. You must learn—you must learn."

"What a bait you're in!" said Stalky. "Keep your hair on, Beetle."

"I've had it done to me," said Beetle. "Now—about my being a beast."

"*Pax*—oh *pax!*" cried Sefton; "make it *pax*. I'll give up! Let me off! I'm broke! I can't stand it!"

"Ugh! Just when we were gettin' our hand in!" grunted McTurk. "They didn't let Clewer off, I'll swear."

"Confess—apologise—quick!" said Stalky.

From the floor Sefton made unconditional surrender, more abjectly even than Campbell. He would never touch any one again. He would go softly all the days of his life.

"We've got to take it, I suppose?" said Stalky. "All right, Sefton. You're broke? Very good. Shut up, Beetle! But before we let you up, you an' Campbell will kindly oblige us with 'Kitty of Coleraine'—*à la* Clewer."

"That's not fair," said Campbell; "we've surrendered."

" 'Course you have. Now you're goin' to do what we tell you—same as Clewer would. If you hadn't surrendered you'd ha' been really bullied. Havin' surrendered—do you follow, Seffy?—you sing odes in honour of the conquerors. Hurry up!"

They dropped into chairs luxuriously. Campbell and Sefton looked at each other, and, neither taking comfort from that view, struck up "Kitty of Coleraine."

"Vile bad," said Stalky, as the miserable wailing ended. "If you hadn't surrendered it would have been our painful duty to buzz books at you for singin' out o' tune. Now then."

He freed them from their bonds, but for several minutes they could not rise. Campbell was first on his feet, smiling uneasily. Sefton staggered to the table, buried his head in his arms, and shook with sobs. There was no shadow of fight in either—only amazement, distress, and shame.

"Ca-Can't he shave clean before tea, please?" said Campbell. "It's ten minutes to bell."

Stalky shook his head. He meant to escort the half-shaved one to the meal.

McTurk yawned in his chair and Beetle mopped his face. They were all dripping with excitement and exertion.

"If I knew anything about it, I swear I'd give you a moral lecture," said Stalky, severely.

"Don't jaw; they've surrendered," said McTurk. "This moral suasion biznai takes it out of a chap."

"Don't you see how gentle we've been? We might have called Clewer in to look at you," said Stalky. " 'The bleatin' of the tiger excites the kid.' But we didn't. We've only got to tell a few chaps in Coll about this and you'd be hooted all over the shop. Your life wouldn't be worth havin'. But we aren't goin' to do that, either. We're strictly moral suasers, Campbell; so, unless you or Seffy split about this, no one will."

"I swear you're a brick," said Campbell. "I suppose I was rather a brute to Clewer."

"It looked like it," said Stalky. "But I don't think Seffy need come into hall with cock-eye whiskers. Horrid bad for the fags if they saw him. He can shave. Ain't you grateful, Sefton?"

The head did not lift. Sefton was deeply asleep.

"That's rummy," said McTurk, as a snore mixed with a sob. " 'Cheek, *I* think; or else he's shammin'.' "

"No, 'tisn't," said Beetle. "When 'Molly' Fairburn had attended to me for an hour or so I used to go bung off to sleep on a form sometimes. Poor devil! But he called me a beastly poet, though."

"Well, come on." Stalky lowered his voice. "Good-by, Campbell. 'Member, if you don't talk, nobody will."

There should have been a war-dance, but that all three were so utterly tired that they almost went to sleep above the tea-cups in their study, and slept till prep.

* * * * *

"A most extraordinary letter. Are *all* parents incurably mad? What do you make of it?" said the Head, handing a closely written eight pages to the Reverend John.

" 'The only son of his mother, and she a widow.' That is the least reasonable sort." The chaplain read with pursed lips.

"If half those charges are true he should be in the sick-house; whereas he is disgustingly well. Certainly he has shaved. I noticed that."

"Under compulsion, as his mother points out. How delicious! How salutary!"

"You haven't to answer her. It isn't often I don't know what has happened in the school; but this is beyond me."

"If you asked me I should say seek not to propitiate. When one is forced to take crammers' pups—"

"He was perfectly well at extra-tuition—with me—this morning," said the Head, absently. "Unusually well behaved, too."

"—they either educate the school, or the school, as in this case, educates them. I prefer our own methods," the chaplain concluded.

"You think it was that?" A lift of the Head's eyebrow.

"I'm sure of it! And nothing excuses his trying to give the College a bad name."

"That's the line I mean to take with him," the Head answered.

The Augurs winked.

* * * * *

A few days later the Reverend John called on Number Five. "Why haven't we seen you before, Padre?" said they.

"I've been watching times and seasons and events and men —and boys," he replied. "I am pleased with my Tenth Legion. I make them my compliments. Clewer was throwing ink-balls in form this morning, instead of doing his work. He is now doing fifty lines for—unheard-of audacity."

"You can't blame us, sir," said Beetle. "You told us to remove the—er—pressure. That's the worst of a fag."

"I've known boys five years his senior throw ink-balls, Beetle. To such an one have I given two hundred lines—not so long ago. And now I come to think of it, were those lines ever shown up?"

"Were they, Turkey?" said Beetle, unblushingly.

"Don't you think Clewer looks a little cleaner, Padre?" Stalky interrupted.

"We're no end of moral reformers," said McTurk.

"It was all Stalky, but it was a lark," said Beetle.

"I have noticed the moral reform in several quarters. Didn't I tell you you had more influence than any boys in the Coll if you cared to use it?"

"It's a trifle exhaustin' to use frequent—our kind of moral suasion. Besides, you see, it only makes Clewer cheeky."

"I wasn't thinking of Clewer; I was thinking of—the other people, Stalky."

"Oh, we didn't bother much about the other people," said McTurk. "Did we?"

"But *I* did—from the beginning."

"Then you knew, sir?"

A downward puff of smoke.

"Boys educate each other, they say, more than we can or dare. If I had used one half of the moral suasion you may or may not have employed—"

"With the best motives in the world. Don't forget our pious motives, Padre," said McTurk.

"—I suppose I should be now languishing in Bideford jail, shouldn't I? Well, to quote the Head, in a little business which we have agreed to forget, that strikes me as flagrant injustice. . . . What are you laughing at, you young sinners? Isn't it true? I will not stay to be shouted at. What I looked into this den of iniquity for was to find out if any one cared to come down for a bathe off the Ridge. But I see you won't."

"Won't we, though! Half a shake, Padre Sahib, till we get our towels, and *nous sommes avec vous!*"

A Little Prep.

THE EASTER TERM was but a month old when Stettson major, a day-boy, contracted diphtheria, and the Head was very angry. He decreed a new and narrower set of bounds—the infection had been traced to an outlying farm-house—urged the prefects severely to lick all trespassers, and promised extra attentions from his own hand. There were no words bad enough for Stettson major, quarantined at his mother's house, who had lowered the school-average of health. This he said in the gymnasium after prayers. Then he wrote some two hundred letters to as many anxious parents and guardians, and bade the school carry on. The trouble did not spread, but, one night, a dog-cart drove to the Head's door, and in the morning the Head had gone, leaving all things in charge of Mr. King, senior house-master. The Head often ran up to town, where the school devoutly believed he bribed officials for early proofs of the Army Examination papers; but this absence was unusually prolonged.

"Downy old bird!" said Stalky to the allies, one wet afternoon, in the study. "He must have gone on a bend an' been locked up, under a false name."

"What for?" Beetle entered joyously into the libel.

"Forty shillin's or a month for hackin' the chucker-out of the Pavvy on the shins. Bates always has a spree when he goes to town. Wish he was back, though. I'm about sick o' King's 'whips an' scorpions' an' lectures on public-school spirit—yah!—and scholarship!"

" 'Crass an' materialised brutality of the middle-classes—readin' solely for marks. Not a scholar in the whole school,' " McTurk quoted, pensively boring holes in the mantelpiece with a hot poker.

"That's rather a sickly way of spending an afternoon. Stinks, too. Let's come out an' smoke. Here's a treat." Stalky held up a long Indian cheroot. " 'Bagged it from my pater

137

last holidays. I'm a bit shy of it, though; it's heftier than a pipe. We'll smoke it palaver-fashion. Hand it round, eh? Let's lie up behind the old harrow on the Monkey-farm Road."

"Out of bounds. Bounds beastly strict these days, too. Besides, we shall cat." Beetle sniffed the cheroot critically. "It's a regular Pomposo Stinkadore."

"You can; I sha'n't. What d'you say, Turkey?"

"Oh, may's well, I s'pose."

"Chuck on your cap, then. It's two to one. Beetle, out you come!"

They saw a group of boys by the notice-board in the corridor; little Foxy, the school-sergeant, among them.

"More bounds, I expect," said Stalky. "Hullo, Foxibus, who are you in mournin' for?" There was a broad band of crape round Foxy's arm.

"He was in my old regiment," said Foxy, jerking his head towards the notices, where a newspaper cutting was thumb-tacked between call-over lists.

"By gum!" quoth Stalky, uncovering as he read. "It's old Duncan—Fat-Sow Duncan— killed on duty at something or other Kotal. '*Rallyin' his men with conspicuous gallantry*.' He would, of course. '*The body was recovered*.' That's all right. They cut 'em up sometimes, don't they, Foxy?"

"Horrid," said the sergeant, briefly.

"Poor old Fat-Sow! I was a fag when he left. How many does that make to us, Foxy?"

"Mr. Duncan, he is the ninth. He come here when he was no bigger than little Grey tertius. My old regiment, too. Yiss, nine to us, Mr. Corkran, up to date."

The boys went out into the wet, walking swiftly.

"Wonder how it feels—to be shot and all that," said Stalky, as they splashed down a lane. "Where did it happen, Beetle?"

"Oh, out in India somewhere. We're always rowin' there. But look here, Stalky, what *is* the good o' sittin' under a hedge an' cattin'? It's be-eastly cold. It's be-eastly wet, and we'll be collared as sure as a gun."

"Shut up! Did you ever know your Uncle Stalky get you

into a mess yet?" Like many other leaders, Stalky did not dwell on past defeats.

They pushed through a dripping hedge, landed among water-logged clods, and sat down on a rust-coated harrow. The cheroot burned with sputterings of saltpetre. They smoked it gingerly, each passing to the other between closed forefinger and thumb.

"Good job we hadn't one apiece, ain't it?" said Stalky, shivering through set teeth. To prove his words he immediately laid all before them, and they followed his example. . . .

"I told you," moaned Beetle, sweating clammy drops. "Oh, Stalky, you *are* a fool!"

"*Je cat, tu cat, il cat. Nous cattons!*" McTurk handed up his contribution and lay hopelessly on the cold iron.

"Something's wrong with the beastly thing. I say, Beetle, have you been droppin' ink on it?"

But Beetle was in no case to answer. Limp and empty, they sprawled across the harrow, the rust marking their ulsters in red squares and the abandoned cheroot-end reeking under their very cold noses. Then—they had heard nothing—the Head himself stood before them—the Head who should have been in town bribing examiners—the Head fantastically attired in old tweeds and a deer-stalker!

"Ah," he said, fingering his moustache. "Very good. I might have guessed who it was. You will go back to the College and give my compliments to Mr King and ask him to give you an extra-special licking. You will then do me five hundred lines. I shall be back to-morrow. Five hundred lines by five o'clock to-morrow. You are also gated for a week. This is not exactly the time for breaking bounds. *Extra*-special, please."

He disappeared over the hedge as lightly as he had come. There was a murmur of women's voices in the deep lane.

"Oh, you Prooshan brute!" said McTurk as the voices died away. "Stalky, it's all your silly fault."

"Kill him! Kill him!" gasped Beetle.

"I ca-an't. I'm going to cat again. . . . I don't mind that, but King'll gloat over us horrid. Extra-special, ooh!"

Stalky made no answer—not even a soft one. They went to College and received that for which they had been sent. King enjoyed himself most thoroughly, for by virtue of their seniority the boys were exempt from his hand, save under special order. Luckily, he was no expert in the gentle art.

" 'Strange, how desire doth outrun performance,' " said Beetle, irreverently, quoting from some Shakespeare play that they were cramming that term. They regained their study and settled down to the imposition.

"You're quite right, Beetle," Stalky spoke in silky and propitiating tones. "Now, if the Head had sent us up to a prefect, we'd have got something to remember!"

"Look here," McTurk began with cold venom, "we aren't goin' to row you about this business, because it's too bad for a row; but we want you to understand you're jolly well excommunicated, Stalky. You're a plain ass."

"How was I to know that the Head 'ud collar us? What was he doin' in those ghastly clothes, too?'

"Don't try to raise a side-issue," Beetle grunted severely.

"Well, it was all Stettson major's fault. If he hadn't gone an' got diphtheria 'twouldn't have happened. But don't you think it rather rummy—the Head droppin' on us that way?"

"Shut up! You're dead!" said Beetle. "We've chopped your spurs off your beastly heels. We've cocked your shield upside down and—and I don't think you ought to be allowed to brew for a month."

"Oh, stop jawin' at me. I want—"

"Stop? Why—why, we're gated for a week." McTurk almost howled as the agony of the situation overcame him. "A lickin' from King, five hundred lines, *and* a gatin'. D'you expect us to kiss you, Stalky, you beast?"

"Drop rottin' for a minute. I want to find out about the Head bein' where he was."

"Well, you have. You found him quite well and fit. Found him makin' love to Stettson major's mother. That was her in the lane—I heard her. And *so* we were ordered a lickin' before a day-boy's mother. Bony old widow, too," said McTurk. "Anything else you'd like to find out?"

"I don't care. I swear I'll get even with him some day," Stalky growled.

"Looks like it," said McTurk. "Extra-special, week's gatin', and five hundred . . . and now you're goin' to row about it! Help scrag him, Beetle!" Stalky had thrown his Virgil at them.

The Head returned next day without explanation, to find the lines waiting for him and the school a little relaxed under Mr. King's viceroyalty. Mr. King had been talking at and round and over the boys' heads, in a lofty and promiscuous style, of public-school spirit and the traditions of ancient seats; for he always improved an occasion. Beyond waking in two hundred and fifty young hearts a lively hatred of all other foundations, he accomplished little—so little, indeed, that when, two days after the Head's return, he chanced to come across Stalky & Co., gated but ever resourceful, playing marbles in the corridor he said that he was not surprised—not in the least surprised. This was what he had expected from persons of their *morale*.

"But there isn't any rule against marbles, sir. Very interestin' game," said Beetle, his knees white with chalk and dust. Then he received two hundred lines for insolence, besides an order to go to the nearest prefect for judgment and slaughter.

This is what happened behind the closed doors of Flint's study, and Flint was then Head of the Games:—

"Oh, I say, Flint. King has sent me to you for playin' marbles in the corridor an' shoutin' 'alley tor' an' 'knuckle down.' "

"What does he suppose I have to do with that?" was the answer.

"Dunno. Well?" Beetle grinned wickedly. "What am I to tell him? He's rather wrathy about it."

"If the Head chooses to put a notice in the corridor forbiddin' marbles, I can do something; but I can't move on a house-master's report. He knows that as well as I do."

The sense of this oracle Beetle conveyed, all unsweetened, to King, who hastened to interview Flint.

Now Flint had been seven and a half years at the College,

counting six months with a London crammer, from whose roof he had returned, homesick, to the Head for the final Army polish. There were four or five other seniors who had gone through much the same mill, not to mention boys, rejected by other establishments on account of a certain overwhelmingness, whom the Head had wrought into very fair shape. It was not a Sixth to be handled without gloves, as King found.

"Am I to understand it is your intention to allow board-school games under your study windows, Flint? If so, I can only say—" He said much, and Flint listened politely.

"Well, sir, if the Head sees fit to call a prefects' meeting we are bound to take the matter up. But the tradition of the school is that the prefects can't move in any matter affecting the whole school without the Head's direct order."

Much more was then delivered, both sides a little losing their temper.

After tea, at an informal gathering of prefects in his study, Flint related the adventure.

"He's been playin' for this for a week, and now he's got it. You know as well as I do that if he hadn't been gassing at us the way he has, that young devil Beetle wouldn't have dreamed of marbles."

"We know that," said Perowne, "but that isn't the question. On Flint's showin' King has called the prefects names enough to justify a first-class row. Crammers' rejections, ill-regulated hobble-de-hoys, wasn't it? Now it's impossible for prefects—"

"Rot," said Flint. "King's the best classical cram we've got; and 'tisn't fair to bother the Head with a row. He's up to his eyes with extra-tu. and Army work as it is. Besides, as I told King, we *aren't* a public school. We're a limited liability company payin' four per cent. My father's a shareholder, too."

"What's that got to do with it?" said Venner, a red-headed boy of nineteen.

"Well, it seems to me that we should be interferin' with ourselves. We've got to get into the Army or—get out, haven't we? King's hired by the Council to teach us. All the rest's flum-diddle. Can't you see?"

It might have been because he felt the air was a little thunderous that the Head took his after-dinner cheroot to Flint's study; but he so often began an evening in a prefect's room that nobody suspected when he drifted in pensively, after the knocks that etiquette demanded.

"Prefects' meeting?" A cock of one wise eyebrow.

"Not exactly, sir; we're just talking things over. Won't you take the easy-chair?"

"Thanks. Luxurious infants, you are." He dropped into Flint's big half-couch and puffed for a while in silence. "Well, since you're all here, I may confess that I'm mute with the bow-string."

The young faces grew serious. The phrase meant that certain of their number would be withdrawn from all further games for extra-tuition. It might also mean future success at Sandhurst; but it was present ruin for the First Fifteen.

"Yes, I've come for my pound of flesh. I ought to have had you out before the Exeter match; but it's our sacred duty to beat Exeter."

"Isn't the Old Boys' match sacred, too, sir?" said Perowne. The Old Boys' match was the event of the Easter term.

"We'll hope they aren't in training. Now for the list. First I want Flint. It's the Euclid that does it. You must work deductions with me. Perowne, extra mechanical drawing. Dawson goes to Mr. King for extra Latin, and Venner to me for German. Have I damaged the First Fifteen much?" He smiled sweetly.

"Ruined it, I'm afraid, sir," said Flint. "Can't you let us off till the end of the term?"

"Impossible. It will be a tight squeeze for Sandhurst this year."

"And all to be cut up by those vile Afghans, too," said Dawson. "Wouldn't think there'd be so much competition, would you?"

"Oh, that reminds me. Crandall is coming down with the Old Boys—I've asked twenty of them, but we sha'n't get more than a weak team. I don't know whether he'll be much use, though. He was rather knocked about, recovering poor old Duncan's body."

"Crandall major—the Gunner?" Perowne asked.

"No, the minor—'Toffee' Crandall—in a native infantry regiment. He was almost before your time, Perowne."

"The papers didn't say anything about him. We read about Fat-Sow, of course. What's Crandall done, sir?"

"I've brought over an Indian paper that his mother sent me. It was rather a—hefty, I think you say—piece of work. Shall I read it?"

The Head knew how to read. When he had finished the quarter-column of close type they thanked him politely.

"Good for the old Coll!" said Perowne. "Pity he wasn't in time to save Fat-Sow, though. That's nine to us, isn't it, in the last three years?"

"Yes. . . . And I took old Duncan off all games for extra-tu. five years ago this term," said the Head. "By the way, who do you hand over the Games to, Flint?"

"Haven't thought yet. Who'd you recommend, sir?"

"No, thank you. I've heard it casually hinted behind my back that the Prooshan Bates is a downy bird, but he isn't going to make himself responsible for a new Head of the Games. Settle it among yourselves. Good night."

"And that's the man," said Flint, when the door shut, "that you want to bother with a dame's school row."

"I was only pullin' your fat leg," Perowne returned hastily. "You're so easy to draw, Flint."

"Well, never mind that. The Head's knocked the First Fifteen to bits, and we've got to pick up the pieces, or the Old Boys will have a walk-over. Let's promote all the Second Fifteen and make Big Side play up. There's heaps of talent somewhere that we can polish up between now and the match."

The case was represented so urgently to the school that even Stalky and McTurk, who affected to despise football, played one Big-Side game seriously. They were forthwith promoted ere their ardor had time to cool, and the dignity of their Caps demanded that they should keep some show of virtue. The match-team was worked at least four days out of seven, and the school saw hope ahead.

With the last week of the term the Old Boys began to arrive, and their welcome was nicely proportioned to their worth. Gentlemen cadets from Sandhurst and Woolwich, who had only left a year ago, but who carried enormous side, were greeted with a cheerful "Hullo! What's the Shop like?" from those who had shared their studies. Militia subalterns had more consideration, but it was understood they were not precisely of the true metal. Recreants who, failing for the Army, had gone into business or banks were received for old sake's sake, but in no way made too much of. But when the real subalterns, officers and gentlemen full-blown—who had been to the ends of the earth and back again and so carried no side—came on the scene strolling about with the Head, the school divided right and left in admiring silence. And when one laid hands on Flint, even upon the Head of the Games, crying, "Good Heavens! What do you mean by growing in this way? You were a beastly little fag when I left," visible haloes encircled Flint. They would walk to and fro in the corridor with the little red school-sergeant, telling news of old regiments; they would burst into form-rooms sniffing the well-remembered smells of ink and whitewash; they would find nephews and cousins in the lower forms and present them with enormous wealth; or they would invade the gymnasium and make Foxy show off the new stock on the bars.

Chiefly, though, they talked with the Head, who was father-confessor and agent-general to them all; for what they shouted in their unthinking youth, they proved in their thoughtless manhood—to wit, that the Prooshan Bates was "a downy bird." Young blood who had stumbled into an entanglement with a pastry-cook's daughter at Plymouth; experience who had come into a small legacy but mistrusted lawyers; ambition halting at cross-roads, anxious to take the one that would lead him farthest; extravagance pursued by the money-lender; arrogance in the thick of a regimental row —each carried his trouble to the Head; and Chiron showed him, in language quite unfit for little boys, a quiet and safe way round, out, or under. So they overflowed his house, smoked his cigars, and drank his health as they had drunk it all the earth over when two or three of the old school had foregathered.

"Don't stop smoking for a minute," said the Head. "The more you're out of training the better for us. I've demoralised the First Fifteen with extra-tu."

"Ah, but we're a scratch lot. Have you told 'em we shall need a substitute even if Crandall can play?" said a Lieutenant of Engineers with a D.S.O. to his credit.

"He wrote me he'd play, so he can't have been much hurt. He's coming down to-morrow morning."

"Crandall minor that was, and brought off poor Duncan's body?" The Head nodded. "Where are you going to put him? We've turned you out of house and home already, Head Sahib." This was a Squadron Commander of Bengal Lancers, home on leave.

"I'm afraid he'll have to go up to his old dormitory. You know Old Boys can claim that privilege. Yes, I think leetle Crandall minor must bed down there once more."

"Bates Sahib"—a Gunner flung a heavy arm round the Head's neck—"you've got something up your sleeve. Confess! I know that twinkle."

"Can't you see, you cuckoo?" a Submarine Miner interrupted. "Crandall goes up to the dormitory as an object-lesson, for moral effect and so forth. Isn't that true, Head Sahib?"

"It is. You know too much, Purvis. I licked you for that in '79."

"You did, sir, and it's my private belief you chalked the cane."

"N-no. But I've a very straight eye. Perhaps that misled you."

That opened the flood-gates of fresh memories, and they all told tales out of school.

When Crandall minor that was—Lieutenant R. Crandall of an ordinary Indian regiment—arrived from Exeter on the morning of the match, he was cheered along the whole front of the College, for the prefects had repeated the sense of that which the Head had read them in Flint's study. When Prout's house understood that he would claim his Old Boy's right to a bed for one night, Beetle ran into King's house next door and executed a public "gloat" up and down the enemy's big form-room, departing in a haze of ink-pots.

"What d'you take any notice of these rotters for?" said Stalky, playing substitute for the Old Boys, magnificent in black jersey, white knickers, and black stockings. "I talked to *him* up in the dormitory when he was changin'. Pulled his sweater down for him. He's cut about all over the arms— horrid purply ones. He's goin' to tell us about it to-night. I asked him to when I was lacin' his boots."

"Well, you *have* got cheek," said Beetle, enviously.

"Slipped out before I thought. But he wasn't a big angry. He's no end of a chap. I swear I'm goin' to play up like beans. Tell Turkey!"

The technique of that match belongs to a by-gone age. Scrimmages were tight and enduring; hacking was direct and to the purpose; and around the scrimmage stood the school, crying, "Put down your heads and shove!" Towards the end everybody lost all sense of decency, and mothers of day-boys too close to the touch-line heard language not included in the bills. No one was actually carried off the field, but both sides felt happier when time was called, and Beetle helped Stalky and McTurk into their overcoats. The two had met in the many-legged heart of things, and, as Stalky said, had "done each other proud." As they swaggered woodenly behind the teams—substitutes do not rank as equals of hairy men— they passed a pony-carriage near the wall, and a husky voice cried, "Well played. Oh, played indeed!" It was Stettson major, white-cheeked and hollow-eyed, who had fought his way to the ground under escort of an impatient coachman.

"Hullo, Stettson," said Stalky, checking. "Is it safe to come near you yet?"

"Oh, yes. I'm all right. They wouldn't let me out before,

but I had to come to the match. Your mouth looks pretty plummy."

"Turkey trod on it accidental-done-a-purpose. Well, I'm glad you're better, because we owe you something. You and your membranes got us into a sweet mess, young man."

"I heard of that," said the boy, giggling. "The Head told me."

"Dooce he did! When?"

"Oh, come on up to Coll. My shin'll stiffen if we stay jawin' here."

"Shut up, Turkey. I want to find out about this. Well?"

"He was stayin' at our house all the time I was ill."

"What for? Neglectin' the Coll that way? 'Thought he was in town."

"I was off my head, you know, and they said I kept on callin' for him."

"Cheek! You're only a day-boy."

"He came just the same, and he about saved my life. I was all bunged up one night—just goin' to croak, the doctor said—and they stuck a tube or somethin' in my throat, and the Head sucked out the stuff."

"Ugh! 'Shot if *I* would!"

"He ought to have got diphtheria himself, the doctor said. So he stayed at our house instead of going back. I'd ha' croaked in another twenty minutes, the doctor says."

Here the coachman, being under orders, whipped up and nearly ran over the three.

"My Hat!" said Beetle. "That's pretty average heroic."

"Pretty average!" McTurk's knee in the small of his back cannoned him into Stalky, who punted him back. "You ought to be hung!"

"And the Head ought to get the V.C.," said Stalky. "Why, he might have been dead *and* buried by now. But he wasn't. But he didn't. Ho! ho! He just nipped through the hedge like a lusty old blackbird. Extra-special, five hundred lines, an' gated for a week—all sereno!"

"I've read o' something like that in a book," said Beetle. "Gummy, what a chap! Just think of it!"

"I'm thinking," said McTurk; and he delivered a wild Irish yell that made the team turn round.

"Shut your fat mouth," said Stalky, dancing with impatience. "Leave it to your Uncle Stalky, and he'll have the Head on toast. If you say a word, Beetle, till I give you leave, I swear I'll slay you. *Habeo Capitem crinibus minimis.* I've got him by the short hairs! Now look as if nothing had happened."

There was no need of guile. The school was too busy cheering the drawn match. It hung round the lavatories regardless of muddy boots while the team washed. It cheered Crandall minor whenever it caught sight of him, and it cheered more wildly than ever after prayers, because the Old Boys in evening dress, openly twirling their moustaches, attended, and instead of standing with the masters, ranged themselves along the wall immediately before the prefects; and the Head called them over, too—majors, minors, and tertiuses, after their old names.

"Yes, it's all very fine," he said to his guests after dinner, "but the boys are getting a little out of hand. There will be trouble and sorrow later, I'm afraid. You'd better turn in early, Crandall. The dormitory will be sitting up for you. I don't know to what dizzy heights you may climb in your profession, but I do know you'll never get such absolute adoration as you're getting now."

"Confound the adoration. I want to finish my cigar, sir."

"It's all pure gold. Go where glory waits, Crandall—minor."

The setting of that apotheosis was a ten-bed attic dormitory, communicating through doorless openings with three others. The gas flickered over the raw pine washstands. There was an incessant whistling of draughts, and outside the naked windows the sea beat on the Pebbleridge.

"Same old bed—same old mattress, I believe," said Crandall, yawning. "Same old everything. Oh, but I'm lame! I'd no notion you chaps could play like this." He caressed a battered shin. "You've given us all something to remember you by."

It needed a few minutes to put them at their ease; and, in

some way they could not understand, they were more easy when Crandall turned round and said his prayers—a ceremony he had neglected for some years.

"Oh, I *am* sorry. I've forgotten to put out the gas."

"Please don't bother," said the prefect of the dormitory. "Worthington does that."

A nightgowned twelve-year-old, who had been waiting to show off, leaped from his bed to the bracket and back again, by way of a washstand.

"How d'you manage when he's asleep?" said Crandall, chuckling.

"Shove a cold cleek down his neck."

"It was a wet sponge when *I* was junior in the dormitory. . . . Hullo! What's happening?"

The darkness had filled with whispers, the sound of trailing rugs, bare feet on bare boards, protests, giggles, and threats such as:

"Be quiet, you ass! . . . *Squattez-vous* on the floor, then! . . . I swear you aren't going to sit on *my* bed! . . . Mind the tooth-glass," etc.

"Sta—Corkran said," the prefect began, his tone showing his sense of Stalky's insolence, "that perhaps you'd tell us about that business with Duncan's body."

"Yes—yes—yes," ran the keen whispers. "Tell us."

"There's nothing to tell. What on earth are you chaps hoppin' about in the cold for?"

"Never mind us," said the voices. "Tell about Fat-Sow."

So Crandall turned on his pillow and spoke to the generation he could not see.

"Well, about three months ago he was commanding a treasure-guard—a cart full of rupees to pay troops with—five thousand rupees in silver. He was comin' to a place called Fort Pearson, near Kalabagh."

"I was born there," squeaked a small fag. "It was called after my uncle."

"Shut up—you and your uncle! Never mind *him*, Crandall."

"Well, ne'er mind. The Afridis found out that this treasure was on the move, and they ambushed the whole show a couple of miles before he got to the fort, and cut up the escort. Duncan was wounded, and the escort hooked it. There weren't more than twenty Sepoys all told, and there were any amount of Afridis. As things turned out, I was in charge at Fort Pearson. Fact was, I'd heard the firing and was just going to see about it, when Duncan's men came up. So we all turned back together. They told me something about an officer, but I couldn't get the hang of things till I saw a chap under the wheels of the cart out in the open, propped up on one arm, blazing away with a revolver. You see, the escort had abandoned the cart, and the Afridis—they're an awfully suspicious gang—thought the retreat was a trap—sort of draw, you know—and the cart was the bait. So they had left poor old Duncan alone. 'Minute they spotted how few *we* were, it was a race across the flat who should reach old Duncan first. We ran and they ran, and we won, and after a little hackin' about they pulled off. I never knew it was one of us till I was right on top of him. There are heaps of Duncans in the service, and of course the name didn't remind me. He wasn't changed at all hardly. He'd been shot through the lungs, poor old man, and he was pretty thirsty. I gave him a drink and sat down beside him, and—funny thing, too—he said, 'Hullo, Toffee!' and I said, 'Hullo, Fat-Sow! hope you aren't hurt,' or something of the kind. But he died in a minute or two—never lifted his head off by knees. . . . I say, you chaps out there will get your death of cold. Better go to bed."

"All right. In a minute. But your cuts—your cuts. How did you get wounded?"

"That was when we were taking the body back to the Fort. They came on again, and there was a bit of a scrimmage."

"Did you kill any one?"

"Yes. Shouldn't wonder. Good night."

"Good night. Thank you, Crandall. Thanks awf'ly, Crandall. Good night."

The unseen crowds withdrew. His own dormitory rustled into bed and lay silent for a while.

"I say, Crandall"—Stalky's voice was tuned to a wholly foreign reverence.

"Well, what?"

"Suppose a chap found another chap croaking with diphtheria—all bunged up with it—and they stuck a tube in his throat and the chap sucked the stuff out, what would you say?"

"Um," said Crandall, reflectively. "I've only heard of one case, and that was a doctor. He did it for a woman."

"Oh, this wasn't a woman. It was just a boy."

"Makes it all the finer, then. It's about the bravest thing a man can do. Why?"

"Oh, I heard of a chap doin' it. That's all."

"Then he's a brave man."

"Would *you* funk it?"

"Ra-ather. Anybody would. Fancy dying of diphtheria in cold blood."

"Well—ah! Er! Look here!" The sentence ended in a grunt, for Stalky had leaped out of bed and with McTurk was sitting on the head of Beetle, who would have sprung the mine there and then.

Next day, which was the last of the term and given up to a few wholly unimportant examinations, began with wrath and war. Mr. King had discovered that nearly all his house—it lay, as you know, next door but one to Prout's in the long range of buildings—had unlocked the doors between the dormitories and had gone in to listen to a story by Crandall. He went to the Head, clamorous, injured, appealing; for he never approved of allowing so-called young men of the world to contaminate the morals of boyhood. Very good, said the Head. He would attend to it.

"Well, I'm awf'ly sorry," said Crandall, guiltily. "I don't think I told 'em anything they oughtn't to hear. Don't let them get into trouble on my account."

"Tck!" the Head answered, with the ghost of a wink. "It isn't the boys that make trouble; it's the masters. However, Prout and King don't approve of dormitory gatherings on this scale, and one must back up the house-masters. Moreover, it's hopeless to punish two houses only, so late in the term. We

must be fair and include everybody. Let's see. They have a
holiday task for the Easters, which, of course, none of them
will ever look at. We will give the whole school, except prefects and study-boys, regular prep. to-night; and the Common-
room will have to supply a master to take it. We must be fair
to all."

"Prep. on the last night of the term. Whew!" said Crandall,
thinking of his own wild youth. "I fancy there will be larks."

The school, frolicking among packed trunks, whooping
down the corridor, and "gloating" in form-rooms, received
the news with amazement and rage. No school in the world
did prep. on the last night of the term. This thing was mon-
strous, tyrannical, subversive of law, religion, and morality.
They would go into the form-rooms, and they would take
their degraded holiday task with them, but—here they smiled
and speculated what manner of man the Common-room would
send up against them. The lot fell on Mason, credulous and
enthusiastic, who loved youth. No other master was anxious
to take that "prep.," for the school lacked the steadying influence of tradition; and men accustomed to the ordered routine
of ancient foundations found it occasionally insubordinate.
The four long form-rooms, in which all below the rank of
study-boys worked, received him with thunders of applause.
Ere he had coughed twice they favoured him with a metrical
summary of the marriage-laws of Great Britain, as recorded
by the High Priest of the Israelites and commented on by the
leader of the host. The lower forms reminded him that it was
the last day, and that therefore he must "take it all in play."
When he dashed off to rebuke them, the Lower Fourth and
Upper Third began with one accord to be sick, loudly and
realistically. Mr. Mason tried, of all vain things under heaven,
to argue with them, and a bold soul at a back desk bade him
"take fifty lines for not 'olding up 'is 'and before speaking."
As one who prided himself upon the precision of his English
this cut Mason to the quick, and while he was trying to
discover the offender, the Upper and Lower Second, three
form-rooms away, turned out the gas and threw ink-pots. It

was a pleasant and stimulating "prep." The study-boys and prefects heard the echoes of it far off, and the Common-room at dessert smiled.

Stalky waited, watch in hand, till half-past eight.

"If it goes on much longer the Head will come up," said he. "We'll tell the studies first, and then the form-rooms. Look sharp!"

He allowed no time for Beetle to be dramatic or McTurk to drawl. They poured into study after study, told their tale, and went again so soon as they saw they were being understood, waiting for no comment; while the noise of that unholy "prep." grew and deepened. By the door of Flint's study they met Mason flying towards the corridor.

"He's gone to fetch the Head. Hurry up! Come on!"

They broke into Number Twelve form-room abreast and panting.

"The Head! The Head! The Head!" That call stilled the tumult for a minute, and Stalky, leaping to a desk, shouted, "He went and sucked the diphtheria stuff out of Stettson major's throat when we thought he was in town. Stop rotting, you asses! Stettson major would have croaked if the Head hadn't done it. The Head might have died himself. Crandall says it's the bravest thing any livin' man can do, and I"—his voice cracked—"the Head don't know we know!"

McTurk and Beetle, jumping from desk to desk, drove the news home among the junior forms. There was a pause, and then, Mason behind him, the Head entered. It was in the established order of things that no boy should speak or move under his eye. He expected the hush of awe. He was received with cheers—steady, ceaseless cheering. Being a wise man, he went away, and the forms were silent and a little frightened.

"It's all right," said Stalky. "He can't do much. 'Tisn't as if you'd pulled the desks up like we did when old Carleton took prep. once. Keep it up! Hear 'em cheering in the studies!" He rocketed out with a yell, to find Flint and the prefects lifting the roof off the corridor.

When the Head of a limited liability company, paying four per cent., is cheered on his saintly way to prayers, not only by four form-rooms of boys waiting punishment, but by his trusted prefects, he can either ask for an explanation or go his road with dignity, while the senior house-master glares like an excited cat and points out to a white and trembling mathematical master that certain methods—not his, thank God— usually produce certain results. Out of delicacy the Old Boys did not attend that call-over; and it was to the school drawn up in the gymnasium that the Head spoke icily.

"It is not often that I do not understand you; but I confess I do not to-night. Some of you, after your idiotic performances at prep., seem to think me a fit person to cheer. I am going to show you that I am not."

Crash—crash—crash—came the triple cheer that disproved it, and the Head glowered under the gas.

"That is enough. You will gain nothing. The little boys [the Lower School did not like that form of address] will do me three hundred lines apiece in the holidays. I shall take no further notice of them. The Upper School will do me one thousand lines apiece in the holidays, to be shown up the evening of the day they come back. And further—"

"Gummy, what a glutton!" Stalky whispered.

"For your behaviour towards Mr. Mason I intend to lick the whole of the Upper School to-morrow when I give you your journey-money. This will include the three study-boys I found dancing on the form-room desks when I came up. Prefects will stay after call-over."

The school filed out in silence, but gathered in groups by the gymnasium door waiting what might befall.

"And now, Flint," said the Head, "will you be good enough to give me some explanation of your conduct?"

"Well, sir," said Flint, desperately, "if you save a chap's life at the risk of your own when he's dyin' of diphtheria, and the Coll finds it out, wha-what *can* you expect, sir?"

"Um, I see. Then that noise was not meant for—ah, cheek. I can connive at immorality, but I cannot stand impudence. However, it does not excuse their insolence to Mr. Mason. I'll forego the lines this once, remember; but the lickings hold good."

When this news was made public, the school, lost in wonder and admiration, gasped at the Head as he went to his house. Here was a man to be reverenced. On the rare occasions when he caned he did it very scientifically, and the execution of a hundred boys would be epic—immense.

"It's all right, Head Sahib. *We* know," said Crandall, as the Head slipped off his gown with a grunt in his smoking-room. "I found out just now from our substitute. He was gettin' my opinion of your performance last night in the dormitory. I didn't know then that it was you he was talkin' about. Crafty young animal. Freckled chap with eyes—Corkran, I think his name is."

"Oh, I know *him*, thank you," said the Head, and reflectively. "Ye-es, I should have included them even if I hadn't seen 'em."

"If the old Coll weren't a little above themselves already, we'd chair you down the corridor," said the Engineer. "Oh, Bates, how could you? You might have caught it yourself, and where would we have been, then?"

"I always knew you were worth twenty of us any day. Now I'm sure of it," said the Squadron Commander, looking round for contradictions.

"He isn't fit to manage a school, though. Promise you'll never do it again, Bates Sahib. We—we can't go away comfy in our minds if you take these risks," said the Gunner.

"Bates Sahib, you aren't ever goin' to cane the whole Upper School, are you?" said Crandall.

"I can connive at immorality, as I said, but I can't stand impudence. Mason's lot is quite hard enough even when I back him. Besides, the men at the Golf-club heard them singing 'Aaron and Moses.' I shall have complaints about that from the parents of day-boys. Decency must be preserved."

"We're coming to help," said all the guests.

* * * * * * * *

The Upper School were caned one after the other, their overcoats over their arms, the brakes waiting in the road below to take them to the station, their journey-money on the table.

The Head began with Stalky, McTurk, and Beetle. He dealt faithfully by them.

"And here's your journey-money. Good-by, and pleasant holidays."

"Good-by. Thank you, sir. Good-by."

They shook hands.

"Desire don't outrun performance—*much*—this mornin'. We got the cream of it," said Stalky. "Now wait till a few chaps come out, and we'll really cheer him."

"Don't wait on our account, please," said Crandall, speaking for the Old Boys. "We're going to begin now."

It was very well so long as the cheering was confined to the corridor, but when it spread to the gymnasium, when the boys awaiting their turn cheered, the Head gave it up in despair, and the remnant flung themselves upon him to shake hands.

Then they seriously devoted themselves to cheering till the brakes were hustled off the premises in dumb-show.

"Didn't I say I'd get even with him?" said Stalky on the box-seat, as they swung into the narrow Northam street. "Now all together—takin' time from your Uncle Stalky:

> "*It's a way we have in the Army,*
> *It's a way we have in the Navy,*
> *It's a way we have at the Public Schools,*
> *Which nobody can deny!*"

The Flag of Their Country

IT WAS WINTER and bitter cold of mornings. Consequently Stalky and Beetle—McTurk being of the offensive type that makes ornate toilet under all circumstances—drowsed till the last moment before turning out to call-over in the gas-lit gymnasium. It followed that they were often late; and since every unpunctuality earned them a black mark, and since three black marks a week meant defaulters' drill, equally it followed that they spent hours under the Sergeant's hand. Foxy drilled the defaulters with all the pomp of his old parade-ground.

"Don't think it's any pleasure to me" (his introduction never varied). "I'd much sooner be smoking a quiet pipe in my own quarters—but I see we 'ave the Old Brigade on our 'ands this afternoon. If I only 'ad you regular, Muster Corkran," said he, dressing the line.

"You've had me for nearly six weeks, you old glutton. Number off from the right!"

"Not *quite* so previous, please. I'm taking this drill. Left, half—turn! Slow—march." Twenty-five sluggards, all old offenders, filed into the gymnasium. "Quietly provide yourselves with the requisite dumb-bells; returnin' quietly to your place. Number off from the right, in *a* low voice. Odd numbers one pace to the front. Even numbers stand fast. Now, leanin' forward from the 'ips, takin' your time from me."

The dumb-bells rose and fell, clashed and were returned as one. The boys were experts at the weary game.

"Ve-ry good. I shall be sorry when any of you resume your 'abits of punctuality. Quietly return dumb-bells. We will now try some simple drill."

"Ugh! I know that simple drill."

"It would be 'ighly to your discredit if you did not, Muster Corkran. *At* the same time, it is not so easy as it looks."

"Bet you a bob, I can drill as well as you, Foxy."

"We'll see later. Now try to imagine you ain't defaulters at

159

all, but an 'arf company on parade, me bein' your commandin' officer. There's no call to laugh. If you're lucky, most of you will 'ave to take drills 'arf your life. Do me a little credit. You've been at it long enough, goodness knows."

They were formed into fours, marched, wheeled, and countermarched, the spell of ordered motion strong on them. As Foxy said, they had been at it a long time.

The gymnasium door opened, revealing McTurk in charge of an old gentleman.

The Sergeant, leading a wheel, did not see. "Not so bad," he murmured. "Not 'arf so bad. The pivot-man of the wheel *honly* marks time, Muster Swayne. Now, Muster Corkran, you say you know the drill? Oblige me by takin' over the command and, reversin' my words step by step, relegate them to their previous formation."

"What's this? What's this?" cried the visitor, authoritatively.

"A—a little drill, sir," stammered Foxy, saying nothing of first causes.

"Excellent—excellent. I only wish there were more of it," he chirruped. "Don't let me interrupt. You were just going to hand over to some one, weren't you?" He sat down, breathing frostily in the chill air.

"I shall muck it. I know I shall," whispered Stalky, uneasily; and his discomfort was not lightened by a murmur from the rear rank that the old gentleman was General Collinson, a member of the College Board of Council.

"Eh—what?" said Foxy.

"Collinson, K.C.B.—He commanded the Pompadours—my father's old regiment," hissed Swayne major.

"Take your time," said the visitor. "*I* know how it feels. Your first drill—eh?"

"Yes, sir." He drew an unhappy breath. " 'Tention. Dress!" The echo of his own voice restored his confidence.

The wheel was faced about, flung back, broken into fours, and restored to line without a falter. The official hour of punishment was long past, but no one thought of that. They were backing up Stalky—Stalky in deadly fear lest his voice should crack.

"He does you credit, Sergeant," was the visitor's comment. "A good drill—and good material to drill. Now, it's an extraordinary thing: I've been lunching with your head-master and he never told me you had a cadet-corps in the College."

"We 'aven't, sir. This is only a little drill," said the Sergeant.

"But aren't they keen on it?" said McTurk, speaking for the first time, with a twinkle in his deep-set eyes.

"Why aren't *you* in it, though, Willy?"

"Oh, I'm not punctual enough," said McTurk. "The Sergeant only takes the pick of us."

"Dismiss! Break off!" cried Foxy, fearing an explosion in the ranks. "I—I ought to have told you, sir, that—"

"But you should have a cadet-corps." The General pursued his own line of thought. "You *shall* have a cadet-corps, too, if my recommendation in Council is any use. I don't know when I've been so pleased. Boys animated by a spirit like yours should set an example to the whole school."

"They do," said McTurk.

"Bless my soul! Can it be so late? I've kept my fly waiting half an hour. Well, I must run away. Nothing like seeing things for one's self. Which end of the buildings does one get out at? Will you show me, Willy? Who was that boy who took the drill?"

"Corkran, I think his name is."

"You ought to know him. That's the kind of boy you should cultivate. Evidently an unusual sort. A wonderful sight. Five-and-twenty boys, who, I dare say, would much sooner be playing cricket—" (it was the depth of winter; but grown people, especially those who have lived long in foreign parts, make these little errors, and McTurk did not correct him)—"drilling for the sheer love of it. A shame to waste so much good stuff; but I think I can carry my point."

"An' who's your friend with the white whiskers?" demanded Stalky, on McTurk's return to the study.

"General Collinson. He comes over to shoot with my father sometimes. Rather a decent old bargee, too. He said I ought to cultivate your acquaintance, Stalky."

"Did he tip you?"

McTurk exhibited a blessed whole sovereign.

"Ah," said Stalky, annexing it, for he was treasurer. "We'll have a hefty brew. You'd pretty average cool cheek, Turkey, to jaw about our keenness an' punctuality."

"Didn't the old boy know we were defaulters?" said Beetle.

"Not him. He came down to lunch with the Head. I found him pokin' about the place on his own hook afterwards, an' I thought I'd show him the giddy drill. When I found he was so pleased, I wasn't goin' to damp his giddy ardour. He mightn't ha' given me the quid if I had."

"Wasn't old Foxy pleased? Did you see him get pink behind the ears?" said Beetle. "It was an awful score for him. Didn't we back him up beautifully? Let's go down to Keyte's and get some cocoa and sassingers."

They overtook Foxy, speeding down to retail the adventure to Keyte, who in his time had been Troop Sergeant-Major in a cavalry regiment, and now, a war-worn veteran, was local postmaster and confectioner.

"You owe us something," said Stalky, with meaning.

"I'm 'ighly grateful, Muster Corkran. I've 'ad to run against you pretty hard in the way o' business, now and then, but I *will* say that outside o' business—bounds an' smokin', an' such like—I don't wish to have a more trustworthy young gentleman to 'elp me out of a hole. The way you 'andled the drill was beautiful, though I say it. Now, if you come regular henceforth—"

"But he'll have to be late three times a week," said Beetle. "You can't expect a chap to do that—just to please you, Foxy."

"Ah, that's true. Still, if you could manage it—and you, Muster Beetle—it would give you a big start when the cadet-corps is formed. I expect the General will recommend it."

They raided Keyte's very much at their own sweet will, for the old man, who knew them well, was deep in talk with Foxy.

"I make what we've taken seven and six," Stalky called at last over the counter; "but you'd better count for yourself."

"No—no. I'd take your word any day, Muster Corkran.—

In the Pompadours, was he, Sergeant? We lay with them once —at Umballa, I think it was."

"I don't know whether this ham-and-tongue tin is eighteen-pence or one an' four."

"Say one an' fourpence, Muster Corkran. . . . Of course, Sergeant, if it was any use to give my time, I'd be pleased to do it, but I'm too old. I'd like to see a drill again."

"Oh, come on, Stalky," cried McTurk. "He isn't listenin' to you. Chuck over the money."

"I want the quid changed, you ass. Keyte! Private Keyte! Corporal Keyte! Terroop-Sergeant-Major Keyte, will you give me change for a quid?"

"Yes—yes, of course. Seven an' six." He stared abstractedly, pushed the silver over, and melted away into the darkness of the back room.

"Now those two'll jaw about the Mutiny till tea-time," said Beetle.

"Old Keyte was at Sobraon," said Stalky. "Hear him talk about that sometimes! Beats Foxy hollow."

* * * * * * * *

The Head's face, inscrutable as ever, was bent over a pile of letters.

"What do you think?" he said at last to the Reverend John Gillett.

"It's a good idea. There's no denying that—an estimable idea."

"We concede that much. Well?"

"I have my doubts about it—that's all. The more I know of boys the less do I profess myself capable of following their moods; but I own I shall be very much surprised if the scheme takes. It—it isn't the temper of the school. We prepare for the Army."

"My business—in *this* matter—is to carry out the wishes of the Council. They demand a volunteer cadet-corps. A volunteer cadet-corps will be furnished. I have suggested, however, that we need not embark upon the expense of uniforms till we are drilled. General Collinson is sending us fifty lethal weapons—cut-down Sniders, he calls them—all carefully plugged."

"Yes, that is necessary in a school that uses loaded saloon-pistols to the extent we do." The Reverend John smiled.

"Therefore there will be no outlay except the Sergeant's time."

"But if he fails you will be blamed."

"Oh, assuredly. I shall post a notice in the corridor this afternoon, and—"

"I shall watch the result."

* * * * * * * *

"Kindly keep your 'ands off the new arm-rack."

Foxy wrestled with a turbulent crowd in the gymnasium. "Nor it won't do even a condemned Snider any good to be continual snappin' the lock, Mr. Swayne.—Yiss, the uniforms will come later, when we're more proficient; at present we will confine ourselves to drill. I am 'ere for the purpose of takin' the names o' those willin' to join.—Put down that Snider, Muster Hogan!"

"What are you goin' to do, Beetle?" said a voice.

"I've had all the drill *I* want, thank you."

"What! After all you've learned? Come on. Don't be a scab! They'll make you corporal in a week," cried Stalky.

"I'm not goin' up for the Army." Beetle touched his spectacles.

"Hold on a shake, Foxy," said Hogan. "Where are you goin' to drill us?"

"Here—in the Gym—till you are fit an' capable to be taken out on the road." The Sergeant threw a chest.

"For all the Northam cads to look at? Not good enough, Foxibus."

"Well, we won't make a point of it. You learn your drill first, an' later we'll see."

"Hullo," said Ansell of Macrea's, shouldering through the mob. "What's all this about a giddy cadet-corps?"

"It will save you a lot o' time at Sandhurst," the Sergeant replied promptly. "You'll be dismissed your drills early if you go up with a good groundin' before'and."

"Hm! 'Don't mind learnin' my drill, but I'm not goin' to ass about the country with a toy Snider. Perowne, what are you goin' to do? Hogan's joinin'."

"Don't know whether I've the time," said Perowne. "I've got no end of extra-tu. as it is."

"Well, call this extra-tu.," said Ansell. " 'Twon't take us long to mug up the drill."

"Oh, that's right enough, but what about marchin' in public?" said Hogan, not foreseeing that three years later he should die in the Burmese sunlight outside Minhla Fort.

"Afraid the uniform won't suit your creamy complexion?" McTurk asked with a villainous sneer.

"Shut up, Turkey. You aren't goin' up for the Army."

"No, but I'm goin' to send a substitute. Hi! Morrell an' Wake! You two fags by the arm-rack, you've got to volunteer."

Blushing deeply—they had been too shy to apply before—the youngsters sidled towards the Sergeant.

"But I don't want the little chaps—not at first," said the Sergeant, disgustedly. "I want—I'd like some of the Old Brigade—the defaulters—to stiffen 'em a bit."

"Don't be ungrateful, Sergeant. They're nearly as big as you get 'em in the Army now." McTurk read the papers of those years and could be trusted for general information, which he used as he used his "tweaker." Yet he did not know that Wake minor would be a bimbashi of the Egyptian Army ere his thirtieth year.

Hogan, Swayne, Stalky, Perowne, and Ansell were deep in consultation by the vaulting-horse, Stalky as usual laying down the law. The Sergeant watched them uneasily, knowing that many waited on their lead.

"Foxy don't like my recruits," said McTurk, in a pained tone, to Beetle. "You get him some."

Nothing loath, Beetle pinioned two more fags—each no taller than a carbine.

"Here you are, Foxy. Here's food for powder. Strike for your hearths an' homes, you young brutes—an' be jolly quick about it."

"Still he isn't happy," said McTurk.

> *"For the way we have with our Army*
> *Is the way we have with our Navy."*

Here Beetle joined in. They had found the poem in an old volume of "Punch," and it seemed to cover the situation:

> *"An' both of 'em led to adversity,*
> *Which nobody can deny!"*

"You be quiet, young gentlemen. If you can't 'elp—don't 'inder." Foxy's eye was still on the council by the horse. Carter, White, and Tyrrell, all boys of influence, had joined it. The rest fingered the rifles irresolutely.

"Half a shake," cried Stalky. "Can't we turn out those rotters before we get to work?"

"Certainly," said Foxy. "Any one wishful to join will stay 'ere. Those who do not so intend will go out, quietly closin' the door be'ind 'em."

Half a dozen of the earnest-minded rushed at them, and they had just time to escape into the corridor.

"Well, why don't you join?" Beetle asked, resettling his collar.

"Why didn't you?"

"What's the good? We aren't goin' up for the Army. Besides, I know the drill—all except the manual, of course. 'Wonder what they're doin' inside?"

"Makin' a treaty with Foxy. Didn't you hear Stalky say: 'That's what we'll do—an' if he don't like it he can lump it'? They'll use Foxy for a cram. Can't you see, you idiot? They're goin' up for Sandhurst or the Shop in less than a year. They'll learn their drill an' then they'll drop it like a shot. D'you suppose chaps with their amount of extra-tu. are takin' up volunteerin' for fun?"

"Well, I don't know. I thought of doin' a poem about it—rottin' 'em, you know—'The Ballad of the Dog-Shooters'—eh?"

"I don't think you can, because King'll be down on the corps like a cart-load o' bricks. He hasn't been consulted. He's sniffin' round the notice-board now. Let's lure him." They strolled up carelessly towards the house-master—a most meek couple.

"How's this?" said King, with a start of feigned surprise. "Methought you would be learning to fight for your country."

"I think the company's full, sir," said McTurk.

"It's a great pity," sighed Beetle.

"Forty valiant defenders, have we, then? How noble! What devotion! I presume that it is possible that a desire to evade their normal responsibilities may be at the bottom of this zeal. Doubtless they will be accorded special privileges, like the Choir and the Natural History Society—one must not say Bug-hunters."

"Oh, I suppose so, sir," said McTurk, cheerily. "The Head hasn't said anything about it yet, but he will, of course."

"Oh, sure to."

"It is just possible, my Beetle," King wheeled on the last speaker, "that the house-masters—a necessary but somewhat neglected factor in our humble scheme of existence—may have a word to say on the matter. Life, for the young at least, is not all weapons and munitions of war. Education is incidentally one of our aims."

"What a consistent pig he is!" cooed McTurk, when they were out of ear-shot. "One always knows where to have him. Did you see how he rose to that draw about the Head and special privileges?"

"Confound him, he might have had the decency to have backed the scheme. I could do such a lovely ballad, rottin' it; and now I'll have to be a giddy enthusiast. It don't bar our pulling Stalky's leg in the study, does it?"

"Oh, no; but in the Coll we must be pro-cadet-corps like anything. Can't you make up a giddy epigram, à la Catullus, about King objectin' to it?"

Beetle was at this noble task when Stalky returned all hot from his first drill.

"Hello, my ramrod-bunger!" began McTurk. "Where's your dead dog? Is it Defence or Defiance?"

"Defiance," said Stalky, and leaped on him at that word.

"Look here, Turkey, you mustn't rot the corps. We've arranged it beautifully. Foxy swears he won't take us out into the open till we say we want to go."

"*Dis*-gustin' exhibition of immature infants apin' the idiosyncrasies of their elders. Snff!"

"Have you drawn King, Beetle?" Stalky asked in a pause of the scuffle.

"Not exactly; but that's his genial style."

"Well, listen to your Uncle Stalky—who is a great man. Moreover and subsequently, Foxy's goin' to let us drill the corps in turn—*privatim et seriatim*—so that we'll all know how to handle a half company anyhow. *Ergo,* an' *propter hoc,* when we go to the Shop we shall be dismissed drill early; thus, my beloved 'earers, combinin' education with wholesome amusement."

"I knew you'd make a sort of extra-tu. of it, you cold-blooded brute," said McTurk. "Don't you want to die for your giddy country?"

"Not if I can jolly well avoid it. So you mustn't rot the corps."

"We've decided on that, years ago," said Beetle, scornfully. "King'll do the rottin'."

"Then you've got to rot King, my giddy poet. Make up a good catchy Limerick, and let the fags sing it."

"Look here, you stick to volunteerin', and don't jog the table."

"He won't have anything to take hold of," said Stalky, with dark significance.

They did not know what that meant till, a few days later, they proposed to watch the corps at drill. They found the gymnasium door locked and a fag on guard.

"This is sweet cheek," said McTurk, stooping.

"Mustn't look through the key-hole," said the sentry.

"I like that. Why, Wake, you little beast, I made you a volunteer."

"Can't help it. My orders are not to allow any one to look."

"S'pose we do?" said McTurk. "S'pose we jolly well slay you?"

"My orders are, I am to give the name of anybody who interfered with me on my post to the corps, an' they'd deal with him after drill, accordin' to martial law."

"What a brute Stalky is!" said Beetle. They never doubted for a moment who had devised that scheme.

"You esteem yourself a giddy centurion, don't you?" said Beetle, listening to the crash and rattle of grounded arms within.

"My orders are, not to talk except to explain my orders—they'll lick me if I do."

McTurk looked at Beetle. The two shook their heads and turned away.

"I swear Stalky *is* a great man," said Beetle after a long pause. "One consolation is that this sort of secret-society biznai will drive King wild."

It troubled many more than King, but the members of the corps were muter than oysters. Foxy, being bound by no vow, carried his woes to Keyte.

"I never come across such nonsense in my life. They've tiled the lodge, inner and outer guard all complete, and then they get to work, keen as mustard."

"But what's it all for?" asked the ex-Troop-Sergeant-Major.

"To learn their drill. You never saw anything like it. They begin after I've dismissed 'em—practisin' tricks; but out into the open they will *not* come—not for ever so. The 'ole thing is preposterous. If you're a cadet-corps, *I* say, be a cadet-corps, instead o' hidin' be'ind locked doors."

"And what do the authorities say about it?"

"That beats me again." The Sergeant spoke fretfully. "I go to the 'Ead an' 'e gives me no help. There's times when I think he's makin' fun o' me. I've never been a Volunteer-sergeant, thank God—but I've always had the consideration to pity 'em. I'm glad o' that."

"I'd like to see 'em," said Keyte. "From your statements, Sergeant, I can't get at what they're after."

"Don't ask me, Major! Ask that freckle-faced young Corkran. He's their generalissimo."

One does not refuse a warrior of Sobraon, or deny the only

pastry-cook within bounds. So Keyte came, by invitation, leaning upon a stick, tremulous with old age, to sit in a corner and watch.

"They shape well. They shape uncommon well," he whispered between evolutions.

"Oh, *this* isn't what they're after. Wait till I dismiss 'em."

At the "break-off" the ranks stood fast. Perowne fell out, faced them, and, refreshing his memory by glimpses at a red-bound, metal-clasped book, drilled them for ten minutes. (This is that Perowne who was shot in Equatorial Africa by his own men.)

Ansell followed him, and Hogan followed Ansell. All three were implicitly obeyed.

Then Stalky laid aside his Snider, and, drawing a long breath, favoured the company with a blast of withering invective.

" 'Old 'ard, Muster Corkran. That ain't in any drill," cried Foxy.

"All right, Sergeant. You never know what you may have to say to your men.—For pity's sake, try to stand up without leanin' against each other, you blear-eyed, herrin'-gutted gutter-snipes. It's no pleasure to me to comb you out. That ought to have been done before you came here, you—you militia broom-stealers."

"The old touch—the old touch. *We* know it," said Keyte, wiping his rheumy eyes. "But where did he pick it up?"

"From his father—or his uncle. Don't ask me! Half of 'em must have been born within ear-shot o' the barracks." (Foxy was not far wrong in his guess.) "I've heard more back talk since this volunteerin' nonsense began than I've heard in a year in the service."

"There's a rear-rank man lookin' as though his belly were in the pawn-shop. Yes, you, Private Ansell," and Stalky tongue-lashed the victim for three minutes, in gross and in detail.

"Hullo!" He returned to his normal tone. "First blood to me. You flushed, Ansell. You wriggled."

"Couldn't help flushing," was the answer. "Don't think I wriggled, though."

"Well, it's your turn now." Stalky resumed his place in the ranks.

"Lord, Lord! It's as good as a play," chuckled the attentive Keyte.

Ansell, too, had been blessed with relatives in the service, and slowly, in a lazy drawl—his style was more reflective than Stalky's—descended the abysmal depths of personality.

"Blood to me!" he shouted triumphantly. "You couldn't stand it, either." Stalky was a rich red, and his Snider shook visibly.

"I didn't think I would," he said, struggling for composure, "but after a bit I got in no end of a bait. Curious, ain't it?"

"Good for the temper," said the slow-moving Hogan, as they returned arms to the rack.

"Did you ever?" said Foxy, hopelessly, to Keyte.

"I don't know much about volunteers, but it's the rummiest show I ever saw. I can see what they're gettin' at, though. Lord! how often I've been told off an' dressed down in my day! They shape well—extremely well they shape."

"If I could get 'em out into the open, there's nothing I couldn't do with 'em, Major. Perhaps when the uniforms come down, they'll change their mind."

Indeed, it was time that the corps made some concession to the curiosity of the school. Thrice had the guard been maltreated and thrice had the corps dealt out martial law to the offender. The school raged. What was the use, they asked, of a cadet-corps which none might see? Mr. King congratulated them on their invisible defenders, and they could not parry his thrusts. Foxy was growing sullen and restive. A few of the corps expressed openly doubts as to the wisdom of their course; and the question of uniforms loomed on the near horizon. If these were issued, they would be forced to wear them.

But, as so often happens in this life, the matter was suddenly settled from without.

The Head had duly informed the Council that their recommendation had been acted upon, and that, so far as he could learn, the boys were drilling.

He said nothing of the terms on which they drilled. Naturally, General Collinson was delighted and told his friends. One of his friends rejoiced in a friend, a Member of Parliament—a zealous, an intelligent, and, above all, a patriotic person, anxious to do the most good in the shortest possible time. But we cannot answer, alas! for the friends of our friends. If Collinson's friend had introduced him to the General, the latter would have taken his measure and saved much. But the friend merely spoke of his friend; and since no two people in the world see eye to eye, the picture conveyed to Collinson was inaccurate. Moreover, the man was an M.P., an impeccable Conservative, and the General had the English soldier's lurking respect for any member of the Court of Last Appeal. He was going down into the West country, to spread light in somebody's benighted constituency. Wouldn't it be a good idea if, armed with the General's recommendations, he, taking the admirable and newly established cadet-corps for his text, spoke a few words—"Just talked to the boys a little—eh? You know the kind of thing that would be acceptable; and he'd be the very man to do it. The sort of talk that boys understand, you know."

"They didn't talk to 'em much in my time," said the General, suspiciously.

"Ah! but times change—with the spread of education and so on. The boys of to-day are the men of to-morrow. An impression in youth is likely to be permanent. And in these times, you know, with the country going to the dogs?"

"You're quite right." The island was then entering on five years of Mr. Gladstone's rule; and the General did not like what he had seen of it. He would certainly write to the Head, for it was beyond question that the boys of to-day made the men of to-morrow. That, if he might say so, was uncommonly well put.

In reply, the Head stated that he should be delighted to welcome Mr. Raymond Martin, M. P., of whom he had heard so much; to put him up for the night, and to allow him to address the school on any subject that he conceived would interest them. If Mr. Martin had not yet faced an audience of this particular class of British youth, the Head had no doubt that he would find it an interesting experience.

"And I don't think I am very far wrong in that last," he confided to the Reverend John. "Do you happen to know anything of one Raymond Martin?"

"I was at College with a man of that name," the chaplain replied. "He was without form and void, so far as I remember, but desperately earnest."

"He will address the Coll on 'Patriotism' next Saturday."

"If there is one thing our boys detest more than another it is having their Saturday evenings broken into. Patriotism has no chance beside 'brewing.' "

"Nor art either. D'you remember our 'Evening with Shakespeare'?" The Head's eyes twinkled. "Or the humorous gentleman with the magic lantern?"

*　*　*　*　*　*　*　*

"An' who the dooce is this Raymond Martin, M.P.?" demanded Beetle, when he read the notice of the lecture in the corridor. "Why do the brutes always turn up on a Saturday?"

"Ouh! Reomeo, Reomeo. Wherefore art thou Reomeo?" said McTurk over his shoulder, quoting the Shakespeare *artiste* of last term. "Well, he won't be as bad as *her*, I hope. Stalky, are you properly patriotic? Because if you ain't, this chap's goin' to make you."

"Hope he won't take up the whole of the evening. I suppose we've got to listen to him."

"Wouldn't miss him for the world," said McTurk. "A lot of chaps thought that Romeo-Romeo woman was a bore. *I* didn't. I liked her! 'Member when she began to hiccough in the middle of it? P'r'aps he'll hiccough. Whoever gets into the Gym first, bags seats for the other two."

*　*　*　*　*　*　*　*

There was no nervousness, but a brisk and cheery affability about Mr. Raymond Martin, M.P., as he drove up, watched by many eyes, to the Head's house.

"Looks a bit of a bargee," was McTurk's comment. "Shouldn't be surprised if he was a Radical. He rowed the driver about the fare. I heard him."

"That was his giddy patriotism," Beetle explained.

After tea they joined the rush for seats, secured a private and invisible corner, and began to criticise. Every gas-jet was lit. On the little dais at the far end stood the Head's official desk, whence Mr. Martin would discourse, and a ring of chairs for the masters.

Entered then Foxy, with official port, and leaned something like a cloth rolled round a stick against the desk. No one in authority was yet present, so the school applauded, crying: "What's that, Foxy? What are you stealin' the gentleman's brolly for?—We don't birch here. We cane! Take away that bauble!—Number off from the right"—and so forth, till the entry of the Head and the masters ended all demonstrations.

"One good job—the Common-room hate this as much as we do. Watch King wrigglin' to get out of the draught."

"Where's the Raymondiferous Martin? Punctuality, my beloved 'earers, is the image o' war—"

"Shut up. Here's the giddy Dook. Golly, what a dewlap!" Mr. Martin, in evening dress, was undeniably throaty—a tall, generously designed, pink-and-white man. Still, Beetle need not have been coarse.

"Look at his back while he's talkin' to the Head. Vile bad form to turn your back on the audience! He's a Philistine—a Bopper—a Jebusite—an' a Hivite." McTurk leaned back and sniffed contemptuously.

In a few colourless words, the Head introduced the speaker and sat down amid applause. When Mr. Martin took the applause to himself, they naturally applauded more than ever. It was some time before he could begin. He had no knowledge of the school—its tradition or heritage. He did not know that the last census showed that eighty per cent. of the boys had been born abroad—in camp, cantonment, or upon the high seas; or that seventy-five per cent. were sons of officers in one or other of the services—Willoughbys, Paulets, De Castros, Maynes, Randalls, after their kind—looking to follow their fathers' profession. The Head might have told him this, and much more; but, after an hour-long dinner in his company, the Head decided to say nothing whatever. Mr. Raymond Martin seemed to know so much already.

He plunged into his speech with a long-drawn, rasping "Well, boys," that, though they were not conscious of it, set every young nerve ajar. He supposed they knew—hey?—what he had come down for? It was not often that he had an opportunity to talk to boys. He supposed that boys were very much the same kind of persons—some people thought them rather funny persons—as they had been in his youth.

"This man," said McTurk, with conviction, "is the Gadarene Swine."

But they must remember that they would not always be boys. They would grow up into men, because the boys of to-day made the men of to-morrow, and upon the men of to-morrow the fair fame of their glorious native land depended.

"If this goes on, my beloved 'earers, it will be my painful duty to rot this bargee." Stalky drew a long breath through his nose.

"Can't do that," said McTurk. "He ain't chargin' anything for his Romeo."

And so they ought to think of the duties and responsibilities of the life that was opening before them. Life was not all—he enumerated a few games, and, that nothing might be lacking to the sweep and impact of his fall, added "marbles." "Yes, life was not," he said, "all marbles."

There was one tense gasp—among the juniors almost a shriek—of quivering horror. He was a heathen—an outcast—beyond the extremest pale of toleration—self-damned before all men. Stalky bowed his head in his hands. McTurk, with a bright and cheerful eye, drank in every word, and Beetle nodded solemn approval.

Some of them, doubtless, expected in a few years to have the honour of a commission from the Queen, and to wear a sword. Now, he himself had had some experience of these duties, as a Major in a volunteer regiment, and he was glad to learn that they had established a volunteer corps in their midst. The establishment of such an establishment conduced to a proper and healthy spirit, which, if fostered, would be of great benefit to the land they loved and were so proud to belong to. Some of those now present expected, he had no doubt—some of them anxiously looked forward to leading their men against the bullets of England's foes; to confronting the stricken field in all the pride of their youthful manhood.

Now the reserve of a boy is tenfold deeper than the reserve of a maid, she being made for one end only by blind Nature, but man for several. With a large and healthy hand, he tore down these veils, and trampled them under the well-intentioned feet of eloquence. In a raucous voice, he cried aloud little matters, like the hope of Honour and the dream of Glory, that boys do not discuss even with their most intimate equals, cheerfully assuming that, till he spoke, they had never considered these possibilities. He pointed them to shining goals, with fingers which smudged out all radiance on all horizons. He profaned the most secret places of their souls with outcries and gesticulations. He bade them consider the deeds of their ancestors in such a fashion that they were flushed to their tingling ears. Some of them—the rending voice cut a frozen stillness—might have had relatives who perished in defence of their country. They thought, not a few of them, of an old sword in a passage, or above a breakfast-room table, seen and fingered by stealth since they could walk. He adjured them to emulate those illustrious examples; and they looked all ways in their extreme discomfort.

Their years forbade them even to shape their thoughts clearly to themselves. They felt savagely that they were being outraged by a fat man who considered marbles a game.

And so he worked towards his peroration—which, by the way, he used later with overwhelming success at a meeting of electors—while they sat, flushed and uneasy, in sour disgust. After many, many words, he reached for the cloth-wrapped stick and thrust one hand in his bosom. This—this was the concrete symbol of their land—worthy of all honour and reverence! Let no boy look on this flag who did not purpose to worthily add to its imperishable lustre. He shook it before them—a large calico Union Jack, staring in all three colours, and waited for the thunder of applause that should crown his effort.

They looked in silence. They had certainly seen the thing before—down at the coast-guard station, or through a telescope, half-mast high when a brig went ashore on Braunton Sands; above the roof of the Golf-club, and in Keyte's window, where a certain kind of striped sweetmeat bore it in paper on each box. But the College never displayed it; it was no part of the scheme of their lives; the Head had never alluded to it; their fathers had not declared it unto them. It was a matter shut up, sacred and apart. What, in the name of everything caddish, was he driving at, who waved that horror before their eyes? Happy thought! Perhaps he was drunk.

The Head saved the situation by rising swiftly to propose a vote of thanks, and at his first motion, the school clapped furiously, from a sense of relief.

"And I am sure," he concluded, the gaslight full on his face, "that you will all join me in a very hearty vote of thanks to Mr. Raymond Martin for the most enjoyable address he has given us."

To this day we shall never know the rights of the case. The Head vows that he did no such thing; or that, if he did, it must have been something in his eye; but those who were present are persuaded that he winked, once, openly and solemnly, after the word "enjoyable." Mr. Raymond Martin got his applause full tale. As he said, "Without vanity, I think my few words went to their hearts. I never knew boys could cheer like that."

He left as the prayer-bell rang, and the boys lined up against the wall. The flag lay still unrolled on the desk, Foxy regarding it with pride, for he had been touched to the quick by Mr. Martin's eloquence. The Head and the Common-room, standing back on the dais, could not see the glaring offence, but a prefect left the line, rolled it up swiftly, and as swiftly tossed it into a glove and foil locker.

Then, as though he had touched a spring, broke out the low murmur of content, changing to quick-volleyed hand-clapping.

They discussed the speech in the dormitories. There was not one dissentient voice. Mr. Raymond Martin, beyond question, was born in a gutter, and bred in a board-school, where they played marbles. He was further (I give the barest handful from great store) a Flopshus Cad, an Outrageous Stinker, a Jelly-bellied Flag-flapper (this was Stalky's contribution), and several other things which it is not seemly to put down.

The volunteer cadet-corps fell in next Monday, depressedly, with a face of shame. Even then, judicious silence might have turned the corner.

Said Foxy: "After a fine speech like what you 'eard night before last, you ought to take 'old of your drill with re-newed activity. I don't see how you can avoid comin' out an' marchin' in the open now."

"Can't we get out of it, then, Foxy?" Stalky's fine old silky tone should have warned him.

"No, not with his giving the flag so generously. He told me before he left this morning that there was no objection to the corps usin' it as their own. It's a handsome flag."

Stalky returned his rifle to the rack in dead silence, and fell out. His example was followed by Hogan and Ansell.

Perowne hesitated. "Look here, oughtn't we—?" he began.

"I'll get it out of the locker in a minute," said the Sergeant, his back turned. "Then we can—"

"Come on!" shouted Stalky. "What the devil are you waiting for? Dismiss! Break off."

"Why—what the—where the—?"

The rattle of Sniders, slammed into the rack, drowned his voice, as boy after boy fell out.

"I—I don't know that I sha'n't have to report this to the Head, he stammered.

"Report, then, and be damned to you," cried Stalky, white to the lips, and ran out.

* * * * *

"Rummy thing!" said Beetle to McTurk. "I was in the study, doin' a simply lovely poem about the Jelly-bellied Flag-flapper, an' Stalky came in, an' I said 'Hullo!' an' he cursed me like a bargee, an' then he began to blub like anything. Shoved his head on the table and howled. Hadn't we better do something?"

McTurk was troubled. "P'r'aps he's smashed himself up somehow."

They found him, with very bright eyes, whistling between his teeth.

"Did I take you in, Beetle? I thought I would. Wasn't it a good draw? Didn't you think I was blubbin'? Didn't I do it well? Oh, you fat old ass!" And he began to pull Beetle's ears and cheeks, in the fashion that was called "milking."

"I knew you were blubbin'," Beetle replied composedly. "Why aren't you at drill?"

"Drill! What drill?"

"Don't try to be a clever fool. Drill in the Gym."

" 'Cause there isn't any. The volunteer cadet-corps is broke up—disbanded—dead—putrid—corrupt—stinkin'. An' if you look at me like that, Beetle, I'll slay you too. . . . Oh, yes, an' I'm goin' to be reported to the Head for swearin'."

The Last Term

IT WAS WITHIN A FEW DAYS of the holidays, the term-end examinations, and, more important still, the last issue of the College paper which Beetle edited. He had been cajoled into that office by the blandishments of Stalky and McTurk and the extreme rigour of study law. Once installed, he discovered, as others have done before him, that his duty was to do the work while his friends criticised. Stalky christened it the "Swillingford Patriot," in pious memory of Sponge—and McTurk compared the output unfavourably with Ruskin and De Quincey. Only the Head took an interest in the publication, and his methods were peculiar. He gave Beetle the run of his brown-bound, tobacco-scented library; prohibiting nothing, recommending nothing. There Beetle found a fat arm-chair, a silver inkstand, and unlimited pens and paper. There were scores and scores of ancient dramatists; there were Hakluyt, his voyages; French translations of Muscovite authors called Pushkin and Lermontoff; little tales of a heady and bewildering nature, interspersed with unusual songs—Peacock was that writer's name; there was Borrow's "Lavengro"; an odd theme, purporting to be a translation of something, called a "Rubáiyát," which the Head said was a poem not yet come to its own; there were hundreds of volumes of verse—Crashaw; Dryden; Alexander Smith; L. E. L.; Lydia Sigourney; Fletcher and a purple island; Donne; Marlowe's "Faust"; and—this made McTurk (to whom Beetle conveyed it) sheer drunk for three days—Ossian; "The Earthly Paradise"; "Atalanta in Calydon"; and Rossetti—to name only a few. Then the Head, drifting in under pretence of playing censor to the paper, would read here a verse and here another of these poets, opening up avenues. And, slow breathing, with half-shut eyes above his cigar, would he speak of great men living, and journals, long dead, founded in their riotous youth; of years when all the planets were little new-lit stars trying to find their places in the uncaring void, and he, the Head, knew them as young men know one another. So the regular work went to the dogs, Beetle being full of other matters and metres, hoarded in secret and only told to McTurk of an afternoon, on the sands, walking high and disposedly round the wreck of the Armada galleon, shouting and declaiming against the long-ridged seas.

Thanks in large part to their house-master's experienced distrust, the three for three consecutive terms had been passed over for promotion to the rank of prefect—an office that went by merit, and carried with it the honour of the ground-ash, and liberty, under restrictions, to use it.

"*But*," said Stalky, "come to think of it, we've done more giddy jesting with the Sixth since we've been passed over than any one else in the last seven years."

He touched his neck proudly. It was encircled by the stiffest of stick-up collars, which custom decreed could be worn only by the Sixth. And the Sixth saw those collars and said no word. "Pussy" Abanazar or Dick Four of a year ago would have seen them discarded in five minutes or . . . But the Sixth of that term was made up mostly of young but brilliantly clever boys, pets of the house-masters, too anxious for their dignity to care to come to open odds with the resourceful three. So they crammed their càps at the extreme back of their heads, instead of a trifle over one eye as the Fifth should, and rejoiced in patent-leather boots on week-days, and marvellous made-up ties on Sundays—no man rebuking. McTurk was going up for Cooper's Hill, and Stalky for Sandhurst, in the spring; and the Head had told them both that, unless they absolutely collapsed during the holidays, they were safe. As a trainer of colts, the Head seldom erred in an estimate of form.

He had taken Beetle aside that day and given him much good advice, not one word of which did Beetle remember when he dashed up to the study, white with excitement, and poured out the wondrous tale. It demanded a great belief.

"*You* begin on a hundred a year?" said McTurk, unsympathetically. "Rot!"

"*And* my passage out! It's all settled. The Head says he's been breaking me in for this for ever so long, and I never knew—I never knew. One don't begin with writing straight off, y'know. Begin by filling in telegrams and cutting things out o' papers with scissors.

"Oh, Scissors! What an ungodly mess you'll make of it," said Stalky. "But, anyhow, this will be your last term, too. Seven years, my dearly beloved 'earers—though not prefects."

"Not half bad years, either," said McTurk. "I shall be sorry to leave the old Coll; sha'n't you?"

They looked out over the sea creaming along the Pebble-ridge in the clear winter light. "Wonder where we shall all be this time next year?" said Stalky, absently.

"This time five years," said McTurk.

"Oh," said Beetle, "my leavin's between ourselves. The Head hasn't told any one. I know he hasn't, because Prout grunted at me to-day that if I were more reasonable—yah!— I might be a prefect next term. I suppose he's hard up for his prefects."

"Let's finish up with a row with the Sixth," suggested McTurk.

"Dirty little schoolboys!" said Stalky, who already saw himself a Sandhurst cadet. "What's the use?"

"Moral effect," quoth McTurk. "Leave an imperishable tradition, and all the rest of it."

"Better go into Bideford an' pay up our debts," said Stalky. "I've got three quid out of my father—*ad hoc*. Don't owe more than thirty bob, either. Cut along, Beetle and ask the Head for leave. Say you want to correct the 'Swillingford Patriot.'"

"Well, I do," said Beetle. "It'll be my last issue, and I'd like it to look decent. I'll catch him before he goes to his lunch."

Ten minutes later they wheeled out in line, by grace released from five-o'clock call-over, and all the afternoon lay before them. So also unluckily did King, who never passed without witticisms. But brigades of Kings could not have ruffled Beetle that day.

"Aha! Enjoying the study of light literature, my friends," said he, rubbing his hands. "Common mathematics are not for such soaring minds as yours, are they?"

("One hundred a year," thought Beetle, smiling into vacancy.)

"Our open incompetence takes refuge in the flowery paths of inaccurate fiction. But a day of reckoning approaches, Beetle mine. I myself have prepared a few trifling foolish questions in Latin prose which can hardly be evaded even by your practised acts of deception. Ye-es, Latin prose. I think, if I may say so—but we shall see when the papers are set—'Ulpian serves *your* need.' Aha! '*Elucescebat,* quoth our friend.' We shall see! We shall see!"

Still no sign from Beetle. He was on a steamer, his passage paid into the wide and wonderful world—a thousand leagues beyond Lundy Island.

King dropped him with a snarl.

"He doesn't know. He'll go on correctin' exercises an' jawin' an' showin' off before the little boys next term—and next." Beetle hurried after his companions up the steep path of the furze-clad hill behind the College.

They were throwing pebbles on the top of the gasometer, and the grimy gas-man in charge bade them desist. They watched him oil a turncock sunk in the ground between two furze-bushes.

"Cokey, what's that for?" said Stalky.

"To turn the gas on to the kitchens," said Cokey. "If so be I didn't turn her on, yeou young gen'elmen 'ud be larnin' your book by candlelight."

"Um!" said Stalky, and was silent for at least a minute.

"Hullo! Where are you chaps going?"

A bend of the lane brought them face to face with Tulke, senior prefect of King's house—a smallish, white-haired boy, of the type that must be promoted on account of its intellect, and ever afterwards appeals to the Head to support its authority when zeal has outrun discretion.

The three took no sort of notice. They were on lawful pass. Tulke repeated his question hotly, for he had suffered many slights from Number Five study, and fancied that he had at last caught them tripping.

"What the devil is that to you?" Stalky replied, with his sweetest smile.

"Look here, I'm not goin'—I'm not goin' to be sworn at by the Fifth!" sputtered Tulke.

"Then cut along and call a prefects' meeting," said McTurk, knowing Tulke's weakness.

The prefect became inarticulate with rage.

"Mustn't yell at the Fifth that way," said Stalky. "It's vile bad form."

"Cough it up, ducky!" McTurk said calmly.

"I—I want to know what you chaps are doing out of bounds?" This with an important flourish of his ground-ash.

"Ah," said Stalky. "Now we're gettin' at it. Why didn't you ask that before?"

"Well, I ask it now. What are you doing?"

"We're admiring you, Tulke," said Stalky. "We think you're no end of a fine chap, don't we?"

"We do! We do!" A dog-cart with some girls in it swept round the corner, and Stalky promptly kneeled before Tulke in the attitude of prayer; so Tulke turned a colour.

"I've reason to believe—" he began.

"Oyez! Oyez! Oyez!" shouted Beetle, after the manner of Bideford's town crier, "Tulke has reason to believe! Three cheers for Tulke!"

They were given. "It's all our giddy admiration," said Stalky. "You know how we love you, Tulke. We love you so much we think you ought to go home and die. You're too good to live, Tulke."

"Yes," said McTurk. "*Do* oblige us by dyin'. Think how lovely you'd look stuffed!"

Tulke swept up the road with an unpleasant glare in his eye.

"That means a prefects' meeting—sure pop," said Stalky. "Honour of the Sixth involved, and all the rest of it. Tulke'll write notes all this afternoon, and Carson will call us up after tea. They daren't overlook that."

"Bet you a bob he follows us!" said McTurk. "He's King's pet, and it's scalps to both of 'em if we're caught out. We must be virtuous."

"Then I move we go to Mother Yeo's for a last gorge. We owe her about ten bob, and Mary'll weep sore when she knows we're leaving," said Beetle.

"She gave me an awful wipe on the head last time—Mary," said Stalky.

"She does if you don't duck," said McTurk. "But she generally kisses one back. Let's try Mother Yeo."

They sought a little bottle-windowed half dairy, half restaurant, a dark-browned, two-hundred-year-old house, at the head of a narrow side street. They had patronised it from the days of their fagdom, and were very much friends at home.

"We've come to pay our debts, mother," said Stalky, sliding his arm round the fifty-six-inch waist of the mistress of the establishment. "To pay our debts and say good-bye—and —and we're awf'ly hungry."

"Aie!" said Mother Yeo, "makkin' love to me! I'm shaamed of 'ee."

" 'Rackon us wouldn't du no such thing if Mary was here," said McTurk, lapsing into the broad North Devon that the boys used on their campaigns.

"Who'm takin' my name in vain?" The inner door opened, and Mary, fair-haired, blue-eyed, and apple-cheeked, entered with a bowl of cream in her hands. McTurk kissed her. Beetle followed suit, with exemplary calm. Both boys were promptly cuffed.

"Niver kiss the maid when 'ee can kiss the mistress," said Stalky, shamelessly winking at Mother Yeo, as he investigated a shelf of jams.

"Glad to see one of 'ee don't want his head slapped no more?" said Mary, invitingly, in that direction.

"Neu! Reckon I can get 'em give me," said Stalky, his back turned.

"Not by me—yeou little masterpiece!"

"Niver asked 'ee. There's maids to Northam. Yiss—an' Appledore." An unreproducible sniff, half contempt, half reminiscence, rounded the retort.

"Aie! Yeou won't niver come to no good end. Whutt be 'baout, smellin' the cream?"

" 'Tees bad," said Stalky. "Zmell 'un."

Incautiously Mary did as she was bid.

"Bidevoor kiss."

"Niver amiss," said Stalky, taking it without injury.

"Yeou—yeou—yeou—" Mary began, bubbling with mirth.

"They'm better to Northam—more rich, laike—an' us gets them give back again," he said, while McTurk solemnly waltzed Mother Yeo out of breath, and Beetle told Mary the sad news, as they sat down to clotted cream, jam, and hot bread.

"Yiss. Yeou'll niver zee us no more, Mary. We'm goin' to be passons an' missioners."

"Steady the Buffs!" said McTurk, looking through the blind. "Tulke *has* followed us. He's comin' up the street now."

"They've niver put us out o' bounds," said Mother Yeo. "Bide yeou still, my little dearrs." She rolled to the inner room to make the score.

"Mary," said Stalky, suddenly, with tragic intensity. "Do 'ee lov' me, Mary?"

"Iss—fai! Talled 'ee zo since yeou was zo high!" the damsel replied.

"Zee 'un comin' up street, then?" Stalky pointed to the unconscious Tulke. "He've niver been kissed by no sort or manner o' maid in hees borned laife, Mary. Oh, 'tees shaamful!"

"Whutt's to do with me? 'Twill come to 'un in the way o' nature, I rackon." She nodded her head sagaciously. "Yeou niver want me to kiss 'un—sure-*ly?*"

"Give 'ee half-a-crown if 'ee will," said Stalky, exhibiting the coin.

Half-a-crown was much to Mary Yeo, and a jest was more; but—

"Yeou'm afraid," said McTurk, at the psychological moment.

"Aie!" Beetle echoed, knowing her weak point. "There's not a maid to Northam 'ud think twice. An' yeou such a fine maid, tu!"

McTurk planted one foot firmly against the inner door lest Mother Yeo should return inopportunely, for Mary's face was set. It was then that Tulke found his way blocked by a tall daughter of Devon—that county of easy kisses, the pleasantest under the sun. He dodged aside politely. She reflected a moment, and laid a vast hand upon his shoulder.

"Where be 'ee gwaine tu, my dearr?" said she.

Over the handkerchief he had crammed into his mouth Stalky could see the boy turn scarlet.

"Gie I a kiss! Don't they larn 'ee manners to College?"

Tulke gasped and wheeled. Solemnly and conscientiously Mary kissed him twice, and the luckless prefect fled.

She stepped into the shop, her eyes full of simple wonder.

"Kissed 'un?" said Stalky, handing over the money.

"Iss, fai! But, oh, my little body, *he'm* no Colleger. 'Zeemed tu minded to cry, laike."

"Well, we won't. You couldn't make us cry that way," said McTurk. "Try."

Whereupon Mary cuffed them all round.

As they went out with tingling ears, said Stalky generally, "Don't think there'll be much of a prefects' meeting."

"Won't there, just!" said Beetle. "Look here. If he kissed her—which is our tack—he is a cynically immoral hog, and his conduct is blatant indecency. *Confer orationes Regis furiosissimi,* when he collared me readin' 'Don Juan.' "

" 'Course he kissed her," said McTurk. "In the middle of the street. With his house-cap on!"

"Time, 3:57 P.M. Make a note o' that. What d'you mean, Beetle?" said Stalky.

"Well! He's a truthful little beast. He may say he was kissed."

"And then?"

"Why, then!" Beetle capered at the mere thought of it. "Don't you see? The corollary to the giddy proposition is that the Sixth can't protect 'emselves from outrages an' ravishin's. Want nurse-maids to look after 'em! We've only got to whisper that to the Coll. Jam for the Sixth! Jam for us! Either way it's jammy!"

"By gum!" said Stalky. "Our last term's endin' well. Now you cut along an' finish up your old rag, and Turkey and me will help. We'll go in the back way. No need to bother Randall."

"Don't play the giddy garden-goat, then?" Beetle knew what help meant, though he was by no means averse to showing his importance before his allies. The little loft behind Randall's printing-office was his own territory, where he saw himself already controlling the "Times." Here, under the guidance of the inky apprentice, he had learned to find his way more or less circuitously about the case, and considered himself an expert compositor.

The school paper in its locked forms lay on a stone-topped table, a proof by the side; but not for worlds would Beetle have corrected from the mere proof. With a mallet and a pair of tweezers, he knocked out mysterious wedges of wood that released the form, picked a letter here and inserted a letter there, reading as he went along and stopping much to chuckle over his own contributions.

"You won't show off like that," said McTurk, "when you've got to do it for your living. Upside down and backwards, isn't it? Let's see if I can read it."

"Get out!" said Beetle. "Go and read those forms in the rack there, if you think you know so much."

"Forms in a rack! What's that? Don't be so beastly professional."

McTurk drew off with Stalky to prowl about the office. They left little unturned.

"Come here a shake, Beetle. What's this thing?" said Stalky, in a few minutes. "Looks familiar."

Said Beetle, after a glance: "It's King's Latin prose exam. paper. *In—In Verrem: actio prima*. What a lark!"

"Think o' the pure-souled, high-minded boys who'd give their eyes for a squint at it!" said McTurk.

"No, Willie dear," said Stalky; "that would be wrong and painful to our kind teachers. You wouldn't crib, Willie, would you?"

"Can't read the beastly stuff, anyhow," was the reply. "Besides, we're leavin' at the end o' the term, so it makes no difference to us."

" 'Member what the Considerate Bloomer did to Spraggon's account of the Puffin'ton Hounds? We must sugar Mr. King's milk for him," said Stalky, all lighted from within by a devilish joy. "Let's see what Beetle can do with those forceps he's so proud of."

"Don't see how you can make Latin prose much more cockeye than it is, but we'll try," said Beetle, transposing an *aliud* and *Asiae* from two sentences. "Let's see! We'll put that fullstop a little further on, and begin the sentence with the next capital. Hurrah! Here's three lines that can move up all in a lump."

" 'One of those scientific rests for which this eminent huntsman is so justly celebrated.' " Stalky knew the Puffington run by heart.

"Hold on! Here's a *vol—voluntate quidnam* all by itself," said McTurk.

"I'll attend to her in a shake. *Quidnam* goes after *Dolabella.*"

"Good old Dolabella," murmured Stalky. "Don't break him. Vile prose Cicero wrote, didn't he? He ought to be grateful for—"

"Hullo!" said McTurk, over another form. "What price a giddy ode? *Qui—quis—*oh, it's *Quis multa gracilis,* o' course."

"Bring it along. We've sugared the milk here," said Stalky, after a few minutes' zealous toil. "Never thrash your hounds unnecessarily."

"*Quis munditiis?* I swear that's not bad," began Beetle, plying the tweezers. "Don't that interrogation look pretty? *Heu quoties fidem!* That sounds as if the chap were anxious an' excited. *Cui flavam religas in rosa*—Whose flavour is relegated to a rose. *Mutatosque Deos flebit in antro.*"

"Mute gods weepin' in a cave," suggested Stalky. " 'Pon my Sam, Horace needs as much lookin' after as—Tulke."

They edited him faithfully till it was too dark to see.

* * * * *

" 'Aha! *Elucescebat,* quoth our friend.' Ulpian serves my need, does it? If King can make anything out of *that,* I'm a blue-eyed squatteroo," said Beetle, as they slid out of the loft window into a back alley of old acquaintance and started on a three-mile trot to the College. But the revision of the classics had detained them too long. They halted, blown and breathless, in the furze at the back of the gasometer, the College lights twinkling below, ten minutes at least late for tea and lock-up.

"It's no good," puffed McTurk. "Bet a bob Foxy is waiting for defaulters under the lamp by the Fives Court. It's a nuisance, too, because the Head gave us long leave, and one doesn't like to break it."

" 'Let me now from the bonded ware'ouse of my knowledge,' " began Stalky.

"Oh, rot! Don't Jorrock. Can we make a run for it?" snapped McTurk.

" 'Bishops' boots Mr. Radcliffe also condemned, an' spoke 'ighly in favour of tops cleaned with champagne an' abricot jam.' Where's that thing Cokey was twiddlin' this afternoon?"

They heard him groping in the wet, and presently beheld a great miracle. The lights of the coast-guard cottages near the sea went out; the brilliantly illuminated windows of the Golf-club disappeared, and were followed by the frontages of the two hotels. Scattered villas dulled, twinkled, and vanished. Last of all, the College lights died also. They were left in the pitchy darkness of a windy winter's night.

" 'Blister my kidneys. It *is* a frost. The dahlias are dead!' " said Stalky. "Bunk!"

They squattered through the dripping gorse as the College hummed like an angry hive and the dining-rooms chorussed, "Gas! gas! gas!" till they came to the edge of the sunk path that divided them from their study. Dropping that ha-ha like bullets, and rebounding like boys, they dashed to their study, in less than two minutes had changed into dry trousers and coat, and, ostentatiously slippered, joined the mob in the dining-hall, which resembled the storm-centre of a South American revolution.

" 'Hellish dark and smells of cheese.' " Stalky elbowed his way into the press, howling lustily for gas. "Cokey must have gone for a walk. Foxy'll have to find him."

Prout, as the nearest house-master, was trying to restore order, for rude boys were flicking butter-pats across chaos, and McTurk had turned on the fags' tea-urn, so that many were parboiled and wept with an unfeigned dolour. The Fourth and Upper Third broke into the school song, the "*Vive la Compagnie*," to the accompaniment of drumming knife-handles; and the junior forms shrilled bat-like shrieks and raided one another's victuals. Two hundred and fifty boys in high condition, seeking for more light, are truly earnest inquirers.

When a most vile smell of gas told them that supplies had been renewed, Stalky, waistcoat unbuttoned, sat gorgedly over what might have been his fourth cup of tea. "And that's all right," he said. "Hullo! 'Ere's Pomponius Ego!"

It was Carson, the head of the school, a simple, straight-minded soul, and a pillar of the First Fifteen, who crossed over from the prefects' table and in a husky, official voice invited the three to attend in his study in half an hour.

"Prefects' meetin'! Prefects' meetin'!" hissed the tables, and they imitated barbarically the actions and effects of the ground-ash.

"How are we goin' to jest with 'em?" said Stalky, turning half-face to Beetle. "It's your play this time!"

"Look here," was the answer, "all I want you to do is not to laugh. I'm goin' to take charge o' young Tulke's immorality —*à la* King—and it's goin' to be serious. If you can't help laughin' don't look at me, or I'll go pop."

"I see. All right," said Stalky.

McTurk's lank frame stiffened in every muscle and his eyelids dropped half over his eyes. That last was a war-signal.

The eight or nine seniors, their faces very set and sober, were ranged in chairs round Carson's severely Philistine study. Tulke was not popular among them, and a few who had had experience of Stalky and Company doubted that he might, perhaps, have made an ass of himself. But the dignity of the Sixth was to be upheld. So Carson began hurriedly:

"Look here, you chaps, I've—we've sent for you to tell you you're a good deal too cheeky to the Sixth—have been for some time—and—and we've stood about as much as we're goin' to, and it seems you've been cursin' and swearin' at Tulke on the Bideford road this afternoon, and we're goin' to show you you can't do it. That's all."

"Well, that's awfully good of you," said Stalky, "but we happen to have a few rights of our own, too. You can't, just because you happen to be made prefects, haul up seniors and jaw 'em on spec., like a house-master. *We* aren't fags, Carson. This kind of thing may do for Davies tertius, but it won't do for us."

"It's only old Prout's lunacy that we weren't prefects long ago. You know that," said McTurk. "You haven't any tact."

"Hold on," said Beetle. "A prefects' meetin' has to be reported to the Head. I want to know if the Head backs Tulke in this business?"

"Well—well, it isn't exactly a prefects' meeting," said Carson. "We only called you in to warn you."

"But all the prefects are here," Beetle insisted. "Where's the difference?"

"My gum!" said Stalky. "Do you mean to say you've just called us in for a jaw—after comin' to us before the whole school at tea an' givin' 'em the impression it was a prefects' meeting? 'Pon my Sam, Carson, you'll get into trouble, you will."

"Hole-an'-corner business—hole-an'-corner business," said McTurk, wagging his head. "Beastly suspicious."

The Sixth looked at each other uneasily. Tulke had called three prefects' meetings in two terms, till the Head had informed the Sixth that they were expected to maintain discipline without the recurrent menace of his authority. Now, it seemed that they had made a blunder at the outset, but any right-minded boy would have sunk the legality and been properly impressed by the Court. Beetle's protest was distinct "cheek."

"Well, you chaps deserve a lickin'," cried one Naughten incautiously. Then was Beetle filled with a noble inspiration.

"For interferin' with Tulke's amours, eh?" Tulke turned a rich sloe colour. "Oh, no, you don't!" Beetle went on. "You've had your innings. We've been set up for cursing and

swearing at you, and we're goin' to be let off with a warning!
Are we? Now then, you're goin' to catch it."

"I—I—I—" Tulke began. "Don't let that young devil start
jawing."

"If you've anything to say you must say it decently," said
Carson.

"Decently? I will. Now look here. When we went into
Bideford we met this ornament of the Sixth—is that decent
enough?—hanging about on the road with a nasty look in his
eye. We didn't know *then* why he was so anxious to stop us,
but at five minutes to four, when we were in Yeo's shop, we
saw Tulke *in* broad daylight, *with* his house-cap on, kissin' an'
huggin' a woman *on* the pavement. Is that decent enough for
you?"

"I didn't—I wasn't."

"We saw you!" said Beetle. "And now—I'll be decent,
Carson—you sneak back with her kisses" (not for nothing had
Beetle perused the later poets) "hot on your lips and call prefects' meetings, which aren't prefects' meetings, to uphold
the honour of the Sixth." A new and heaven-cleft path opened
before him that instant. "And how do we know," he shouted
—"how do we know how many of the Sixth are mixed up in
this abominable affair?"

"Yes, that's what we want to know," said McTurk, with
simple dignity.

"We meant to come to you about it quietly, Carson, but you
would have the meeting," said Stalky, sympathetically.

The Sixth were too taken aback to reply. So, carefully
modelling his rhetoric on King, Beetle followed up the attack,
surpassing and surprising himself.

"It—it isn't so much the cynical immorality of the biznai,
as the blatant indecency of it, that's so awful. As far as we
can see, it's impossible for us to go into Bideford without run-
nin' up against some prefect's unwholesome amours. There's
nothing to snigger over, Naughten. *I* don't pretend to know
much about these things—but it sems to me a chap must be
pretty far dead in sin" (that was a quotation from the school-
chaplain) "when he takes to embracing his paramours" (that

was Hakluyt) "before all the city" (a reminiscence of Milton). "He might at least have the decency—you're authorities on decency, I believe—to wait till dark. But he didn't. You didn't! Oh, Tulke! You—you incontinent little animal!"

"Here, shut up a minute. What's all this about, Tulke?" said Carson.

"I—look here. I'm awfully sorry. I never thought Beetle would take this line."

"Because—you've—no decency—you—thought—I hadn't," cried Beetle all in one breath.

"Tried to cover it all up with a conspiracy, did you?" said Stalky.

"Direct insult to all three of us," said McTurk. "A most filthy mind you have, Tulke."

"I'll shove you fellows outside the door if you go on like this," said Carson, angrily.

"That proves it's a conspiracy," said Stalky, with the air of a virgin martyr.

"I—I was goin' along the street—I swear I was," cried Tulke, "and—and I'm awfully sorry about it—a woman came up and kissed me. I swear I didn't kiss her."

There was a pause, filled by Stalky's long, liquid whistle of contempt, amazement, and derision.

"On my honour," gulped the persecuted one. "Oh, do stop him jawing."

"Very good," McTurk interjected. "We are compelled, of course, to accept your statement."

"Confound it!" roared Naughten. "You aren't head-prefect here, McTurk."

"Oh, well," returned the Irishman, "you know Tulke better than we do. I am only speaking for ourselves. *We* accept Tulke's word. But all I can say is that if I'd been collared in a similarly disgustin' situation, and had offered the same explanation Tulke has, I—I wonder what you'd have said. However, it seems on Tulke's word of honour—"

"And Tulkus—beg pardon—*kiss*, of course—Tulkiss is an honourable man," put in Stalky.

"—that the Sixth can't protect 'emselves from bein' kissed

when they go for a walk!" cried Beetle, taking up the running with a rush. "Sweet business, isn't it? Cheerful thing to tell the fags, ain't it? We aren't prefects, of course, but we aren't kissed very much. Don't think that sort of thing ever enters our heads; does it, Stalky?"

"Oh, no!" said Stalky, turning aside to hide his emotions. McTurk's face merely expressed lofty contempt and a little weariness.

"Well, you seem to know a lot about it," interposed a prefect.

"Can't help it—when you chaps shove it under our noses." Beetle dropped into a drawling parody of King's most biting colloquial style—the gentle rain after the thunder-storm. "Well, it's all very sufficiently vile and disgraceful, isn't it? I don't know who comes out of it worst; Tulke, who happens to have been caught; or the other fellows who haven't. And we—" here he wheeled fiercely on the other two— "we've got to stand up and be jawed by them because we've disturbed their intrigues."

"Hang it! I only wanted to give you a word of warning," said Carson, thereby handing himself bound to the enemy.

"Warn? You?" This with the air of one who finds loathsome gifts in his locker. "Carson, would you be good enough to tell us what conceivable thing there is that you are entitled to warn us about after this exposure? Warn? Oh, it's a little too much! Let's go somewhere where it's clean."

The door banged behind their outraged innocence.

"Oh, Beetle! Beetle! Beetle! Golden Beetle!" sobbed Stalky, hurling himself on Beetle's panting bosom as soon as they reached the study. "However did you do it?"

"Dear-r man!" said McTurk, embracing Beetle's head with both arms, while he swayed it to and fro on the neck, in time to this ancient burden—

> "Pretty lips—sweeter than—cherry or plum,
> Always look—jolly and—never look glum;
> Seem to say—Come away. Kissy!—come, come!
> Yummy-yum! Yummy-yum! Yummy-yum-yum!"

"Look out. You'll smash my gig-lamps," puffed Beetle, emerging. "Wasn't it glorious? Didn't I 'Eric' 'em splendidly? Did you spot my cribs from King? Oh, blow!" His countenance clouded. "There's one adjective I didn't use—'obscene.' Don't know how I forgot that. It's one of King's pet ones, too."

"Never mind. They'll be sendin' ambassadors round in half a shake to beg us not to tell the school. It's a deuced serious business for them," said McTurk. "Poor Sixth—poor old Sixth!"

"Immoral young rips," Stalky snorted. "What an example to pure-souled boys like you and me!"

And the Sixth in Carson's study sat aghast, glowering at Tulke, who was on the edge of tears.

"Well," said the head-prefect, acidly. "You've made a pretty average ghastly mess of it, Tulke."

"Why—why didn't you lick that young devil Beetle before he began jawing?" Tulke wailed.

"I knew there'd be a row," said a prefect of Prout's house. "But you would insist on the meeting, Tulke."

"Yes, and a fat lot of good it's done us," said Naughten. "They come in here and jaw our heads off when we ought to be jawin' them. Beetle talks to us as if we were a lot of blackguards and—and all that. And when they've hung us up to dry, they go out and slam the door like a house-master. All your fault, Tulke."

"But I didn't kiss her."

"You ass! If you'd said you *had* and stuck to it, it would have been ten times better than what you did," Naughten retorted. "Now they'll tell the whole school—and Beetle'll make up a lot of beastly rhymes and nicknames."

"But, hang it, she kissed me!" Outside of his work, Tulke's mind moved slowly.

"I'm not thinking of you. I'm thinking of *us*. I'll go up to their study and see if I can make 'em keep quiet!"

"Tulke's awf'ly cut up about this business—" Naughten began, ingratiatingly, when he found Beetle.

"Who's kissed him this time?"

"—and I've come to ask you chaps, and especially you,

Beetle, not to let the thing be known all over the school. Of course, fellows as senior as you are can easily see why."

"Um!" said Beetle, with the cold reluctance of one who foresees an unpleasant public duty. "I suppose I must go and talk to the Sixth again."

"Not the least need, my dear chap, I assure you," said Naughten, hastily. "I'll take any message you care to send."

But the chance of supplying the missing adjective was too tempting. So Naughten returned to that still undissolved meeting, Beetle, white, icy, and aloof, at his heels.

"There seems," he began with laboriously crisp articulation —"there seems to be a certain amount of uneasiness among you as to the steps we may think fit to take in regard to this last revelation of the—ah—obscene. If it is any consolation to you to know that we have decided—for the honour of the school, you understand—to keep our mouths shut as to these —ah—obscenities, you—ah—have it."

He wheeled, his head among the stars, and strode statelily back to his study, where Stalky and McTurk lay side by side upon the table wiping their tearful eyes—too weak to move.

* * * * *

The Latin prose paper was a success beyond their wildest dreams. Stalky and McTurk were, of course, out of all examinations (they did extra-tuition with the Head), but Beetle attended with zeal.

"This, I presume, is a par-ergon on your part," said King, as he dealt out the papers. "One final exhibition ere you are translated to loftier spheres? A last attack on the classics? It seems to confound you already."

Beetle studied the print with knit brows. "*I* can't make head or tail of it," he murmured. "What does it mean?"

"No, no!" said King, with scholastic coquetry. "We depend upon *you* to give us the meaning. This is an examination, Beetle mine, not a guessing-competition. You will find your associates have no diffculty in—"

Tulke left his place and laid the paper on the desk. King looked, read, and turned a ghastly green.

"Stalky's missing a heap," thought Beetle. "Wonder how King'll get out of it?"

"There seems," King began with a gulp, "a certain modicum of truth in our Beetle's remark. I am—er—inclined to believe that the worthy Randall must have dropped this in form—if you know what that means. Beetle, you purport to be an editor. Perhaps you can enlighten the form as to forms."

"What, sir? Whose form? I don't see that there's any verb in this sentence at all, an'—an'—the Ode is all different, somehow."

"I was about to say, before you volunteered your criticism, that an accident must have befallen the paper in type, and that the printer reset it by the light of nature. No—" he held the thing at arm's length— "our Randall is not an authority on Cicero or Horace."

"Rather mean to shove it off on Randall," whispered Beetle to his neighbour. "King must ha' been as screwed as an owl when he wrote it out."

"But we can amend the error by dictating it."

"No, sir." The answer came pat from a dozen throats at once. "That cuts the time for the exam. Only two hours allowed, sir. 'Tisn't fair. It's a printed-paper exam. How're we goin' to be marked for it? It's all Randall's fault. It isn't *our* fault, anyhow. An exam.'s an exam.," etc., etc.

Naturally Mr. King considered this was an attempt to undermine his authority, and, instead of beginning dictation at once, delivered a lecture on the spirit in which examinations should be approached. As the storm subsided, Beetle fanned it afresh.

"Eh? What? What was that you were saying to MacLagan?"

"I only said I thought the papers ought to have been looked at before they were given out, sir."

"Hear, hear!" from a back bench.

Mr. King wished to know whether Beetle took it upon himself personally to conduct the traditions of the school. His zeal for knowledge ate up another fifteen minutes, during which the prefects showed unmistakable signs of boredom.

"Oh, it was a giddy time," said Beetle, afterwards, in dismantled Number Five. "He gibbered a bit, and I kept him on the gibber, and then he dictated about a half of Dolabella & Co."

"Good old Dolabella! Friend of mine. Yes?" said Stalky, pensively.

"Then we had to ask him how every other word was spelt, of course, and he gibbered a lot more. He cursed me and Mac-Lagan (Mac played up like a trump) and Randall, and the 'materialised ignorance of the unscholarly middle classes,' 'lust for mere marks,' and all the rest. It was what you might call a final exhibition—a last attack—a giddy par-ergon."

"But o' course he was blind squiffy when he wrote the paper. I hope you explained *that?*" said Stalky.

"Oh, yes. I told Tulke so. I said an immoral prefect an' a drunken house-master were legitimate inferences. Tulke nearly blubbed. He's awfully shy of us since Mary's time."

Tulke preserved that modesty till the last moment—till the journey-money had been paid, and the boys were filling the brakes that took them to the station. Then the three tenderly constrained him to wait awhile.

"You see, Tulke, you may be a prefect," said Stalky, "but I've left the Coll. Do you see, Tulke, dear?"

"Yes, I see. Don't bear malice, Stalky."

"Stalky? Curse your impudence, you young cub," shouted Stalky, magnificent in top-hat, stiff collar, spats, and high-waisted snuff-coloured ulster. "I want you to understand that *I'm* Mister Corkran, an' you're a dirty little schoolboy."

"Besides bein' frabjously immoral," said McTurk. "Wonder you aren't ashamed to foist your company on pure-minded boys like us."

"Come on, Tulke," cried Naughten, from the prefects' brake.

"Yes, we're comin'. Shove up and make room, you Collegers. You've all got to be back next term, with your 'Yes, sir,' an' 'O, sir,' an' 'No, sir,' an' 'Please sir'; but before we say good-by we're going to tell you a little story. Go on, Dickie" (this to the driver); "we're quite ready. Kick that hat-box under the seat, an' don't crowd your Uncle Stalky."

"As nice a lot of high-minded youngsters as you'd wish to see," said McTurk, gazing round with bland patronage. "A trifle immoral, but then—boys will be boys. It's no good tryin' to look stuffy, Carson. *Mister* Corkran will now oblige with the story of Tulke an' Mary Yeo!"

Slaves of the Lamp—Part II

THAT VERY INFANT who told the story of the capture of Boh Na Ghee[1] to Eustace Cleaver, novelist, inherited an estateful baronetcy with vast revenues, resigned the service, and became a landholder, while his mother stood guard over him to see that he married the right girl. But, new to his position, he presented the local volunteers with a full-sized magazine-rifle range, two miles long, across the heart of his estate, and the surrounding families, who lived in savage seclusion among woods full of pheasants, regarded him as an erring maniac. The noise of the firing disturbed their poultry, and Infant was cast out from the society of J. P.'s and decent men till such time as a daughter of the county might lure him back to right thinking. He took his revenge by filling the house with choice selections of old schoolmates home on leave—affable detrimentals, at whom the bicycle-riding maidens of the surrounding families were allowed to look from afar. I knew when a troop-ship was in port by the Infant's invitations. Sometimes he would produce old friends of equal seniority; at others, young and blushing giants whom I had left small fags far down in the Lower Second; and to these Infant and the elders expounded the whole duty of man in the Army.

"I've had to cut the service," said the Infant; "but that's no reason why my vast stores of experience should be lost to posterity." He was just thirty, and in that same summer an imperious wire drew me to his baronial castle: "Got good haul; ex-*Tamar*. Come along."

It was an unusually good haul, arranged with a single eye to my benefit. There was a baldish, broken-down captain of Native Infantry, shivering with ague behind an indomitable red nose—and they called him Captain Dickson. There was another captain, also of Native Infantry, with a fair moustache; his face was like white glass, and his hands were fragile, but

[1] "A conference of the Powers": "Many Inventions."

he answered joyfully to the cry of Tertius. There was an enormously big and well-kept man, who had evidently not campaigned for years, clean-shaved, soft-voiced, and cat-like, but still Abanazar for all that he adorned the Indian Political Service; and there was a lean Irishman, his face tanned blue-black with the suns of the Telegraph Department. Luckily the baize doors of the bachelors' wing fitted tight, for we dressed promiscuously in the corridor or in each other's rooms, talking, calling, shouting, and anon waltzing by pairs to songs of Dick Four's own devising.

There were sixty years of mixed work to be sifted out between us, and since we had met one another from time to time in the quick scene-shifting of India—a dinner, camp, or a race-meeting here; a dak-bungalow or railway-station up-country somewhere else—we had never quite lost touch. Infant sat on the banisters, hungrily and enviously drinking it in. He enjoyed his baronetcy, but his heart yearned for the old days.

It was a cheerful babel of matters personal, provincial, and imperial, pieces of old call-over lists, and new policies, cut short by the roar of a Burmese gong, and we went down not less than a quarter of a mile of stairs to meet Infant's mother, who had known us all in our school-days and greeted us as if those had ended a week ago. But it was fifteen years since, with tears of laughter, she had lent me a grey princess-skirt for amateur theatricals.

That was a dinner from the "Arabian Nights," served in an eighty-foot hall full of ancestors and pots of flowering roses, and, what was more impressive, heated by steam. When it was ended and the little mother had gone away—("You boys want to talk, so I shall say good night now")—we gathered about an apple-wood fire, in a gigantic polished steel grate, under a mantelpiece ten feet high, and the Infant compassed us about with curious liqueurs and that kind of cigarette which serves best to introduce your own pipe.

"Oh, bliss!" grunted Dick Four from a sofa, where he had been packed with a rug over him. "First time I've been warm since I came home."

We were all nearly on top of the fire, except Infant, who

had been long enough at Home to take exercise when he felt chilled. This is a grisly diversion, but much affected by the English of the Island.

"If you say a word about cold tubs and brisk walks," drawled McTurk, "I'll kill you, Infant. I've got a liver, too. 'Member when we used to think it a treat to turn out of our beds on a Sunday morning—thermometer fifty-seven degrees if it was summer—and bathe off the Pebbleridge? Ugh!"

" 'Thing I don't understand," said Tertius, "was the way we chaps used to go down into the lavatories, boil ourselves pink, and then come up with all our pores open into a young snowstorm or a black frost. Yet none of our chaps died, that I can remember."

" 'Talkin' of baths," said McTurk, with a chuckle, " 'member our bath in Number Five, Beetle, the night Rabbits-Eggs rocked King? What wouldn't I give to see old Stalky now! He is the only one of the two Studies not here."

"Stalky is the great man of his Century," said Dick Four.

"How d'you know?" I asked.

"How do I know?" said Dick Four, scornfully. "If you've ever been in a tight place with Stalky you wouldn't ask."

"I haven't seen him since the camp at Pindi in '87," I said. "He was goin' strong then—about seven feet high and four feet through."

"Adequate chap. Infernally adequate," said Tertius, pulling his moustache and staring into the fire.

"Got dam' near court-martialled and broke in Egypt in '84," the Infant volunteered. "I went out in the same trooper with him—as raw as he was. Only *I* showed it, and Stalky didn't."

"What was the trouble?" said McTurk, reaching forward absently to twitch my dress-tie into position.

"Oh, nothing. His colonel trusted him to take twenty Tommies out to wash, or groom camels, or something at the back of Suakin, and Stalky got embroiled with Fuzzies five miles in the interior. He conducted a masterly retreat and wiped up eight of 'em. He knew jolly well he'd no right to go out so far, so he took the initiative and pitched in a letter to his colonel, who was frothing at the mouth, complaining of the 'paucity of support accorded to him in his operations.' Gad, it might have been òne fat brigadier slangin' another! Then he went into the Staff Corps."

"That—is—entirely—Stalky," said Abanazar from his arm-chair.

"You've come across him, too?" I said.

"Oh, yes," he replied in his softest tones. "I was at the tail of that—that epic. Don't you chaps know?"

We did not—Infant, McTurk, and I; and we called for information very politely.

" 'Twasn't anything," said Tertius. "We got into a mess up in the Khye-Kheen hills a couple o' years ago, and Stalky pulled us through. That's all."

McTurk gazed at Tertius with all an Irishman's contempt for the tongue-tied Saxon.

"Heavens!" he said. "And it's you and your likes govern Ireland. Tertius, aren't you ashamed?"

"Well, I can't tell a yarn. I can chip in when the other fellow starts *bukhing*. Ask him." He pointed to Dick Four, whose nose gleamed scornfully over the rug.

"I knew you wouldn't," said Dick Four. "Give me a whisky-and-soda. I've been drinking lemon-squash and ammoniated quinine while you chaps were bathin' in champagne, and my head's singin' like a top."

He wiped his ragged moustache above the drink; and, his teeth chattering in his head, began:

"You know the Khye-Kheen-Malôt expedition, when we scared the souls out of 'em with a field force they daren't fight against? Well, both tribes—there was a coalition against us—came in without firing a shot; and a lot of hairy villains, who had no more power over their men than I had, promised and vowed all sorts of things. On that very slender evidence, Pussy dear—"

"I was at Simla," said Abanazar, hastily.

"Never mind, you're tarred with the same brush. On the strength of those tuppeny-ha'penny treaties, your asses of Politicals reported the country as pacified, and the Government, being a fool, as usual, began road-makin'—dependin' on local supply for labour. 'Member *that*, Pussy? 'Rest of our chaps who'd had no look-in during the campaign didn't think there'd be any more of it, and were anxious to get back to India. But I'd been in two of these little rows before, and I had my suspicions. I engineered myself, *summo ingenio*, into command of a road-patrol—no shovellin', only marching up and down genteelly with a guard. They'd withdrawn all the troops they could, but I nucleussed about forty Pathans, recruits chiefly, of my regiment, and sat tight at the base-camp while the road-parties went to work, as per Political survey."

"Had some rippin' sing-songs in camp, too," said Tertius.

"My pup"—thus did Dick Four refer to his subaltern—"was a pious little beast. He didn't like the sing-songs, and so he went down with pneumonia. I rootled round the camp, and found Tertius gassing about as a D. A. Q. M. G., which, God knows, he isn't cut out for. There were six or eight of the old Coll at base-camp (we're always in force for a frontier row), but I'd heard of Tertius as a steady old hack, and I told him he had to shake off his D. A. Q. M. G. breeches and help *me*. Tertius volunteered like a shot, and we settled it with the authorities, and out we went—forty Pathans, Tertius, and me, looking up the road-parties. Macnamara's—'member old Mac, the Sapper, who played the fiddle so damnably at Umballa?— Mac's party was the last but one. The last was Stalky's. He was at the head of the road with some of his pet Sikhs. Mac said he believed he was all right."

"Stalky *is* a Sikh," said Tertius. "He takes his men to pray at the Durbar Sahib at Amritsar, regularly as clockwork, when he can."

"Don't interrupt, Tertius. It was about forty miles beyond Mac's before I found him; and my men pointed out gently, but firmly, that the country was risin'. What kind o' country, Beetle? Well, *I'm* no word-painter, thank goodness, but *you* might call it a hellish country! When we weren't up to our necks in snow, we were rolling down the khud. The well-disposed inhabitants, who were to supply labour for the road-making (don't forget that, Pussy dear), sat behind rocks and took pot-shots at us. 'Old, old story! We all legged it in search of Stalky. I had a feeling that he'd be in good cover, and about dusk we found him and his road-party, as snug as a bug in a rug, in an old Malôt stone fort, with a watch-tower at one corner. It overhung the road they had blasted out of the cliff fifty feet below; and under the road things went down pretty sheer, for five or six hundred feet, into a gorge about half a mile wide and two or three miles long. There were chaps on the other side of the gorge scientifically gettin' our range. So I hammered on the gate and nipped in, and tripped over Stalky in a greasy, bloody old poshteen, squatting on the ground, eating with his men. I'd only seen him for half a minute about three months before, but I might have met him yesterday. He waved his hand all sereno.

" 'Hullo, Aladdin! Hullo, Emperor!' he said. 'You're just in time for the performance.'

"I saw his Sikhs looked a bit battered. 'Where's your command? Where's your subaltern?' I said.

" 'Here—all there is of it,' said Stalky. 'If you want young Everett, he's dead, and his body's in the watch-tower. They rushed our road-party last week, and got him and seven men. We've been besieged for five days. I suppose they let you through to make sure of you. The whole country's up. 'Strikes me you've walked into a first-class trap.' He grinned, but neither Tertius nor I could see where the deuce the fun was. We hadn't any grub for our men, and Stalky had only four days' whack for his. That came of dependin' upon your asinine Politicals, Pussy dear, who told us that the inhabitants were friendly.

"To make us *quite* comfy, Stalky took us up to the watch-tower to see poor Everett's body, lyin' in a foot o' drifted snow. It looked like a girl of fifteen—not a hair on the little fellow's face. He'd been shot through the temple, but the Malôts had left their mark on him. Stalky unbuttoned the tunic, and showed it to us—a rummy sickle-shaped cut on the chest. 'Member the snow all white on his eyebrows, Tertius? 'Member when Stalky moved the lamp and it looked as if he was alive?"

"Ye-es," said Tertius, with a shudder. " 'Member the beastly look on Stalky's face, though, with his nostrils all blown out, same as he used to look when he was bullyin' a fag? That was a lovely evening."

"We held a council of war up there over Everett's body. Stalky said the Malôts and Khye-Kheens were up together; havin' sunk their blood-feuds to settle us. The chaps we'd seen across the gorge were Khye-Kheens. It was about half a mile from them to us as a bullet flies, and they'd made a line of sungars under the brow of the hill to sleep in and starve us out. The Malôts, he said, were in front of us promiscuous. There wasn't good cover behind the fort, or they'd have been there, too. Stalky didn't mind the Malôts half as much as he did the Khye-Kheens. He said the Malôts were treacherous curs. What I couldn't understand was, why in the world the two gangs didn't join in and rush us. There must have been at least five hundred of 'em. Stalky said they didn't trust each other very well, because they were ancestral enemies when they were at home; and the only time they'd tried a rush he'd hove a couple of blasting-charges among 'em, and that had sickened 'em a bit.

"It was dark by the time we finished, and Stalky, always sereno, said: 'You command now. I don't suppose you mind my taking any action I may consider necessary to reprovision the fort?' I said, 'Of course not,' and then the lamp blew out. So Tertius and I had to climb down the tower steps (we didn't want to stay with Everett) and got back to our men. Stalky had gone off—to count the stores, I supposed. Anyhow, Tertius and I sat up in case of a rush (they were plugging at us pretty generally, you know), relieving each other till the mornin'.

"Mornin' came. No Stalky. Not a sign of him. I took counsel with his senior native officer—a grand, white-whiskered old chap—Rutton Singh, from Jullunder-way. He only grinned, and said it was all right. Stalky had been out of the fort twice before, somewhere or other, accordin' to him. He said Stalky 'ud come back unchipped, and gave me to understand that Stalky was an invulnerable *Guru* of sorts. All the same, I put the whole command on half rations, and set 'em to pickin' out loopholes.

"About noon there was no end of a snow-storm, and the enemy stopped firing. We replied gingerly, because we were awfully short of ammunition. 'Don't suppose we fired five shots an hour, but we generally got our man. Well, while I was talking with Rutton Singh I saw Stalky coming down from the watch-tower, rather puffy about the eyes, his poshteen coated with claret-coloured ice.

" 'No trustin' these snow-storms,' he said. 'Nip out quick and snaffle what you can get. There's a certain amount of friction between the Khye-Kheens and the Malôts just now.'

"I turned Tertius out with twenty Pathans, and they bucked about in the snow for a bit till they came on to a sort of camp about eight hundred yards away, with only a few men in charge and half a dozen sheep by the fire. They finished off the men, and snaffled the sheep and as much grain as they could carry, and came back. No one fired a shot at 'em. There didn't seem to be anybody about, but the snow was falling pretty thick.

" 'That's good enough,' said Stalky when we got dinner ready and he was chewin' mutton-kababs off a cleanin'-rod. 'There's no sense riskin' men. They're holding a powwow between the Khye-Kheens and the Malôts at the head of the gorge. I don't think these so-called coalitions are much good.'

"Do you know what that maniac had done? Tertius and I shook it out of him by instalments. There was an underground granary cellar-room below the watch-tower, and in blasting the road Stalky had blown a hole into one side of it. Being no one else *but* Stalky, he'd kept the hole open for his own ends; and laid poor Everett's body slap over the well of the stairs that led down to it from the watch-tower. He'd had to move and replace the corpse every time he used the passage. The Sikhs wouldn't go near the place, of course. Well, he'd got out of this hole, and dropped on to the road. Then, in the night *and* a howling snow-storm, he'd dropped over the edge of the khud, made his way down to the bottom of the gorge, forded the nullah, which was half frozen, climbed up on the other

side along a track he'd discovered, and come out on the right
flank of the Khye-Kheens. He had then—listen to this!—
crossed over a ridge that paralleled their rear, walked half a
mile behind that, and come out on the left of their line where
the gorge gets shallow and where there was a regular track
between the Malôt and the Khye-Kheen camps. That was
about two in the morning, and, as it turned out, a man spotted
him—a Khye-Kheen. So Stalky abolished him quietly, and left
him—*with* the Malôt mark on his chest, same as Everett had.

" 'I was just as economical as I could be,' Stalky said to us.
'If he'd shouted I should have been slain. I'd never had to do
that kind of thing but once before, and that was the first time
I tried that path. It's perfectly practicable for infantry, you
know.'

" 'What about your first man?' I said.

" 'Oh, that was the night after they killed Everett, and I
went out lookin' for a line of retreat for my men. A man
found me. I abolished him—*privatim*—scragged him. But on
thinkin' it over it occurred to me that if I could find the body
(I'd hove it down some rocks) I might decorate it with the
Malôt mark and leave it to the Khye-Kheens to draw inferences. So I went out again the next night and did. The Khye-
Kheens are shocked at the Malôts perpetratin' these two
dastardly outrages after they'd sworn to sink all blood-feuds. I
lay up behind their sungars early this morning and watched
'em. They all went to confer about it at the head of the gorge.
Awf'ly annoyed they are. Don't wonder.' You know the way
Stalky drops out his words, one by one."

"My God!" said the Infant, explosively, as the full depth of
the strategy dawned on him.

"Dear-r man!" said McTurk, purring rapturously.

"Stalky stalked," said Tertius. "That's all there is to it."

"No, he didn't," said Dick Four. "Don't you remember how
he insisted that he had only applied his luck? Don't you remember how Rutton Singh grabbed his boots and grovelled
in the snow, and how our men shouted?"

"None of our Pathans believed that was luck," said Tertius.
"They swore Stalky ought to have been born a Pathan, and

—'member we nearly had a row in the fort when Rutton Singh said Stalky was a Pathan? Gad, how furious the old chap was with my Jamadar! But Stalky just waggled his finger and they shut up."

"Old Rutton Singh's sword was half out, though, and he swore he'd cremate every Khye-Kheen and Malôt he killed. That made the Jamadar pretty wild, because he didn't mind fighting against his own creed but he wasn't going to crab a fellow Mussulman's chances of Paradise. Then Stalky jabbered Pushtu and Punjabi in alternate streaks. Where the deuce did he pick up his Pushtu from, Beetle?"

"Never mind his language, Dick," said I. "Give us the gist of it."

"I flatter myself I can address the wily Pathan on occasion, but, hang it all, I can't make puns in Pushtu, or top off my arguments with a smutty story, as he did. He played on those two old dogs o' war like a—like a concertina. Stalky said— and the other two backed up his knowledge of Oriental nature —that the Khye-Kheens and the Malôts between 'em would organise a combined attack on us that night, as a proof of good faith. They wouldn't drive it home, though, because neither side would trust the other on account, as Rutton Singh put it, of the little accidents. Stalky's notion was to crawl out at dusk with his Sikhs, manœuvre 'em along this ungodly goat-track that he'd found, to the back of the Khye-Kheen position, and then lob in a few long shots at the Malôts when the attack was well on. 'That'll divert their minds and help to agitate 'em,' he said. 'Then you chaps can come out and sweep up the pieces, and we'll rendezvous at the head of the gorge. After that, I move we get back to Mac's camp and have something to eat.'"

"*You* were commandin'?" the Infant suggested.

"I was about three months senior to Stalky, and two months Tertius's senior," Dick Four replied. "*But* we were all from the same old Coll. I should say ours was the only little affair on record where some one wasn't jealous of some one else."

"*We* weren't," Tertius broke in, "but there was another row between Gul Sher Khan and Rutton Singh. Our Jamadar said

—he was quite right—that no Sikh living could stalk worth a damn; and that Koran Sahib had better take out the Pathans, who understood that kind of mountain work. Rutton Singh said that Koran Sahib jolly well knew every Pathan was a born deserter, and every Sikh was a gentleman, even if he couldn't crawl on his belly. Stalky struck in with some woman's proverb or other, that had the effect of doublin' both men up with a grin. He said the Sikhs and the Pathans could settle their claims on the Khye-Kheens and Malôts later on, but he was going to take his Sikhs along for this mountain-climbing job, because Sikhs could shoot. They can, too. Give 'em a mule-load of ammunition apiece, and they're perfectly happy."

"And out he gat," said Dick Four. "As soon as it was dark, and he'd had a bit of a snooze, him and thirty Sikhs went down through the staircase in the tower, every mother's son of 'em salutin' little Everett where It stood propped up against the wall. The last I heard him say was, 'Kubbadar! tumbleinga!' [2] and they tumbleingaed over the black edge of nothing. Close upon 9 P.M. the combined attack developed; Khye-Kheens across the valley, and Malôts in front of us, pluggin' at long range and yellin' to each other to come along and cut our infidel throats. Then they skirmished up to the gate, and began the old game of callin' our Pathans renegades, and invitin' 'em to join the holy war. One of our men, a young fellow from Dera Ismail, jumped on the wall to slang 'em back, and jumped down, blubbing like a child. He'd been hit smack in the middle of the hand. 'Never saw a man yet who could stand a hit in the hand without weepin' bitterly. It tickles up all the nerves. So Tertius took his rifle and smote the others on the head to keep them quiet at the loopholes. The dear children wanted to open the gate and go in at 'em generally, but that didn't suit our book.

"At last, near midnight, I heard the wop, wop, wop, of Stalky's Martinis across the valley, and some general cursing

[2] "Look out; you'll fall!"

among the Malôts whose main body was hid from us by a fold in the hillside. Stalky was brownin' 'em at a great rate, and very naturally they turned half right and began to blaze at their faithless allies, the Khye-Kheens—regular volley firin'. In less than ten minutes after Stalky opened the diversion they were going it hammer and tongs, both sides the valley. When we could see, the valley was rather a mixed-up affair. The Khye-Kheens had streamed out of their sungars above the gorge to chastise the Malôts, and Stalky—I was watching him through my glasses—had slipped in behind 'em. Very good. The Khye-Kheens had to leg it along the hillside up to where the gorge got shallow and they could cross over to the Malôts, who were awfully cheered to see the Khye-Kheens taken in the rear.

"Then it occurred to me to comfort the Khye-Kheens. So I turned out the whole command, and we advanced à la pas de charge, doublin' up what, for the sake of argument, we'll call the Malôts' left flank. Even then, if they'd sunk their differences, they could have eaten us alive; but they'd been firin' at each other half the night, and they went on firin'. Queerest thing you ever saw in your born days! As soon as our men doubled up to the Malôts, they'd blaze at the Khye-Kheens more zealously than ever, to show they were on our side, run up the valley a few hundred yards, and halt to fire again. The moment Stalky saw our game he duplicated it his side the gorge; and, by Jove! the Khye-Kheens did just the same thing."

"Yes, but," said Tertius, "you've forgot him playin' 'Arrah, Patsy, mind the baby' on the bugle to hurry us up."

"Did he?" roared McTurk. Somehow we all began to sing it, and there was an interruption.

"Rather," said Tertius, when we were quiet. No one of the Aladdin company could forget that tune. "Yes, he played 'Patsy.' Go on, Dick."

"Finally," said Dick Four, "we drove both mobs into each other's arms on a bit of level ground at the head of the valley, and saw the whole crew whirl off, fightin' and stabbin' and swearin' in a blindin' snow-storm. They were a heavy, hairy lot, and we didn't follow 'em.

"Stalky had captured one prisoner—an old pensioned Sepoy of twenty-five years' service, who produced his discharge—an awf'ly sportin' old card. He had been tryin' to make his men rush us early in the day. He was sulky—angry with his own side for their cowardice—and Rutton Singh wanted to bayonet him—Sikhs don't understand fightin' against the Government after you've served it honestly—but Stalky rescued him, and froze on to him tight—with ulterior motives, I believe. When we got back to the fort, we buried young Everett—Stalky wouldn't hear of blowin' up the place—and bunked. We'd only lost ten men, all told."

"Only ten, out of seventy. How did you lose 'em?" I asked.

"Oh, there was a rush on the fort early in the night, and a few Malôts got over the gate. It was rather a tight thing for a minute or two, but the recruits took it beautifully. Lucky job we hadn't any badly wounded men to carry, because we had forty miles to Macnamara's camp. By Jove, how we legged it! Half-way in, old Rutton Singh collapsed, so we slung him across four rifles and Stalky's overcoat; and Stalky, his prisoner, and a couple of Sikhs were his bearers. After that I went to sleep. You can, you know, on the march, when your legs get properly numbed. Mac swears we all marched into his camp snoring and dropped where we halted. His men lugged us into the tents like gram-bags. I remember wakin' up and seein' Stalky asleep with his head on old Rutton Singh's chest. *He* slept twenty-four hours. I only slept seventeen, but then I was coming down with dysentery."

"Coming down? What rot! He had it on him before we joined Stalky in the fort," said Tertius.

"Well, *you* needn't talk! You hove your sword at Macnamara and demanded a drum-head court-martial every time you saw him. The only thing that soothed you was putting you under arrest every half-hour. You were off your head for three days."

"Don't remember a word of it," said Tertius, placidly. "I remember my orderly giving me milk, though."

"How did Stalky come out?" McTurk demanded, puffing hard over his pipe.

"Stalky? Like a serene Brahmini bull. Poor old Mac was at his Royal Engineers' wits' end to know what to do. You see I was putrid with dysentery, Tertius was ravin', half the men had frost-bite, and Macnamara's orders were to break camp and come in before winter. So Stalky, who hadn't turned a hair, took half his supplies to save him the bother o' luggin' 'em back to the plains, and all the ammunition he could get at, and, *consilio et auxilio Rutton Singhi*, tramped back to his fort with all his Sikhs and his precious prisoner, *and* a lot of dissolute hangers-on that he and the prisoner had seduced into service. He had sixty men of sorts—and his brazen cheek. Mac nearly wept with joy when he went. You see there weren't any explicit orders to Stalky to come in before the passes were blocked: Mac is a great man for orders, and Stalky's a great man for orders—when they suit his book."

"He told me he was goin' to the Engadine," said Tertius. "Sat on my cot smokin' a cigarette, and makin' me laugh till I cried. Macnamara bundled the whole lot of us down to the plains next day. We were a walkin' hospital."

"Stalky told me that Macnamara was a simple godsend to him," said Dick Four. "I used to see him in Mac's tent listenin' to Mac playin' the fiddle, and, between the pieces, wheedlin' Mac out of picks and shovels and dynamite cartridges hand-over-fist. Well, that was the last we saw of Stalky. A week or so later the passes were shut with snow, and I don't think Stalky wanted to be found particularly just then."

"He didn't" said the fair and fat Abanazar. "He didn't. Ho, ho!"

Dick Four threw up his thin, dry hand with the blue veins at the back of it. "Hold on a minute, Pussy; I'll let you in at the proper time. I went down to my regiment, and that spring, five months later, I got off with a couple of companies on detachment: nominally to look after some friends of ours across the border; actually, of course, to recruit. It was a bit unfortunate, because an ass of a young Naick carried a frivolous blood-feud he'd inherited from his aunt into those hills, and the local gentry wouldn't volunteer into my corps. Of course, the Naick had taken short leave to manage the business; that was all regular enough; *but* he'd stalked my pet orderly's uncle. It was an infernal shame, because I knew Harris of the Ghuznees would be covering that ground three months later, and he'd snaffle all the chaps I had my eyes on. Everybody was down on the Naick, because they felt he ought to have had the decency to postpone his—his disgustful amours till our companies were full strength.

"Still the beast had a certain amount of professional feeling left. He sent one of his aunt's clan by night to tell me that, if I'd take safeguard, he'd put me on to a batch of beauties. I nipped over the border like a shot, and about ten miles the other side, in a nullah, my rapparee-in-charge showed me about seventy men variously armed, but standing up like a Queen's company. Then one of 'em stepped out and lugged round an old bugle, just like—who's the man?—Bancroft, ain't it?—feeling for his eye-glass in a farce, and played 'Arrah, Patsy, mind the baby. Arrah, Patsy, mind'—that was as far as he could get."

That, also, was as far as Dick Four could get, because we had to sing the old song through twice, again and once more, and subsequently, in order to repeat it.

"He explained that if I knew the rest of the song he had a note for me from the man the song belonged to. Whereupon, my children, I finished that old tune on that bugle, and *this* is what I got. I knew you'd like to look at it. Don't grab." (We were all struggling for a sight of the well-known unformed handwriting.) "I'll read it aloud.

" 'FORT EVERETT, February 19.

" 'DEAR DICK OR TERTIUS: The bearer of this is in charge of seventy-five recruits, all pukka devils, but desirous of leading new lives. They have been slightly polished, and after being boiled may shape well. I want you to give thirty of them to my adjutant, who, though God's own ass, will need men this spring. The rest you can keep. You will be interested to learn that I have extended my road to the end of the Malôt country. All headmen and priests concerned in last September's affair worked one month each, supplying road metal from their own houses. Everett's grave is covered by a forty-foot mound, which should serve well as a base for future triangulations. Rutton Singh sends his best salaams. I am making some treaties, and have given my prisoner—who also sends his salaams—local rank of Khan Bahadur.

"'A. L. COCKRAN.'"

"Well, that was all," said Dick Four, when the roaring, the shouting, the laughter, and, I think, the tears had subsided. "I chaperoned the gang across the border as quick as I could. They were rather homesick but they cheered up when they recognised some of my chaps, who had been in the Khye-Kheen row, and they made a rippin' good lot. It's rather more than three hundred miles from Fort Everett to where I picked 'em up. Now, Pussy, tell 'em the latter end o' Stalky as you saw it."

Abanazar laughed a little nervous, misleading, official laugh.

"Oh, it wasn't much. I was at Simla in the spring, when our Stalky, out of his snows, began corresponding direct with the Government."

"After the manner of a king," suggested Dick Four.

"My turn now, Dick. He'd done a whole lot of things he shouldn't have done, and constructively pledged the Government to all sorts of action."

"Pledged the State's ticker, eh?" said McTurk, with a nod to me.

"About that; but the embarrassin' part was that it was all so thunderin' convenient, so well reasoned, don't you know? Came in as pat as if he'd had access to all sorts of information—which he couldn't, of course."

"Pooh!" said Tertius, "I back Stalky against the Foreign Office any day."

"He'd done pretty nearly everything he could think of, except strikin' coins in his own image and superscription, all under cover of buildin' this infernal road and bein' blocked by the snow. His report was simply amazin'. Von Lennaert tore his hair over it at first, and then he gasped, 'Who the dooce is this unknown Warren Hastings? He must be slain. He must be slain officially! The Viceroy'll never stand it. It's unheard of. He must be slain by His Excellency in person. Order him up here and pitch in a stinger.' Well, I sent him no end of an official stinger, and I pitched in an unofficial telegram at the same time."

"You!" This with amazement from the Infant, for Abanazar resembled nothing so much as a fluffy Persian cat.

"Yes—me," said Abanazar. " 'Twasn't much, but after what you've said, Dicky, it was rather a coincidence, because I wired:

> " 'Aladdin now has got his wife,
> Your Emperor is appeased.
> I think you'd better come to life:
> We hope you've all been pleased.'

"Funny how that old song came up in my head. That was fairly non-committal and encouragin'. The only flaw was that his Emperor wasn't appeased by very long chalks. Stalky extricated himself from his mountain fastnesses and loafed up to Simla at his leisure, to be offered up on the horns of the altar."

"But," I began, "surely the Commander-in-Chief is the proper—"

"His Excellency had an idea that if he blew up one single junior captain—same as King used to blow us up—he was holdin' the reins of empire, and, of course, as long as he had that idea, Von Lennaert encouraged him. I'm not sure Von Lennaert didn't put that notion into his head."

"They've changed the breed, then, since my time," I said.

"P'r'aps. Stalky was sent up for his wiggin' like a bad little boy. I've reason to believe that His Excellency's hair stood on end. He walked into Stalky for one hour—Stalky at attention in the middle of the floor, and (so he vowed) Von Lennaert pretending to soothe down His Excellency's topknot in dumb-show in the background. Stalky didn't dare to look up, or he'd have laughed."

"Now, wherefore was Stalky not broken publicly?" said the Infant, with a large and luminous leer.

"Ah, wherefore?" said Abanazar. "To give him a chance to retrieve his blasted career, and not to break his father's heart. Stalky hadn't a father, but that didn't matter. He behaved like a—like the Sanawar Orphan Asylum, and His Excellency graciously spared him. Then he came round to my office and sat opposite me for ten minutes, puffing out his nostrils. Then he said, 'Pussy, if I thought that basket-hanger—' "

"Hah! He remembered *that*," said McTurk.

" '—that two-anna basket-hanger governed India, I swear I'd become a naturalised Muscovite to-morrow. I'm a *femme incomprise*. This thing's broken my heart. It'll take six months' shootin'-leave in India to mend it. Do you think I can get it, Pussy?'

"He got it in about three minutes and a half, and seventeen days later he was back in the arms of Rutton Singh—horrid disgraced—with orders to hand over his command, etc., to Cathcart MacMonnie."

"Observe!" said Dick Four. "One colonel of the Political Department in charge of thirty Sikhs, on a hilltop. Observe, my children!"

"Naturally, Cathcart not being a fool, even if he *is* a Political, let Stalky do his shooting within fifteen miles of Fort Everett for the next six months, and I always understood they and Rutton Singh *and* the prisoner were as thick as thieves. Then Stalky loafed back to his regiment, I believe. I've never seen him since."

"I have, though," said McTurk, swelling with pride.

We all turned as one man.

"It was at the beginning of this hot weather. I was in camp in the Jullunder doab and stumbled slap on Stalky in a Sikh village; sitting on the one chair of state, with half the population grovellin' before him, a dozen Sikh babies on his knees, an old harridan clappin' him on the shoulder, and a garland o' flowers round his neck. Told me he was recruitin'. We dined together that night, but he never said a word of the business at the Fort. Told me, though, that if I wanted any supplies I'd better say I was Koran Sahib's *bhai;* and I did, and the Sikhs wouldn't take my money."

"Ah! That must have been one of Rutton Singh's villages," said Dick Four; and we smoked for some time in silence.

"I say," said McTurk, casting back through the years, "did Stalky ever tell you *how* Rabbits-Eggs came to rock King that night?"

"No," said Dick Four.

Then McTurk told.

"I see," said Dick Four, nodding. "Practically he duplicated that trick over again. There's nobody like Stalky."

"That's just where you make the mistake," I said. "India's full of Stalkies—Cheltenham and Haileybury and Marlborough chaps—that we don't know anything about, and the surprises will begin when there is really a big row on."

"Who will be surprised?" said Dick Four.

"The other side. The gentlemen who go to the front in first-class carriages. Just imagine Stalky let loose on the south side of Europe with a sufficiency of Sikhs and a reasonable prospect of loot. Consider it quietly."

"There's something in that, but you're too much of an optimist, Beetle," said the Infant.

"Well, I've a right to be. Ain't I responsible for the whole thing? You needn't laugh. Who wrote 'Aladdin now has got his wife'—eh?"

"What's that got to do with it?" said Tertius.

"Everything," said I.

"Prove it," said the Infant.

And I have.